ISLAND OF LAST RESORTS

ISLAND OF LAST RESORTS

Mary Ellis

This first world edition published 2019
in Great Britain and the USA by
SEVERN HOUSE PUBLISHERS LTD of
Eardley House, 4 Uxbridge Street, London W8 7SY.
Trade paperback edition first published
in Great Britain and the USA 2020 by
SEVERN HOUSE PUBLISHERS LTD.

British Library Cataloguing in Publication Data
A CIP catalogue record for this title is available from the British Library.

ISBN-13: 978-0-7278-8934-8 (cased)
ISBN-13: 978-1-78029-626-5 (trade paper)
ISBN-13: 978-1-4483-0319-9 (e-book)

All Severn House titles are printed on acid-free paper.

Severn House Publishers support the Forest Stewardship Council™ [FSC™],
the leading international forest certification organisation. All our titles that
are printed on FSC certified paper carry the FSC logo.

Typeset by Palimpsest Book Production Ltd.,
Falkirk, Stirlingshire, Scotland.
Printed and bound in Great Britain by
TJ International, Padstow, Cornwall.

ACKNOWLEDGMENTS

I would like to thank the Cumberland Island National Seashore which ferries visitors back and forth to Cumberland Island, along with Yvonne Grovner of the Sapelo Island Visitors Center and National Estuarine Research Reserve. Although Cumberland Island and Sapelo Island are very real and gorgeous places off the coast of Georgia, Elysian Island is purely a figment of the author's imagination and has no basis in reality.

ONE

K ate Weller shifted her load of boxes to her other arm, held the screen door open with her backside, and turned the knob. When the door swung wide, she thought she might be able to move into the upstairs apartment without a major commotion. No such luck.

'A little bird told me you were coming back.' The squeaky voice emanating from the shadows belonged to a white-haired, wren-sized woman, clad in a cotton dress and white apron, who stepped into Kate's path.

'Would that "little bird" be your grandson, Eric?' Kate smiled at the ridiculousness of describing someone who was six foot three inches tall as *little*.

'It would.' Angelica Donatella Manfredi, better known as Nonni, crossed her arms over her chest.

Kate shifted the heavy load of books, CDs, and work para-phernalia to her other arm. 'Would my moving back be OK with you? If I remember correctly, you really liked me and wanted Eric to marry me.' She bit the inside of her cheek to keep from smiling.

'True, but that was before you set my kitchen on fire, blew up my grandson's car, and then vanished in the dead of night.' Nonni's brows knitted together above the bridge of her nose.

'It was morning when I moved out, and the fire and car bomb weren't exactly my fault. May I please set my boxes on the counter?'

'Not until you answer a few questions.' Nonni stepped closer and peered up. 'Do you have honest intentions toward my Enrique?'

'You bet I do.'

'Do you promise not to cook without a fire extinguisher handy?'

'I promise.' Kate held up her right hand as the boxes began to slip.

'Then put down your junk and give me a hug.' Nonni stretched out both arms.

Kate reached across her heap of boxes and hugged the matriarch of the clan. Donatella and her husband had emigrated from Sicily to South Carolina and opened a small trattoria on the first floor of their home. Now the Manfredi family owned one of the most successful upscale restaurants in Charleston, one that was favorably reviewed in every travel guide. 'I missed you, Nonni.'

'And I, you.' The woman hugged with a fierceness that belied her small stature. 'Go upstairs and rest. Eric didn't like the so-called fresh seafood that they delivered.' Nonni's nose crinkled as she winced. 'He went to the market to select his own fresh catch of the day. I'll have the busboys unpack your car and carry up these boxes.' Nonni's face had flushed and her eyes were moist when she finally released the hug.

Kate knew better than to argue with her about anything. She kissed the top of the octogenarian's head, grabbed her tote bag, and climbed the steep staircase. When she opened the door of the suite reserved for out-of-town relatives, a wave of nostalgia washed over her, despite having lived here only a few months. Her refrigerator would be fully stocked, gratis; her bed linens would be Egyptian cotton, and the quilt handmade. As the only non-relative ever to rent the room, Kate had been made to feel like a family member by Nonni Manfredi. Yet she had held Eric at arm's length so many times she'd almost ruined any chance of a relationship. Without a doubt, he was the best thing that had ever happened to her.

Since packing and moving from Pensacola, Florida to Charleston had left her out of touch with her boss and co-workers for several days, Kate unpacked her laptop and signed into Bella Trattoria's Wi-Fi. Among the emails, a subject line of WHERE ARE YOU!!!, all in caps and followed by several exclamation points caught her immediate attention. Kate clicked on the email from her boss, Nate Price, wherein he repeated his question a second time: *Where are you? You still haven't responded to the notice about our company's retreat.* Then Nate had cut and pasted an invitation from a previous email: *One week, all-expenses-paid getaway – casual attire, championship golf, shopping, hiking, swimming in either heated pool or Atlantic Ocean, bird-watching – you name it! Employee, plus spouse or significant other. Yes, you will be paid for your time out of the field. Please tell me yes or no within the next few days, because we'll be convening on St Simons Island in Georgia in one week.*

Then Nate added at the bottom of the email: *You must have gotten back to Charleston by now. Are you and Eric coming on the retreat? I have a special surprise to announce once everyone gets here. St Simons Island is only a couple hours away and you don't have a case right now!* Then her boss had added an emoji of a skull and crossbones.

Kate experienced several different emotions: fear, because the newest PI in the company had just annoyed the boss; joy, because a week's vacation sounded fabulous; and hope, because Eric might decide unequivocally that he wanted to be a PI. Not taking a chance with an email going unread for days, Kate punched in the boss's number.

Nate Price picked up immediately. 'Good grief, Weller, I was starting to worry about you.'

'I'm fine, but I had to make a few stops between the Gulf and the city of Charleston. I'm unpacking and settling into my old suite right now. Oh, I saw the invite. The retreat sounds wonderful. Thanks for Eric too.'

'Does that mean you're coming?' he asked.

Kate heard a baby crying in the background and remembered Nate and his wife had a two-year-old. 'I am, for sure, but I don't know about Eric. He just got back to work. His family might not want him leaving again so soon. Bella Trattoria is super busy this time of year.'

'I understand, but this is the only time Nicki can get a babysitter for a full week and Izzy can take time off too. Plus, there's a surprise waiting for everyone who shows up on St Simons.' He imbued the words with tantalizing significance. 'Try to talk Eric into it. Even if you have to promise his family you'll work in the restaurant too when you get back.'

'That might not do the trick. The Manfredis know I can't

cook.' She laughed. 'You can expect me for sure in three days and I'll do my best with Eric.'

'Sounds good. We'll be staying at my friend's condo on St Simons Island while he's in Europe. It's a really nice place. I'll text you John's address to punch into the GPS. Be prepared for anything in terms of weather. Bring sturdy shoes, rain gear, sunblock and jungle-strength bug spray, besides all your beach gear.'

'What is your surprise – a private jet to the Amazon rainforest with a stopover in Rio?' she asked.

'Even better than that, because you won't need your passport or typhoid fever shots. Make sure you check your email during the next couple days in case I give you more info. I'm telling you, Weller, this will be the trip of a lifetime. So work your magic with your "significant other."'

When Nate hung up, Kate ran to the window that overlooked the employee parking lot. No black Ford Expedition. Eric hadn't returned, so she unpacked her boxes and one suitcase until wheels crunched the gravel below her window. Then she bolted down the stairs to work her magic. This would be one time Eric couldn't say no.

But of course, he did. At least initially.

Eric listened to her read the entire invitation as attentively and patiently as any boyfriend down through the ages ever had. Then he tipped up her chin and kissed her sweetly. 'Sorry, Kate. As much as I'd love to join you on this getaway, I have to pass.'

'But why?' she asked, unable to hide her disappointment.

'Because the getaway is for spouses and *significant* others. I'm not a spouse and you and I just started dating seriously.'

'What does the number of days or weeks have to do with it?' Kate tried her best to sound seductive. 'Didn't I tell you I loved you?' she added in a whisper.

'And I love you.' Eric kissed her a second time. 'But this company retreat is for private investigators and I'm not one . . . at least, not yet.'

'Hunter Galen isn't a PI; he's a stockbroker. And neither is Isabelle Price, Nate's wife. Besides, you said you wanted to learn investigative work. A retreat would be a great place to learn in a casual setting.'

'These kinds of job-related vacations can strain long-married couples. Do you want to subject our new relationship to so much pressure?' Eric leaned back against the counter and crossed his arms, his biceps straining the fabric of his sleeves.

'That's a bunch of hooey,' Kate argued. 'There won't be any seminars or training sessions. We'll be doing fun stuff like hiking and swimming, maybe deep-sea fishing and a little shopping. Then we'll chow down on free food. What sounds high pressure about that?' Kate was taking a chance by mentioning Eric's favorite pastime, fishing, since she had no clue if that would be available, but she was desperate.

Eric smiled kindly. 'I know your boss intimidates you. So maybe if you just hang out with your friends, without the added drama of me being there, you will relax more.'

Kate resisted the immature impulse to stomp her foot. 'Truly, Nate Price no longer intimidates me. I'm hoping if you hang out with a bunch of private investigators, you'll gain a better feel for the job.' She dropped her voice to a whisper in case Nonni was eavesdropping, one of her favorite pastimes. 'You don't want to give up your position as head chef until you know for sure what you want career-wise.'

The love of her life picked up the recently purveyed seafood to check over and clean. 'You're sweet to worry, but when your family owns the place, they can't slam the door in my face if I change my mind down the road. How would that look at Christmastime?'

Kate decided to join him at the sink. After rolling up her sleeves and washing her hands, she pulled the tails and shells off shrimp that would be used in sauces and casseroles. 'That's true,' she said. 'Even though your family adores you, they recently put up with your absence while you were my bodyguard in Pensacola.'

'And I helped get your brother's capital murder conviction amended.' He rubbed his knuckles against his shirt. 'When Liam is finally released on parole, he'll have a job waiting at Bella Trattoria.'

'And for that, I'm eternally grateful.' Kate reached for another handful of shrimp. 'But don't you think your family should know if you're willing to take the reins when your dad retires or if your sister will be at the helm? This week might give you a better insight as to what a PI does, not just the fun parts.'

'What exactly are the fun parts?' Eric teased. 'But I see your point. Dad has been at the restaurant more than my mother likes, plus my sister needs more help than just her teenage daughter and Nonni. Bernadette needs someone who's invested in the future of Bella.'

Kate paused to organize her thoughts. 'So why not lay your cards on the table? Tell them what you're considering and ask for one more week of time off. After that, you'll come back to work with the intention of remaining permanently. *Or* you'll tell them you'll stay only long enough to hire and train another chef to assist Bernadette. That way you can be true to yourself without leaving your family in the lurch.'

Eric remained quiet as he deveined shrimp after shrimp with an expert's precision. 'That makes sense. I'll talk to my sister and dad tonight to see what they think, but I still can't promise to go on the retreat. I can't leave unless I can cover my position in the kitchen. I'm sure my dad is exhausted.'

'But will you seriously try?' Kate held her colander of shrimp under cold water.

Eric washed his hands of shrimp entrails and wrapped an arm around her shoulder. 'You bet I will. I've only seen you in a swimsuit a handful of times. Is it a pink bikini with white polka dots?'

She chuckled. 'Don't be ridiculous. It's a one-piece racing suit like those worn by professional athletes. And I have a matching swim shirt which I seldom take off.'

'Let's hope my family agrees and for plenty of stifling hot weather.' He kissed the top of her head. 'Now get out of here and let me work. Bella has plenty of reservations for tonight.'

'Thank you, Eric. If your ducks line up, be ready to go Saturday morning with every kind of clothes and footwear. Nate said we should be prepared for anything.'

'Should I bring my Swiss Army knife and Maglite?' he asked.

'Absolutely bring them.' Kate dried her hands and padded across the tile floor in a kitchen that smelled of garlic, rosemary, basil, and grilled onions. She loved the aroma of Italian food. And she loved the family who owned the restaurant. And, most

of all, she loved one man of Italian heritage more than life
itself. So whether Eric would be able to get away or not, she
would behave like a mature adult.

For the next few hours Kate finished unpacking and then
answered every email, one by one. She sent her new best friend
and mentor, Beth Preston, a full update on where she stood
with the retreat. Beth had trained Kate to be a PI after she had
trained Michael, who ended up becoming her new husband.
Truth be told, Michael had been a lot easier to mold than she
had been. But all that was behind them. During this getaway,
she would get to know Beth and Michael better, in addition to
the boss and his wife, Isabelle. And Kate would finally meet
Nicki Price, Nate's cousin, who also worked for the agency.
Nicki, who hailed from a small town in Mississippi, had married
a stockbroker from a very rich, very old New Orleans family.
Kate couldn't wait to meet her since, according to Nate, Nicki
had been worse than her when she first started.

Promptly at nine o'clock, Kate refreshed her makeup, put on
a dress, and headed downstairs. After the last reservation had
been served, the Manfredi clan always sat down to a family-
style dinner in the kitchen, while the wait staff executed their
duties with customary precision. Then the night staff would
clean the kitchen and dining rooms from top to bottom. When
Kate stepped off the bottom rung, everyone was already clus-
tered around the table, chatting and wearing nothing but smiles.

'A pleasure to see you again, Miss Weller,' murmured Irena
Manfredi in her cultured Milanese voice. Warming up to Kate
had taken Eric's mother some time, but nevertheless she'd finally
done so.

'Welcome back, Kate,' boomed the patriarch, Alfonzo
Manfredi. 'You'll be happy to hear I haven't been accused of
any capital crimes while you've been gone.' Alfonzo lifted a
glass of well-aged red wine in salute.

'Thank you, Mr and Mrs Manfredi. I'm grateful that the
upstairs suite was still available.' Kate took her place next to
Eric, who was grinning like a recent lottery winner.

'Ach, so what if I had to kick out a great-nephew doing
postgraduate work?' Alfonzo filled a glass with wine and handed
it to Kate. 'That boy needs to stand on his own two feet.'

Aghast, she peered up at Eric for confirmation.

'Worry not, my sweet.' Eric slid his arm around her waist. 'My cousin had already decided to move in with his girlfriend. A win-win, I'd say.'

'Welcome back, Kate,' greeted Bernadette, entering the kitchen from the back door. Eric's sister usually went home to change clothes and pick up her husband and daughter, Danielle, before eating dinner. 'My brother is never quite right in the head when you're not around.'

'Aunt Kate!' Danielle pushed her uncle aside and locked both arms around Kate's waist. 'I'm so glad to see you. I need *somebody* on my side.'

'If I even hear the words "spring break" once at this table, young lady, I'll drag you to the car by your hair.' Bernadette gritted out the words through clenched teeth.

Everyone at the table except Danielle and her parents laughed.

Kate hugged the seventeen-year-old fondly. 'I'll do my best,' she whispered. 'Good to see all three of you.' She nodded at the parents over Danielle's head.

'Enough of the hellos already!' Nonni approached the table with a steaming platter of food. 'The veal parmesan is done, and the pasta with a Portobello mushroom sauce is getting cold. Everyone, sit down and eat!'

Whenever Nonni speaks, everyone listens . . . and eventually abides by her wishes. Unlike American culinary customs, salad came *after* both the pasta course and the entrée. But because it was an ordinary Wednesday with family, Nonni served the pasta along with the entrée. A huge bowl of salad sat within easy reach for those who wished to partake early.

'Did you miss the merry band of lunatics?' Eric asked next to Kate's ear.

'You bet I did,' she whispered. 'You have no idea what family means to someone who's lived without one for a long time.' Kate passed her plate to Alfonzo for a piece of veal. He then passed her plate to Nonni who loaded it with pasta.

Eric looked at her for a long moment. 'I have taken my family for granted,' he said in a clear voice. 'Thank you for reminding me. Welcome back, Kate.' He lifted his glass of red wine in salute.

Everyone at the table did the same. 'Welcome back,' they chimed.

Kate hadn't meant for her true confession to go public. Speechlessly, she took a sip of Chianti, but couldn't taste it. She stared at a burn mark in the table from when the family had allowed relatives to smoke inside the kitchen. Then everyone started eating and talking, and Kate's embarrassing moment passed.

That night before she fell asleep in a remarkably comfortable bed, Kate whispered a short prayer as sounds of the city drifted in on the breeze: 'Thank you for bringing me back to Charleston. And please don't let me mess things up with Eric again.'

Friday p.m.

Kate rechecked everything in her suitcase for the third time. She'd packed shorts, tank tops, T-shirts, jeans, long-sleeved sweatshirts, and three silky dresses in case they were expected to dress up for dinner, along with sneakers, hiking boots, flip-flops, and one pair of high-heeled sandals. She then added two bathing suits, cover-ups, sunblock, sunglasses, and bug spray, along with her regular toiletries, makeup, and hairdryer. Before she zipped the bulging bag closed, she tossed in several paper-back mysteries and a magazine, just in case she couldn't sleep. Kate debated whether or not she should take her handgun. *Who in their right mind takes a weapon on vacation?* But her mentor, Beth Preston, insists that anyone licensed to carry like they were should go nowhere unarmed. So into her purse went the gun with an extra clip of ammo. After all, the world had become an increasingly dangerous place.

Unlike the other private investigators in the agency, Kate had no one to notify regarding her vacation destination. Her brother remained incarcerated in Santa Rosa Correctional in Florida, and her last foster mother had her hands full with the current group of kids. So after checking her email for any last-minute instructions, Kate set her bag by the door and stretched out for a few minutes of relaxation. Tomorrow she and Eric would head to St Simons for seven fun-filled days and nights. Since arriving back home, Eric had worked non-stop to make sure Bella

Trattoria would run smoothly in his absence. Kate hadn't been around when Eric told his family about the company retreat, which was probably a good thing. Alfonzo had insisted on helping Bernadette in the kitchen, despite his wife's concern for his health. And tonight, after the last customer had been served, Eric promised her a quiet dinner for just the two of them. Kate didn't care if they ate outside in the shaded courtyard or down the street at a burger joint, just as long as they had a few minutes by themselves.

Just as Kate started to doze off, the jangle of her cell phone woke her up. 'Hi, Eric,' she greeted, spotting caller ID. 'Why didn't you just holler up the steps if you needed my help?'

'Because I'm not down in the kitchen, sweet thing.'

Hearing the forced calmness in his voice sent a shiver up Kate's spine. She bolted upright and swung her legs over the side of the bed. 'Then where are you?'

'I'm checking on my sister at Roper Hospital. Bernadette called me from the ambulance because Michael went to Columbia on business.'

A rather selfish thought popped into Kate's head, but she did her best to squash it. 'How is she and what the heck happened?'

'Right now I don't know because the doctors are still examining her. Soon they will send her upstairs for a CAT scan or some X-rays.' Eric exhaled a weary sigh. 'Somebody mugged my sister in the church parking lot, of all places. Bernadette had been dropping off meals for the homeless when some . . . miscreant hit her on the head, pushed her to the ground, and took off with her purse.' His voice rose in volume with each word.

'Oh, Eric, that is just awful,' Kate murmured. 'Want me to sit and wait with you? Isn't Roper Hospital over on Calhoun?'

Eric thought for a moment before answering. 'What I really need is for you to help my dad and Nonni in the kitchen. I already called Aunt Estelle, our pastry chef, to come in for tonight, but it'll take time for her to get downtown.'

The last of Kate's fog vanished. 'You really think I could help in a four-star restaurant? My repertoire of recipes consists of mac-and-cheese from a blue box and tomato soup from a can.'

'Not to worry, my parents will probably just have you clean vegetables and fix salads. Uh-oh, one of the doctors just walked out of Bernadette's exam room. I want to catch him before he heads into another room.'

'Sure, Eric, you can count on me.' Kate tried to sound convincing.

'I know I can. Thanks, Kate. Tonight I'll make *your* dinner extra special.' Then he hung up without another word.

Kate went into the bathroom to wash her face and hands and then headed downstairs. That evening as she scrubbed carrots and cucumbers, chopped celery, grated onions, and artistically arranged heirloom greens on chilled plates for Bella Trattoria customers, Kate had to force away thoughts of tomorrow so many times that she finally concluded she was hopelessly self-centered. Irena Manfredi showed up at six to take over grilling and sautéing duties. Alfonzo manned the five different saucepots, each made fresh every day. Nonni boiled each order of pasta to *al dente* perfection, while Aunt Estelle handled steamed vegetables and appetizers. All in all, dinner for tonight's reservations was pulled off with only a few minor glitches.

When Eric walked in around nine o'clock with his niece trailing behind him, everyone felt exhausted but proud of what they had accomplished. The last two hours had been so hectic without the head and sous chefs that everyone briefly forgot why those two weren't there. But one glance at Eric's tight and drawn face brought everyone back to reality.

Irena Manfredi was the first to speak. 'What is it, son? How is Bernadette?'

'She'll be fine, Ma.' Eric slumped into a chair at the table next to his niece. 'The CAT scan showed a small concussion, but no major head injury. She has cuts, scrapes, bruising, and one chipped tooth, but Bernadette will be discharged tomorrow and should make a complete recovery. Before I left the hospital, the police called to say they found her purse with credit cards and driver's license in the church dumpster. Apparently the thief only wanted cash and her cell phone.' Briefly, Eric let his gaze flicker over Kate, who'd had the sense to take off her stained white apron at the sink.

'Thank God,' said Nonni, Irena, and Aunt Estelle in unison, followed by a simultaneous sign of the cross.

Danielle lifted her sleepy head off the table long enough to add, 'Mom was mostly upset about her favorite casserole dish getting smashed and her dinner going to waste.'

Irena wrapped her slender arms around her granddaughter and nuzzled the top of her blonde head. 'Casserole dishes can be easily replaced, but people cannot be. After we eat, would you like to come home tonight with me and Papa?'

'Thanks, Granny, but Uncle Eric already called my dad. He's on his way back from Columbia. Dad plans to spend the night in the chair in Mom's room. He's coming to get me first thing in the morning, so I'd better stay here.'

'As you wish, *amour mio*.' Irena kissed the top of the girl's head before she walked to the stove to check the simmering sauces. 'It's time for this family to eat and then get some rest. Al, would you pour the wine and iced tea? Estelle, please re-rinse the last batch of pasta that Nonni cooked.' Irena spoke with dignity and a matriarch's authority, now that Nonni had fixed a plate and retired to her room, exhausted.

Eric pushed to his feet. 'Thank you, Mama, but I promised Kate we would dine *al fresco* tonight.' To her, he said, 'Kate, would you carry the wine outdoors while I reheat our dinners?'

Kate didn't have to be asked twice. As her fatigue vanished, she picked up two full glasses and headed for the back door. Over her shoulder she heard one of the waiters say: 'Go with Miss Weller, Mr Manfredi. I'll deliver your dinners as soon as they are warm.'

Eric also didn't have to be told twice. Once outside on the flagstone patio, he slumped in a chair and downed half his glass of Pinot Grigio. 'I'm so sorry, Kate,' he whispered in the waning moonlight. A warm breeze stirred the trees, dropping leaves and spent flowers around their table.

Kate took a tiny sip of wine. 'Sorry for what, exactly?'

'For sticking you with my family in the kitchen tonight when you'd expected a romantic evening before our big trip.'

Kate took another sip and swallowed hard. 'Do you think the retreat on St Simons is still possible?' she asked in a barely audible voice.

'It definitely is for you, sweet girl, and maybe even for me.'
Eric took another swallow of wine. 'Bernadette insists she is
fine and wants us to go. But even if she comes home tomorrow
and rests on Sunday when the restaurant is closed, the earliest
she can return to work is Monday. And that means only standing
over her husband's shoulder and directing everything he does.
I spoke to Michael on the way home. He's taking a week off
to be with his family.'

They both leaned back from the table as their dinners were
delivered on a silver tray, including salads, slices of tiramisu,
and another bottle of wine. The young waiter also brought a
silver candlestick and then lit the taper with a flourish.

'Thank you, Jason,' said Eric. 'Now get on home to your
family.'

'You got it. Goodnight, sir, ma'am.' The young waiter pulled
off his apron and headed for the parking lot.

Eric and Kate leaned over their plates and breathed in
the lemony aroma of chicken piccata over linguini.

'Eat, Kate, before the food gets cold,' he said. 'You must be
starving.'

'Don't be silly. For every baby carrot I washed, I popped
one in my mouth.' Kate's reply was more truth than jest. 'Finish
telling me about the situation with your sister.' Kate swirled
some linguini around her fork.

Eric cut into his tender chicken breast and sampled a bite.
'I think you should join your cohorts tomorrow as planned.
You can explain to everyone what happened here with my
sister. Then tell them that I hope to join you on Sunday or
Monday at the latest, once I'm certain the restaurant can
manage without Bernadette being at one hundred percent.' He
forked up a larger piece of chicken. 'This is quite good, don't
you think?'

Kate set down her wine glass and swallowed a bite of her
cutlet. 'It's wonderful,' she declared, 'like every dish served at
Bella Trattoria. You might be able to leave as early as Sunday?'

'Maybe. Everything depends on how my sister feels and if
my mother will allow Dad another week in the kitchen.'

'Your father loves to cook.' Kate swirled another forkful
of pasta.

'I know he does, but Mom wants him to slow down. You know . . . smell the roses she grows instead of Portobello mushroom sauce all day long.' Eric refilled their glasses from the new bottle.

'This wine is really good,' she said after one sip. 'Is this from upstate New York or Napa Valley, California?' she teased, knowing Eric drank only Italian wine.

Eric grinned over the rim of his wine glass. 'I adore your sense of humor, Kate. And I adore you. Go meet your friends and have a great time. I'll be there before you have a chance to miss me.'

She set down her fork and dabbed her mouth. 'And I adore you, Mr Manfredi. If you can't leave until Sunday, that's when we'll both go. If we must wait until Monday, so be it. I'm not abandoning you.'

He laughed. 'Bella Trattoria is not the *Titanic*.'

'I know, but I've made up my mind, so don't think about trying to change it.' Kate picked up her knife and fork and attacked the chicken in earnest. 'Goodness, Eric, who made this piccata? I believe it tastes even better than yours.' She chewed slowly to savor the delicate blend of herbs and spices.

Eric growled low in his throat. 'You shall pay dearly for that comment, Miss Weller. You won't know where or when, but you shall pay.'

'Do I look worried?' Kate leaned back in her chair and sipped her wine. 'Let's not finish dinner too quickly. We want the dishes already done and the kitchen clean when we carry our plates inside.'

'Spoken like a true Bella Trattoria salad girl.' He lifted his glass in salute. 'I truly do want to attend this retreat with you. We'll leave the moment I feel my responsibilities are covered.'

Kate smiled, knowing that he meant what he said and that she'd made the right choice. After all, what's a getaway without your significant other? Just another work meeting.

TWO

St Simons Island, Georgia. Saturday a.m.

'Why on earth are you pacing back and forth?' asked Isabelle Price. 'You told people to be here between noon and one and it's barely eleven thirty.'

'I'm not worried about the time. I'm just plain . . . excited.' Nate lowered himself to the arm of the sofa in his friend's comfortable condo. 'This is a once-in-a-lifetime opportunity, not usually offered to ordinary folks like us.'

Isabelle pushed to her feet. 'I don't understand why we can't remain exactly where we are for the retreat. Your friend offered his condo for the week while he's in Europe, and St Simons offers everything vacationers want – beaches, great restaurants, shopping, a historic lighthouse, and a bike trail all around the island. You can rent paddleboards and anything else here too.'

'But the condo only has three bedrooms and two bathrooms for four couples.'

'I don't mind if we slept on the pullout couch.' Izzy ran her fingers through his hair.

'That means anyone who's raiding the refrigerator or heading to the pool at midnight must walk by my snoring and you talking in your sleep.'

'I do *not* talk in my sleep,' Isabelle pulled on his earlobe.

'OK, just my snoring then.' Nate winked at his wife. 'I agree there's nothing wrong with St Simons and I'm very grateful to John for letting us come. But Mr Frazier invited us to his *private* island a couple of days ago. We'll have the run of his mansion with private rooms, all meals and drinks, plus his butler, chef, and housekeeper at our disposal for five nights. Mr Frazier has skeet-shooting for his guests, bicycles and horses to ride on the trails, and a pristine beach. Then we'll come back to St Simons for the last two days to recover from all that non-stop luxury.' Nate decided to turn the argument around. 'Why *don't* you want to go to Elysian Island? On a clear day you can see Mr Frazier's island from the top of the lighthouse.'

Izzy took a turn at pacing the room. 'Because I don't like being inaccessible while our son is with a babysitter. St Simons is connected to the mainland by a causeway, but the only way to get to Elysian is on his private yacht. There's no regular ferry boat going back and forth.'

Nate held his ground. 'I still don't see the problem. Our babysitter is Maxine, my secretary, and someone we would both trust with our lives. Maxine can handle any emergency that comes up. And she already promised to check in regularly on our cell phones.'

'You have never met this Mr Frazier or seen this Elysian Island.' Izzy rested one hand on her hip.

'I've never been to Monte Carlo either, but I'd bet a C-note the place is rather elegant.'

She laughed. 'Let's see this C-note you would so recklessly wager.'

Nate put his hands on her waist and smiled. 'Mr Frazier is a friend of Mr and Mrs Baer, the couple we met on vacation in Mobile. Remember them?'

'Oh, when you heroically chased down a purse-snatcher and returned the purse to the rightful owner?' Izzy squeezed his upper arm. 'Show me your muscle, Popeye.'

'Joke all you want, but Mrs Baer has referred plenty of her rich friends to our agency. For that I'm grateful.' Nate headed to the refrigerator for a Coke. 'If Mrs Baer talked so highly of us that Mr Frazier invited the agency to his island, he can't be some kind of nutcase.'

'I'm sure he isn't, but he must want something in return. Entertaining and feeding eight adults won't be cheap.'

'Money is less important to those who have tons than to folks like us.' Nate gulped a mouthful of Coke and set down the can. 'But there is one little thing he wants us to do,' he added.

Izzy, who'd been watching the driveway from the window, marched to where he stood. 'You tell me right now what he wants, Nathan Price. There will be no wife-swapping, bug-eating or being locked in a shark cage underwater!'

Nate shook his head. 'You should stop watching all that

reality TV, but don't worry, it's nothing like that. Mrs Baer said Frazier loves those mystery dinner theatres and he's written his own skit. His employees will perform various roles for our benefit during dinner or maybe over the course of five days. I'm not sure about the timeframe. The Price team has to figure whodunnit in his murder mystery.'

Her mouth dropped open. 'That's it? I love those kinds of dramas. Our local high school sponsors them all the time, but you never want to go.'

'As far as I know, that's it. But no matter how lame his game is, we'd better play our parts well. I don't want Frazier to think we're unappreciative of his generosity.' Nate cocked his head to listen to sounds outside. 'Finally, the first of my agents is here. Let the games begin.'

Nate swept open the door to his cousin, Nicki, and her husband, Hunter Galen, a stockbroker from New Orleans.

'Hey, boss, what's up?' Nicki waltzed into the room in a cloud of expensive perfume and headed straight to Isabelle. With her long auburn hair hanging in stylish curls down her back, this was a much different look from the day Nate had hired her right from PI school. 'Hey, Izzy, who's got your monster for the week?' Nicki asked. 'I practically had to *pay* my mother-in-law to take Evangeline-the-evil for that long. And Clotilde Galen has a staff of household help.' As first-time mothers, they were both figuring things out by trial-and-error and a shelf full of baby books.

'Sit here and tell me all about it.' Izzy handed Nicki a glass of lemonade.

Nate met Hunter's gaze. 'Evangeline-the-*evil*?' he asked, lifting an eyebrow.

Hunter straightened his spine. 'I have no idea to whom my beloved refers. *My* daughter is a perfect angel sent from heaven. I'm not aware of Evie committing a single misdeed.' He turned away to hide his grin. 'Say, Nate. You got anything stronger than lemonade to drink? It was a *long* drive to the Eastern Seaboard with my wife, your cousin.'

'Follow me and we'll find something,' Nate said, heading toward the kitchen. 'Nicki and Izzy will be comparing motherhood notes for a while.'

Forty-five minutes later, Beth and Michael Preston, presently running Nate's Savannah office, knocked at the door.

'It figures that people who live the closest would be last to arrive!' he barked, feigning annoyance. 'You two only live an hour and twenty minutes away.'

'You mean Kate and Eric are already here?' Beth slipped past him in the doorway. 'That Kate will be late to her own funeral.'

'No, but they have a good excuse. Eric can't leave until his sister gets out of the hospital and can replace him in the restaurant. Kate still thinks they will join us, but she doesn't know when.'

'I sure hope so,' said Beth. 'If anybody needs a corporate retreat, it's my protégée. Although I trained her, Kate doesn't always go by the book.' Laughing, she slapped her husband on the back.

'How ya doin', Michael?' Nate asked, extending his hand. 'Or maybe I should ask how's married life with Beth?' Although not as handy with a firearm as his wife, Michael was the agency's forensic accountant. The guy could follow a money trail all the way back to Louis the Fifteenth of France. And since hiring a personal trainer, he could hold his own in hand-to-hand combat.

Michael shook Nate's hand with gusto. 'I'm great, and so is life with Beth. Her bark is so much worse than her bite. We're both looking forward to the vacation. Thanks for the invite.'

'You're welcome. Why not pour yourself something to drink in the kitchen? Then you and Hunter can join us in here.'

Once Michael and Hunter returned with drinks and joined their wives, Nate cleared his throat to get everyone's attention. 'As I told you in my email, I have a special surprise to announce once everyone arrived. You know Kate and Eric will meet us as soon as possible.'

'What happened to Eric's sister?' Beth interrupted.

'She got mugged in her church parking lot and suffered a minor concussion, besides cuts and scrapes. Eric wants to make sure she's well enough to at least supervise the kitchen.'

'A person can't go anywhere these days and feel safe!' muttered Nicki.

'That's why I keep my *little friend* very close.' Beth patted her pant leg where a small Beretta was usually strapped to her ankle.

'That will change once a toddler starts crawling all over you.' Isabelle pointed a finger at Beth's shin, while Nicki heartily agreed.

Nate's focus rotated between his cousin and his wife. 'Getting back to my surprise . . . this condo belongs to an old friend of mine, John Manderly, who's in Europe for a couple weeks.'

'Hip, hip, hooray for John,' said Michael, lifting his can of beer.

'Hip, hip, hooray,' everyone chorused.

'Yes, and as grateful as I am to him, I've been presented with an even better offer for our company retreat.'

Utter silence fell in the room. From the corner of his eye, Nate saw Izzy wringing her hands in her lap.

'What kind of better opportunity?' asked Nicki. Even as a child, she was always the most skeptical of the Price clan.

'Have any of you heard of Elysian Island?' Nate produced his most enthusiastic facial expression.

Nicki, Beth and Michael each shook their head no, as did his wife, even though Nate just told Izzy about the place thirty minutes ago.

'I've heard of it.' Hunter set his empty glass on the table. 'Years ago the place was a playground for the rich and famous . . . or infamous, in some cases. Julian Frazier and his wife used to host celebrity weddings, swimsuit photoshoots, and wild parties that rivaled something from an F. Scott Fitzgerald novel. Lately, the only people invited to step onto his dock are serious poker players.'

Nate jumped to his feet. 'Have you met Mr Frazier?'

Hunter chuckled with amusement. 'No, my notoriety doesn't extend beyond the Big Easy. And the only poker I play is for nickels with my grandmother. I heard this from one of my clients. He told me the buy-in at one of these poker games is half a million. Frazier sends his yacht to pick up invited guests at prearranged rendezvous times. Then no one can leave the island until Frazier decides the game is over.'

'Are poker games even legal in the state of Georgia?' asked Nicki.

Nate frowned. 'I have no idea, but high-stakes poker, legal or otherwise, has nothing to do with us. Mr Frazier has graciously invited my agents and their spouses to his exclusive private island.'

'How much will this cost you, boss?' asked Beth.

'Nothing. Now if you would stop interrupting, I will explain.' Nate glared around the living room. Chastised, Beth shrank down in her chair. Nicki looked confused and Hunter amused. 'Mr Frazier is a good friend of Mrs Baer, that woman from Atlanta who recommends our agency to everyone she meets. And her acquaintances have become some of our best clients.'

'So Frazier wishes to hire your agency?' Hunter placed both hands on his wife's shoulders.

'No, he's offering us full use of his island in exchange for participating in one of those mystery plays. We must solve the crime that his staff will present during dinner.'

'I love those kinds of parties,' Beth exclaimed, forgetting her earlier admonishment.

'And that's it?' asked Hunter. 'That's all Frazier wants from us?'

'That's it. Plus Mr Frazier said the first person to solve the mystery wins a prize.'

Nicki leaned forward on the couch. 'Why can't we just stay here? From what I've seen so far, St Simons Island looks adorable. This way, if Evangeline gets sick or falls on her head, we can jump in our car and drive back to Louisiana. I don't like depending on someone else's yacht to bring me back to dry land.'

Isabelle walked to Nate's side and wrapped an arm around him. But instead of supporting his position, she sided with Nicki. 'I said the same exact thing, Nic. How could we quickly get off an island in an emergency?' Izzy fixed him with her green eyes.

'Good grief. Doesn't anybody see this as the chance of a lifetime? Along with all meals and drinks, Frazier offered us horseback riding, parasailing, deep-sea fishing, and paddleboards at no charge. We would have to shell out plenty for those activities on St Simons.'

Michael Preston lifted his hand. 'I'm game, boss. Beth and I are still broke from our wedding.'

Beth slapped his upraised palm with a high-five. 'If you're going, I am going too.'

Nate reserved his best argument for last. 'This condo is very nice and I'm grateful to John, but there are only three bedrooms and two bathrooms for four couples.'

Hunter stopped scrolling through his phone long enough to comment. 'That won't work if all women take as long as my wife in the bathroom. Besides, I found something that might change Nicki's and Izzy's mind. The Jacksonville airport has helicopters available twenty-four/seven. I could hire a pilot and helicopter if an emergency comes up. How does that sound?' He kissed the top of Nicki's head.

'In that case, I'm in.' Nicki smiled up at him. 'I've always wanted to ride a horse along the beach.'

'The agency will pick up the cost of the helicopter,' Nate offered.

'Absolutely not.' Hunter slashed his hand through the air. 'I've got this should the need arise.'

'Thank you. That's very generous.' Isabelle visibly began to relax. 'Do you think Kate and Eric will like the idea?'

Nate refilled his glass with lemonade from the pitcher. 'I know they will. Since Eric's from Charleston, he may have heard of Elysian Island. Plus, we'll be back here for the last two nights of our vacation. So anyone who wants to go shopping will have a chance. By the way, there are no stores, restaurants or pharmacies on the island, so bring any meds and personal items with you.' Nate waited until everyone nodded their understanding. 'Does anyone have a food allergy that Frazier's chef should be aware of?' No one spoke. 'In that case, I'll call Mr Frazier and arrange for his yacht to pick us up later today. In the meantime, make yourself comfortable. Isabelle will set out a party tray and pizza in the kitchen for our lunch. Help yourself to anything in the fridge. We're welcome to use John's heated pool which is on the other side of those doors.' He pointed in the general direction.

When everyone began talking at once, Nate walked outside to call their host in private. Once he'd confirmed the boat would pick them up at the village pier at five, Nate called Kate. When his newest agent didn't pick up, he left a message as to where she should meet them and, finally, breathed a sigh of relief. Inside, his friends were already eating, drinking, and carrying on. So Nate went inside to make a sandwich too. After all, it should be smooth sailing from this point on.

But as fate would have it, Kate called him exactly at five o'clock, just as Frazier's yacht approached the dock.

'Any update, Weller?' Nate asked.

'Sorry, boss, we're still in Charleston. Eric and I are cooking tonight at Bella Trattoria. Eric's sister came home from the hospital and her husband is at her side, but Bernadette needs to rest today. It looks like the earliest we could get there would be Sunday evening. Should we just skip the retreat?'

Nate hesitated for a moment. 'I'm going to put you on hold, Kate, and call our host. Don't go anywhere.' Five minutes later, he hung up with Frazier's assistant and returned to Kate's call. 'Don't give up yet. Try to get to St Simons Sunday night or Monday morning. I'm texting you the address and security code to the front door of the condo. Call me as soon as you reach St Simons. Mr Frazier will send a boat back to pick you up.'

'Who's Mr Frazier – the guy who owns the condo? And why do we need a boat? According to my map, there's a causeway to the island.'

Nate spotted a well-dressed man waving impatiently on the gangway. 'Plans have changed. The retreat will be on Elysian Island, owned by Mr Frazier. It's off the coast of St Simons. I'll explain more when I see you. Just remember to call me.' As the boat's captain gunned the engine, Nate hung up and climbed aboard.

Kate was a smart girl. She would figure things out.

'I apologize for rushing you, Mr Price, but Mr Frazier is a stickler for schedules.' The well-dressed man bowed low. 'I'm Mr Compton, butler to Julian Frazier. We'll arrive on Elysian in less than thirty minutes. In the meantime, please join the others in the salon for refreshments.'

Nate ducked his head and entered the boat's main cabin, where uniformed maids were filling glasses with champagne and passing round trays of canapés. Already the voices of his employees had ratcheted up a level. Accepting a flute of sparkling wine, Nate slipped into the booth with his wife.

'Check out the label on the bottles. These bubbles are the real thing from Fer-rance.' Izzy pronounced the name of the country as though it had two syllables.

'Like we don't drink the stuff every Friday night with pizza.' Nate took a sip and clinked her glass.

Beth slid into the other side of the booth with a plate of hors d'oeuvres. 'I don't know if these are mini lobster tails or big shrimps.' She held up a prawn on a skewer.

'I'll let you ladies figure out the food. Since I'm not hungry I want to find the captain.' Nate followed a narrow hallway from the salon to the prow, where a circular staircase led to the pilot house. Inside he found Michael and Hunter with stools pulled up next to the captain.

'Hey, boss,' said Michael, sounding very young. 'Isn't this boat gorgeous?'

'How do you do, Mr Price. I'm Captain Mike Burke, retired from Her Majesty's Royal Navy and now a proud citizen of Georgia.' He doffed his cap.

'I'm fine. Pleased to meet you.' Nate pulled up a third stool. 'Looks like you found a great second career.'

'Not bad at all, sir.' Burke winked, deepening the wrinkles around his eyes. 'That's Elysian Island straight ahead. We'll be arriving within the quarter-hour.'

'I'm just curious. Will this boat head back or remain docked on the island?'

'The *Slippery Eel* will head back since I live on St Simons. But rest assured, I'm only a phone call away if Mr Frazier or anyone else needs us.' Burke made eye contact with each of them in succession.

'Gentlemen, champagne?' A woman in a short dress entered the pilot house with a tray of flutes.

No maid's uniform on the topside help, Nate thought as he reached for a glass. *How did a man like Frazier become this rich?* Nate studied the island as they approached at a slight angle. He saw no sandy beaches for swimming or riding horses. In fact, he saw no beach at all. The pier had been anchored between two giant boulders amidst a rocky shoreline. Beyond the rocks loblolly pines shot skyward, interspersed with vine-shrouded oaks and stunted palmetto palms. All in all, the island from this vantage point looked inhospitable.

'Looks like I brought my arm blow-ups and sand bucket for nothing,' muttered Michael.

Captain Burke smiled. 'Don't worry, sir. Like so many people, this island has two faces. You'll find calm water and a pristine beach with white sand on the other side.'

'Then drink up, gentlemen, and let's join our better halves.' Hunter Galen drained his flute and set it on a ledge, like the aristocrat he was. Nate and Michael, however, carried theirs below.

As the group queued to disembark, Izzy whispered next to his ear. 'Nicki said the island looks haunted.'

'My cousin should never drink champagne,' Nate grumbled. 'It feeds Nicki's already overactive imagination. This island will be spectacular.'

'Please, madam, we'll get your luggage.'

When Nate and Izzy turned around, they saw the butler wrestling with Beth over the handle of her suitcase.

'I assure you, it will be delivered to your room,' the butler insisted.

Michael Preston walked up to Beth and whispered something in her ear. Immediately, Beth released the handle and caught up to Nate and Izzy.

'What did Michael say to you?' asked Izzy, laughing uncontrollably.

'That we should act like we've been outside of Natchez before.' Then Beth broke into peals of laughter too.

'And why shouldn't we?' Michael locked his arms around his bride. 'We live in the cultured city of Savannah now.'

Nate watched the butler step from the gangway to the dock and turn to address them. 'Heads up, everyone,' he called.

Compton cleared his throat. 'On behalf of Mr Frazier and the entire staff, welcome to Elysian Island. If I – or anyone in my employ – can help to make this vacation memorable, do not hesitate to ask. Now if you will follow me, we'll continue the cocktail hour in the library. This will give the staff time to deliver luggage to your quarters so you can change for dinner.

Mr Frazier looks forward to making your acquaintance in the grand dining room tonight.'

'Excuse me, Mr Compton?' Hunter stepped out of the crowd. 'I hope Mr Frazier isn't expecting black-tie, because we just learned of the change in plans this afternoon.'

'Of course not, Mr Galen. A pair of Dockers with a collared shirt will suffice. Then after tonight, the dress code will be . . . anything goes.' The butler smiled indulgently.

Hand in hand, Nate and Izzy followed Compton down the dock toward an opening in the rocks. From there a narrow path led into the maritime forest. Noticing that Hunter was right behind him, Nate asked over his shoulder, 'Did you notice the butler already knew your name?'

'I caught that,' Hunter replied. 'So Frazier *assumed* your agents and spouses would agree to the change in plans.'

'Let's keep our eyes wide open.' Nate spoke very softly.

'That was my gut feeling too.' Hunter smiled and then dropped back to Nicki's side.

After twenty minutes of ducking under low branches and tripping over roots, the path opened onto a wide expanse of lawn with flower gardens and fruit trees. French doors opened onto flagstone terraces on the ground floor, while rooms on the second floor had wrought-iron balconies overlooking the gardens. A trellised pergola draped with grapevines covered a long table complete with lace linens and giant candelabras. All in all, Nate had never seen a sight so welcoming.

'Wow,' murmured several of his employees.

'You're not kidding – wow,' Nate agreed.

'Wouldn't this be the perfect wedding venue?' Izzy asked to no one in particular.

'This would be the perfect venue for anything,' Nicki agreed. 'Showers, graduations, even a little girl's birthday party. Couldn't you just imagine pony rides on the lawn?'

'Easy, dear wife. New Orleans is a long way from the Atlantic coast.'

Nicki grabbed his hand. 'Come on, Hunter, stop dragging your feet! Let's catch up to the others.'

Mr Compton guided them into a three-story reception area with an Italian marble floor and a cut-crystal chandelier overhead. From a closet, well concealed in the paneling, the butler pulled out a wicker basket. 'Mr Frazier has one non-negotiable rule in this house,' he intoned. 'All guests must surrender any weapons upon entering.' His eyes slowly scanned each member of the Price team. 'They will be safely stored and returned to you before leaving the house.'

Nate stepped forward. 'I can assure you those employees carrying weapons are well trained and licensed to carry. There will be no accidental or reckless discharge while we're here.'

Compton's expression didn't waver. 'Be that as it may, Mr Price, the rule applies to everyone, including members of law enforcement, private investigators, and bodyguards for celebrities. Your only recourse if you can't comply is to leave the island on the same boat you arrived on.'

Without hesitation, Nate reached under his jacket, pulled the semi-automatic from his shoulder holster and placed it in the basket.

One by one, Michael and Beth did the same. When Compton's gaze fell on the Galens, Nicki opened her lacy cardigan and slowly turned in a circle. 'I never carry a weapon when I'm not working, and my husband doesn't own a gun.'

'Neither does my wife, Isabelle,' Nate added.

'In that case, honored guests, please follow me.' At a brisk pace, Compton marched down a portrait-lined hallway into a library with floor-to-ceiling bookshelves. Frazier's collection must contain at least ten thousand books.

'Did I fall asleep and wake up in *Downton Abbey*?' asked Izzy.

'You've been awake the entire time, dear heart,' murmured Nate, as uniformed maids carried in more trays of canapés, along with more champagne.

'Ah, a pitcher of water.' Izzy marched to the sideboard and filled a glass. Beth and Nicki did the same.

'If I eat another bite, I won't be able to eat dinner,' Nicki moaned. 'But I will have a touch more champagne.' She then filled three flutes.

'You're not kidding.' Beth gulped some water and picked up a flute. 'Doesn't Frazier know people are starving all over the world?'

While the women made humorous assumptions about their host, the men nibbled on canapés and nursed one drink each.

Finally Compton reappeared in the doorway. 'Again, welcome to Elysian Island. Your rooms are ready: Mr and Mrs Galen, room two-twenty-four.' He held out a skeleton key. 'Mr and Mrs Preston, room two-thirty-four.' He produced a second key for Beth and Michael. 'And Mr and Mrs Price, room one-eighteen. You may exit that way. Yours is the only suite down that hallway.' Compton pointed to a narrow door. 'Now if the Galens and Prestons would follow me, I'll take you to the main staircase where the maids will direct you to your quarters. We'll see everyone promptly at eight in the grand dining room.'

'Excuse me, Mr Compton,' said Nate. 'Were you aware that two more guests may arrive tomorrow evening?'

Compton sniffed. 'I am not your host, Mr Price. Please discuss this with Mr Frazier at dinner.' With that, Compton turned on his heel and marched the other two couples away.

Nate exchanged a look with Izzy.

'If there is a grand dining room, is there also a mediocre one?' Izzy burst into a fit of giggles.

'I'll find out, but in the meantime, no more champagne for you tonight.' Nate took his wife's hand and led her through the narrow doorway. 'This house seems to have a maze of hallways.'

'This is just like a game of Clue.' Izzy stifled another giggle as he opened the door to their suite. 'My goodness, Marie Antoinette probably didn't have accommodations so elegant.'

'And we both know what happened to that poor girl's head.'

For a minute they stood admiring the room: four-poster bed, enclosed by filmy curtains; oversized cherry-wood bureaus and armoires; bookcases filled with novels; upholstered chairs grouped around the fireplace, and in the corner a Keurig coffeemaker with every type of coffee and tea known to man. A giant fruit bowl sat on a low table, along with crackers, several cheeses, and another bottle of champagne.

Izzy plucked a grape from the bowl. 'Mr Frazier certainly doesn't want us to starve.'

'Isn't this a bit over-the-top, no?' he asked.

'No, I think the room is beautiful and our host very generous.' Izzy leaped onto the bed like a child.

Nate crossed the room to the French doors and looked out. The view took in the rose garden and tall loblolly pines in the distance. 'This might be a nice spot for morning coffee.' Yet when he tried the door to the patio, it seemed to be bolted from the outside. 'Cancel my idea for morning coffee. We can't get out.'

'Will you please relax?' Izzy slipped her arm around his waist. 'Maybe Mr Frazier hasn't used this guest suite in a while. Security is important, even on private islands.'

'You're right. No big deal.' Nate realized his attitude was less than grateful for the generous gift. 'I'll speak to him this evening about unlocking the door.'

'Good, now let's get dressed for dinner.'

He peered down. 'What's wrong with what I have on? Everything is still clean.'

'Baggy shorts?' Izzy whooshed out an exasperated breath. 'Tonight we meet our host. At least put on chinos and a nice shirt.' She dragged her suitcase to the closet and unpacked with lightning speed. When someone knocked twenty minutes later, Izzy had already refreshed her makeup and changed into a long sheath dress with very high heels.

With his hair still damp, Nate opened the door to the other four, who swarmed into the room like bees.

'Look at you, Izzy,' Beth teased, 'ready for the camera close-ups. And you clean up pretty nice, boss.'

'Thanks. Izzy made me wear these,' Nate said, pointing at his pants. But when he looked at Michael their outfits practically matched, to everyone's great amusement.

With Hunter in a sport coat and Nicki in a silk dress and heels, the Galens were downright spiffy.

Only Beth had remained casual. 'Sorry, I didn't pack any fancy duds,' she said apologetically. 'You two definitely got the biggest room and at least your windows open. Ours seemed to be nailed shut.'

Nate cranked out the casement window. 'Yeah, they open, but we sure can't get out with this iron filigree. And our patio door is barred from the outside.'

Izzy rolled her eyes. 'Then why don't we go to dinner through the hallway door?'

'I'm thinking in case of fire.' Nate tried to rattle the ironwork, to no avail.

'Our windows won't open either. I certainly hope there's no fire.' Nicki looked to her husband for assurance.

Hunter took hold of her hand. 'According to the website, this mansion has stood for a couple hundred years. I'm sure it will stand for another few nights.'

'I can't get a cell signal in here either.' Nicki extracted her phone from a tiny purse.

As the others tried to get a connection with the same result, Nate tried the phone on the bedside table. 'At least the landlines work. It's not surprising our cells don't work, considering the thickness of these stone walls and the distance from the mainland. Do you have phones in your rooms?' Nate looked from Beth to Nicki, who both nodded affirmatively. 'Then let's go down to dinner and not keep Mr Frazier waiting.'

THREE

After one wrong turn after another, Nate and Izzy led the group through a warren of hallways into the three-story foyer.

A grim-faced Compton stood at the bottom of the stairs. 'Ahh, there you are at last, Mr and Mrs Price. If you would all follow me.' He turned on his heel and marched them through a huge living room to the dining room. Opening the tall double doors, he announced in a loud voice, 'Mr and Mrs Nathan Price, Mr and Mrs Hunter Galen, and Mr and Mrs Michael Preston, sir.' Silently, the butler closed the doors behind Michael and Beth.

It took Nate a moment to spot the small, wizened man standing by the fireplace. The guy could be anywhere from seventy to ninety. When he did, he guided Izzy in that direction with the others in tow. 'Mr Frazier? Nate Price, sir, and this is my wife, Isabelle.'

'How do you do, Mr Frazier,' she said. 'Thank you for your gracious invitation.'

'I assure you, madam, the pleasure is mine.' Frazier clasped Izzy's hand between his bony fingers.

'You may call me "Izzy" if you like,' she said.

The corners of Frazier's mouth turned down. 'I wouldn't like that at all, not when the name Isabelle is so beautiful.' Dropping Izzy's hand, he stepped to the next couple in line. 'Mr and Mrs Galen, I presume?'

'Correct, sir, Hunter and Nicki.' Always the gentleman, Hunter shot his cuffs and extended his hand.

After a weak handshake, Frazier turned to Nicki. 'Is your given name "Nicole," Mrs Galen?'

'No, unfortunately, it's "Nicolette," which I no longer like since someone said it sounded like the gum to quit smoking.'

Frazier looked confused, but when the others laughed, so did he. 'Have we met, Hunter? You look so familiar.'

'I don't think so, sir. I would not have forgotten.'

Frazier stared at him a tad longer than polite behavior permitted before turning his attention to the last couple. 'And Mr and Mrs Preston, Michael and—'

'Beth,' she said, not giving him a chance to finish. 'Just Beth, not short for anything.'

Frazier let his gaze travel from the top of Beth's head down to her loafers, frowning at the plaid shirt and jeans in between.

'Sorry, sir, I didn't get the memo regarding the dress code,' she said with a broad grin.

'No worries, Mrs Preston,' he murmured while shaking Michael's hand. 'After all, this is your vacation, is it not?' Before she could respond, Frazier strode to the head of the table. 'Standing by the window is my assistant and head of security, Jonah Creery. He will be dining with us tonight.'

Creery bowed and then walked to the foot of the table.

'Shall we take our seats?' murmured Frazier. 'Isabelle, I'd like you and Nicki on my left and right. I haven't dined with women so beautiful since my late wife passed on.'

As the rest decided on where to sit, Isabelle asked quietly, 'Did your wife pass recently? I hope this visit isn't intruding on your mourning.'

'No, no, it's been quite some time, yet on certain days the wound still feels so fresh. Unfortunately, this is one of those days.'

Nicki patted the arm of their host's brocade dinner jacket. 'You have our sincere condolences.'

'Thank you, my dear.'

Frazier pushed a button on the arm of his chair and soon the double doors swung open. In strode Compton, followed by two maids carrying large trays of food. Compton poured wine, both red and white, at each place setting, while the maids filled water goblets and set serving bowls on the table. Then they stood at attention, waiting for the signal to serve the first course.

'I hope you'll forgive the informality of the dinner. This time of year, I'm operating with just a skeleton crew of staff.'

'Don't worry about not being fancy enough for us,' said Nate. 'If the food tastes as good as it smells, we're in for a treat.'

'This was my wife's favorite menu for a dinner party. She

called it Tuscan land and sea. Let's have a toast and we'll start on fish and salad.' Frazier stood and lifted his glass of white wine, then waited for the others to do the same. 'To a memorable retreat for the Price team of investigators, and may all questions be answered,' he said once everyone did the same.

There was a bevy of replies before everyone sipped and sat down. 'Hear, hear,' chimed Michael, as a maid stopped next to his chair with a platter of smoked salmon and grilled flounder. Once they finished serving the fish, they exited the room while guests passed around bowls of cold salads. Compton watched from the sideboard, ready to refill wine or water glasses as necessary. Conversation consisted mainly of praise for a particular dish, while Price employees generally ate too fast and too much, not considering the other courses yet to come.

Izzy savored another bite of flounder and leaned toward Nate. 'What a shame that Eric and Kate missed the opening night dinner, especially since the recipes honor Tuscany, the land of Eric's ancestors.'

Nate nodded in agreement. Then he noticed for the first time that the table had been set for eight, not ten. While Mr Frazier chatted with Nicki, Nate whispered his observation into Izzy's ear.

She clucked her tongue. 'Don't be ridiculous. The boat captain probably radioed ahead that Eric and Kate missed the proverbial boat. Mr Frazier takes pride in throwing a proper dinner party.'

'Unlike you and me who set out a cooler of Cokes and call for pizza delivery?' Nate wiggled his eyebrows at her.

His common-sense wife smiled and refocused on her food.

Nate took another sip of delicious wine but waved off any attempt to refill his glass. He and Izzy seldom indulged in spirits. Thus, when they did, the effect was usually sudden and dramatic.

Soon Compton ushered in the maids carrying platters of veal cutlets and chicken in a white sauce. Cold salads were removed from the table, replaced by rosemary potatoes, creamed spinach, and an herbed rotini. Again Compton refilled glasses, in some cases while guests weren't looking. Beth and Nicki had to be on their third glasses of wine, not counting any consumed before reaching the dining room. Although neither Michael nor Hunter seemed to be concerned, Hunter was still nursing his first glass of white wine and had refused to switch to red. At least Nate would have one sober companion to solve Frazier's mystery game.

As though the man sensed his apprehension, Hunter cleared his throat, an action which usually commanded the floor. 'I haven't tasted food this delicious in quite some time, Mr Frazier, and we are all grateful.'

'What are you trying to say?' Nicki asked with the smallest of slurs. 'I've been doing all the cooking at home lately.' Even half-in-her-cups, Nicki still managed to look adorable.

Hunter picked up her hand and kissed the back of her fingers. 'Don't be offended, my love. That's not what I meant at all. I'm simply eager for Mr Frazier to introduce the players in tonight's mystery before all that . . . fresh sea air catches up with us.' He pecked Nicki on the cheek and turned his attention to Frazier.

Nate focused on their host too, thinking that if he lived to be a hundred, he would never be as smooth as Hunter.

Frazier, who'd picked at his food all evening, set his knife and fork on the edge of his plate. 'I'd planned to introduce the players over dessert and brandy . . . or coffee for those who prefer.'

'Dessert?' Beth yelped. 'I definitely should have saved room. I'm stuffed to the gills.'

Frazier angled a short but pointed glare in Beth's direction. 'Yes, Mrs Preston, dessert usually follows a meal, but feel free to abstain if that be your desire.' He turned to Nate. 'I'm surprised, Mr Price. Our mutual friend, Mrs Baer, described you as the most gracious of gentlemen with a professional team of investigators. Yet this dinner feels like I'm hosting a sorority or fraternity party.'

The room instantly grew quiet.

Beth flushed to a bright shade of pink. 'I beg your pardon. I didn't mean to—'

But Nate cut her off. 'With all due respect, Mr Frazier, you have practically poured alcohol down our throats since your yacht arrived on St Simons. That might not have been wise with a group of predominantly non-drinkers, if you wished to have docile guests.'

All eyes, which had been on Nate, fixed on Frazier. Almost imperceptibly, Frazier's lip twitched while a knotted cord in his neck appeared. Then, without warning, their host burst into hysterics. 'Relax, Nate. I was joking. Just trying to lighten the mood for the mystery you'll be solving this coming week.'

There was a smattering of laughter around the table, but Nate had to force his teeth to unclench. 'I think now would be a good time to explain how this mystery game works.'

'Of course.' Frazier pushed the button on his chair a second time. 'I'll have the maids bring in coffee and dessert and, as soon as everyone is served, I'll introduce the five potential clues.'

'Like the candlestick, rope and wrench in a game of Clue?' asked Izzy.

'Exactly, but one of these was used in a very real crime, a cold case from eight years ago.' Frazier's dark eyes sparkled with animation. 'Or perhaps *all* were used to commit the crime, sort of like in *Murder on the Orient Express*. It is up to you, my team of ace detectives, to decide.'

'Oh, this is going to be great fun.' Nicki rubbed her palms together.

Frazier pushed himself to his feet. 'I couldn't agree more, Mrs Galen. Now, if you'll relax for a moment, we'll return shortly.'

The maids followed their host and Mr Creery from the room. Once alone, everyone spoke in hushed tones.

'Is this guy for real?' muttered Michael.

'He's probably used to living alone in a quiet house,' offered Izzy.

'We agreed to his terms, so let's just play along,' said Beth.

'I don't think we have much choice,' Hunter muttered, locking gazes with Nate.

When Nate opened his mouth to speak, Frazier and Creery returned, with Creery carrying a serving tray which he set in the center of the table. 'Ladies and gentlemen, may I present the clues in this case.' He held up and identified each object – an iron wrench; an empty whisky bottle; a packet of white powder; a folder of file notes, and, finally, an envelope of photographs. 'You will use whatever you learn from these clues and from the potential suspects to determine the murderer. I went to great lengths to obtain these. Tonight you will be able to look but not touch the clues. Later in the week, you will be free to examine each in detail.'

Everyone scrambled to their feet and crowded around the various objects, even though they were rather ordinary in nature.

Frazier stood like a benevolent grandfather, smiling at his handiwork. 'Very good. Now if you'll take your seats, I'll introduce our cast of suspects.'

There were plenty of amusing conjectures tossed around the table by the Price employees and spouses. Nicki, Isabelle and Beth looked ready to levitate from their shoes. Michael stared at the objects with his analytical mind. Hunter simply focused on eating his raspberry cheesecake. And Nate didn't know what to think.

When Compton opened the double doors again, two armed guards in black tactile vests strode in carrying assault rifles. Behind them five people shuffled forward in leg irons with chains binding their wrists and cloths covering their mouths. Four people wore heavy black robes, while the fifth's robe was white. Before Compton closed the double doors, two more armed guards entered to complete the ensemble.

Nate sprang to his feet. 'See here, Mr Frazier. We were under the impression we were solving a *fictional* mystery. What's with the gags and restraints?'

'Again, Mr Price, I ask you to sit back and relax. The suspects are staff members who are being paid well to act their parts.'

Hunter cleared his throat. 'Even from where I'm sitting, those weapons appear to be real.'

Frazier's grin widened. 'Indeed they are, Mr Galen, but they're not loaded.'

Hunter sipped his coffee without taking his eyes off their host.

'Now, my esteemed guests, may I continue?' Frazier let his gaze land on Izzy, Nicki, and Beth in succession, and his ploy worked.

Nicki pinned Hunter with a warning glance, while Izzy squeezed Nate's upper arm. 'Please continue, Mr Frazier,' murmured Izzy. 'This will be great fun!'

'Thank you, Isabelle.' Frazier motioned to the guards who

prodded forward the first hooded person. 'This is Reuben, our first suspect.' He threw back the hood, revealing a pale, emaciated white male between thirty-five and forty years old.

The guard prodded the second player to step forward. 'This is Charles, also known as Chuck.' When Frazier flipped back the hood, a jowly, overweight male of approximately sixty-five years glared around the room with beady eyes. Nate suspected he possessed an over-fondness for alcohol, judging by his reddened nose.

When the guard prodded forward the third suspect, the thespian resisted. Only when two guards strong-armed the man front and center was Frazier able to reveal a graying blond man of approximately mid-forties. His bloodshot blue eyes flashed with hatred, primarily directed at Frazier.

'This is Bob, who seems to be in a surly mood tonight,' Frazier added with a smile.

Next the guards lifted and carried the fourth person to the forefront. When the hood was thrown back, a pair of brown eyes blinked from a dark complexion. This suspect was a woman of around forty years of age and, by Nate's estimation, didn't seem to be a willing participant.

'Ladies and gentlemen, I'd like you to meet Jennifer.' The woman struggled to no avail against her captors. 'For now our last suspect will remain faceless and nameless. One, two, or maybe all of the suspects are cold-blooded killers. It will be your job, Price employees, to discover the truth.' Frazier pivoted toward his assistant. 'Thank you, Mr Creery. You may take these talented actors back to their quarters. I'm sure they're eager for supper.'

Nate glanced around the table at everyone's expressions. Izzy and Nicki looked terrified. Beth looked confused, while Hunter appeared furious. When Nate exchanged glances with Michael, even his level-headed forensic accountant seemed just as uncomfortable as he felt. *It didn't seem like the five people were acting.* 'When will we hear the details of this cold-case murder?' he asked. 'So far, we have the possible suspects and potential clues, but we have no crime.'

Once the door closed behind the guards and actors, Frazier walked back to the group. 'That will come next.' Their host glanced at his watch. 'But it's dreadfully late now, so I will reveal details of the murder tomorrow at breakfast. Shall we meet here again, say at eight o'clock?'

Following a murmur of discontent around the table, Nate rose to his feet. 'Excuse me, sir, but we have a few concerns. Our cell phones don't seem to work here on the island.'

'Of course, they don't work,' snapped Frazier. 'We're too far from the cell towers on the mainland. But there's a working telephone in every guest's room. The landline phone cable runs underwater.'

Nate nodded. 'Thank you, sir, but could you please ask your maintenance man to unlock the doors to our patio? It would be nice to have coffee outside in the morning.'

'By all means,' Frazier said, exchanging a glance with Creery. 'I'll see that it's done first thing in the morning.'

Hunter stood and helped Nicki to her feet. 'We don't feel comfortable having the windows in our room nailed shut, just in case of an emergency.'

Frazier's eyes narrowed. 'Jumping from your window would be far more dangerous than exiting down the hall, then the staircase, and out the front door. This house is equipped with sprinklers in the unlikely event of a fire. It's hard to believe, but we've had numerous break-ins on the island, hence our heightened security measures. If there's nothing else . . .' He started for the door.

'One more thing,' said Nate. 'My other investigator, Kate, and her boyfriend, Eric, wish to join the retreat either tomorrow night or on Monday. Could you send your yacht back to pick them up on St Simons?'

'It would be my pleasure. I will speak to my yacht captain. Perhaps Captain Burke can more easily get ahold of them and set up a time to meet.'

'Thank you, Mr Frazier, for the lovely dinner . . . and everything else,' Nate added.

'You're welcome, Mr Price, agents.' With that, their host disappeared through the double doors, leaving them alone with an array of dirty dishes and uneaten desserts.

'Well, this was an interesting evening,' said Beth, rising to her feet.

'See everyone in the morning.' Michael guided Beth toward the door.

'The food certainly was delicious,' Izzy concluded, always the peacemaker.

'Yes, it was,' said Hunter, 'but I think it's time we retired for the evening too.' He wrapped his arm firmly around his wife's waist.

'Good night, everyone,' Nicki squeaked. Indeed, she looked downright green around the gills.

Halfway to the door, Hunter stopped and turned. 'Did you mention to Frazier what Kate and Eric's last names were?'

'Yeah, he requested the names of my agents and spouses, and my agents' cell phone numbers after I accepted his invitation.' After he and Izzy were the only ones left in the dining room, Nate asked, 'Would you like me to carry your dessert upstairs?'

'No, I've eaten enough for one day.' Izzy peered up with her luminous green eyes. 'What do you think, sweetie? Have we landed on Fantasy Island or checked into Bates Motel?'

'Come on, Izzy, we're all overtired. This might not be what we expected, but the retreat will be fine. Just wait and see.'

Only Nate didn't really believe that. Not for one minute.

Sunday, a.m.

Nate awoke the following morning to a chilly room and dense fog beyond their casement windows. He tried slipping from their bed without waking his wife, but Izzy bolted upright before his feet hit the floor.

'What's wrong?' she demanded.

'Why would anything be wrong?' Nate reached under the covers to tickle her legs. 'Just because I heard chains rattling in the closet and saw the rocking chair start moving on its own?' He mimicked ghostly noises all the way to the bathroom. When he returned, Izzy was by the window with her bathrobe wrapped tightly around her.

'Make all the jokes you want, Nathan Price, but I saw something spooky last night. Right down there.' Izzy pointed to the area directly below their room.

In a few long strides, Nate was at her side, peering down

where she indicated. 'You can't see twenty feet away in this pea soup.'

'I know that, Mr Obvious, but it was very different at one a.m. I saw two of Mr Frazier's . . . guards dragging one of those performers. They each had one of her arms and her feet were swinging and kicking like she didn't want to go.'

Nate looked down again with the same result. 'In which direction did they go?'

'It looked like they were bringing her back to the house from somewhere.' Izzy pointed down the sloping lawn. 'There is some kind of barn or stable there. I'm not sure, but maybe they were coming from there.'

'Describe what you saw.' Nate was no longer smiling.

'Well, judging by her bare feet, I think it was the one female suspect. She appeared to be black, thin, and of average height. She was wearing a long gown with a white hood pulled up around her face.' Izzy stepped back from the damp windowpane.

'So the woman was dressed head-to-toe in white, while her feet hovered above the ground? Sounds like a female African American ghost. You don't get to see those too often. I always see bony old grannies that are missing most of their teeth.' Nate rubbed his face with his hands.

Izzy stomped her foot. 'Will you please be serious?'

'OK, let's think about this. One of last night's *suspects* happened to be an African American woman. Could it be you were meant to see this as part of Frazier's charade?'

Her face scrunched up. 'How would they have known I would still be awake at that hour? Don't be ridiculous.'

'Maybe because one of the guards saw you pacing back and forth in the front of the French doors?' Nate bit his inner cheek to keep from grinning.

His beautiful, dignified wife of several years stuck out her tongue. 'I'm taking a shower. You'd better make sure this is part of Frazier's game, because our cell phones don't seem to work and he took our firearms.' Izzy closed the door behind her with a bit more force than necessary.

Nate stirred the cold ashes of last night's fire, trying to find a hot ember and to make sense of what Izzy saw. Five minutes later, he gave up on both endeavors. Instead he stalked to the

Keurig machine in the alcove to make coffee. When Izzy opened the bathroom door, makeup on but hair still damp from her shower, he handed her a cup of coffee. 'This is organic hazelnut from Central American farmers, grown under the rainforest canopy.'

'Think this will compensate for you thinking I'm making stuff up?' Izzy clutched the mug with both hands.

'That is my fondest hope.' Nate started a second cup for himself.

'Mmm, this coffee just might.' As Izzy sipped the dark, aromatic brew, the corners of her mouth pulled into a smile. 'Do me a favor. Don't say anything about me seeing a ghost in chains last night. I don't want Beth ducking behind a vase to smirk at me.'

'*What?* You think my crack-shot, ex-cop employee is a *smirker*?' With a laugh, Nate headed to the shower with an armful of clean clothes.

Twenty minutes later, the two of them entered the formal dining room ten minutes before the appointed hour of eight. Except for their host, they were the last to arrive to breakfast.

'Good morning, boss, and boss's better half. Sleep well last night?' These questions came from Beth Preston who, as Izzy implied, was smirking while she poured coffee from a silver carafe.

'Like babies in a mother's arm,' Nate said. 'How about you two?'

Michael held out his cup to be filled. 'I did, but Beth kept waking up with every sound she heard. She doesn't understand that these gorgeous old mansions creak and groan at night. All perfectly normal.' He added two sugars and plenty of cream.

'What I don't understand is why we had to give up our fire-power. What if one of Mr Frazier's guards suddenly goes psycho on us? We're all defenseless.' Beth slumped into a chair at the table.

Michael took the chair next to hers. 'You, my darling, wouldn't be defenseless if you were naked in a cage of wild badgers.' He leaned over and kissed Beth's cheek.

'Ughh.' Nicki Galen sniffed. 'Newly-weds are ridiculous – so uncouth, so tacky.' She feigned a haughty inflection, not in keeping with her rural Mississippi upbringing. 'We were never like *that*, were we, darling?' She draped her arm around Hunter's shoulder.

'Goodness, no, my dear.' Hunter's accent didn't need to be faked. 'We were refined and tasteful even when making out behind a French Quarter dumpster.' He punctuated the sentence with a hearty laugh.

'You two are too much!' Beth threw a packet of sugar at Nicki, who parried to the left. The packet landed on the thick Aubusson rug.

Unfortunately, Mr Julian Frazier chose that moment to join his guests for breakfast. Just for a second, Frazier glared at Beth with as much venom as a facial expression could muster. As Beth rose to retrieve the wayward sweetener, Frazier poured coffee at the sideboard and took his place at the head of the table.

'Good morning, owner and employees of the well-recommended Price team of private investigators. Do you each have your hot beverage of choice? If you would prefer a glass of milk, please just let my butler know.' Frazier's perusal of the table didn't reach the Prestons. 'If so, I'll signal Mr Compton that he may serve breakfast.' He pressed the button on his chair and leaned toward Izzy.

'I trust you slept well, Isabelle?' Frazier asked. 'Before my sweet wife died, your room once was the master suite.'

'It's a lovely room, especially with the wood-burning fireplace and the view of your gardens. But I didn't sleep well at all. I saw your guards dragging one of the suspects, Jennifer, I believe, back to the house.'

Frazier blinked twice. 'When was this, exactly?'

'Around one o'clock, perhaps?'

'Unless my favorite suspect decided to work a little overtime beneath your window, your eyes were playing tricks on you. The house was locked up tight and everyone in bed by that hour.'

'I see, but please see that our French doors are unlocked.'

'Yes, I'll see to that immediately after breakfast.' Frazier studied Izzy over the rim of his cup. 'You do understand how easy it would be for thieves to reach your door? Thieves, or miscreants with worse intentions in mind.' He shuddered.

Izzy didn't hesitate to reply. 'I do understand, but this week I have my husband to keep me safe. He's very good at what he does.'

'Quite right, my dear. Ah, our breakfast is here,' Frazier added as the butler opened the double doors. In marched two maids who delivered to each guest a plate of fresh fruit with two pieces of French toast. One piece was drizzled with caramel syrup and the other covered with fresh sliced strawberries. The third maid carried a platter of breakfast meats to the breakfront, along with a tray of yogurt, granola and cottage cheese for those who wanted healthy fare. 'Mr Price, I hope your team finds something to their liking.'

'It would be impossible not to,' Nate said, rising to his feet. 'Thank you, sir.' He was first to add both bacon and sausage to his plate, followed by Beth and then Michael, who chose cottage cheese with granola.

While they ate, the conversation centered mainly on the food and the rapid change in weather overnight.

'I'm glad there are no televisions in the guest rooms, Mr Frazier.' Nicki sliced a cube of melon in half. 'What a treat *not* to wake up to CNN business news or the Weather Channel.'

'At my age, Mrs Galen, I find business data a colossal bore and not worth watching on television. And regarding the weather? One simply has to look outside for a more accurate forecast than any Atlanta station. After all, this is an island.'

'You have a point there, sir,' said Hunter. 'But I believe we're all eager to hear the particulars of this mystery that you wish us to solve. My wife fell asleep trying to figure out how to use a file folder of papers to solve a murder.'

Everyone, including their host, chuckled. 'Very well, as soon as Mr Compton refreshes everyone's coffee, I will dismiss the staff and get down to business.' Frazier tossed down his napkin, despite having barely touched his food.

Hunter and Izzy did the same, while Nate hurried through his second piece of French toast, along with his last sausage.

Once Frazier had the audience's full attention, he cleared his throat and began. 'As I mentioned, ladies and gentlemen, the case you've been invited here to solve is a cold case murder committed more than eight years ago. I believe one of the perpetrators remains at large. Also the particulars of the crime, especially the motivation, remain unclear. So you are to discover not only whodunnit, but where, when, how, and most importantly, why the crime was committed.'

'I don't feel you're telling us the truth, Mr Frazier, just like it didn't seem like those suspects were acting.'

'You agreed to play by my rules, Mr Price. I'll provide you with the necessary information as needed. Now, are there any questions about the case?'

Isabelle tentatively raised her hand like a schoolgirl and received a nod from Frazier. 'May we assume the murder weapon was one of the five clues shown us last night?'

'You may, Isabelle. Beth, did you also have a question?'

Beth straightened in her chair. 'I do. You implied one of the suspects you paraded after dinner is the murderer. But if this case was never solved, how can you be so certain?'

'Very astute, Mrs Preston. As investigators you're well aware there's a big difference between the certainty of culpability and proving guilt in a court of law. These days, juries are populated with unemployable deadbeats and those usually uneducated with nothing better to do. I'm certain that one of the five is our killer.'

Isabelle opened her mouth, perhaps to refute his low opinion of jurors, but closed it just as quickly.

'There is no statute of limitations on murder,' said Michael. 'Did the police recently uncover new evidence and reopen the case?'

'To the best of my knowledge, no.'

Like Michael, Hunter didn't bother raising his hand like a child. 'How exactly are we to proceed? Cases are usually solved with thorough and accurate research into the background of each possible suspect for opportunity and motive. As of this morning, none of our cell phones works, so accessing the internet is impossible.'

'Hey, I brought my tablet along,' said Nicki. 'I go *nowhere* without access to Candy Crush Saga.'

When the laughter died down, Nate added, 'And I've got my

laptop in my luggage. Thought I'd catch up on paperwork in the evening. Do you have whole house Wi-Fi?'

Frazier's expression was a cross between sadness and contempt. 'No, I do not. May I relay the details of the crime before we consider the avenues available to you?' After several heads nodded, Frazier continued.

'I have invited all of you here not to play some silly parlor game, but to solve a real-life homicide, a cold case, that the Atlanta homicide department never closed. At least, not to my satisfaction.'

FOUR

t was silent around the breakfast table until Nate asked, 'May we assume you have a personal interest in the murder investigation?'

'You may indeed, Mr Price. The murder victim was my wife, Ariana, who was an accomplished artist and an avid bird enthusiast. We had just bought this natural paradise and looked forward to a long retirement in which I could read classic literature and Ari could paint and watch birds to her heart's content.'

Several employees murmured words of condolence, but Frazier cut them off with the wave of his hand. 'I don't need your sympathy eight years after the fact,' he thundered. 'I need to find those responsible. And not just the thug who caved in my beloved's skull with a wrench, but the person behind the killing.'

Izzy seemed to shrink smaller in her chair as Frazier painted a vivid picture of his wife's death. Nate reached for her hand under the table. 'Please give us the details of the crime, sir, so we could help you,' he said.

Frazier sipped some water and straightened in his chair. 'It was around eleven o'clock on a night in December. My wife had just gone up to bed. I programmed the coffeemaker and set the alarm system like I did every night, then I followed her up the stairs. Ariana was in the bathroom. I had just turned down the bedspread and was about to climb in bed when someone hit me from behind and knocked me unconscious for several minutes.' From the concise nature of his explanation, Frazier must have given his statement many times to the police . . . or he had rehearsed it endlessly.

'You didn't hear anyone on the stairs or someone sneak up behind you?' Nate asked.

'I did not. As part of my evening ritual, I removed my hearing aids and placed them next to my watch on the nightstand.'

Frazier paused a moment and then resumed. 'When I regained consciousness, I found my wife bleeding profusely next to the bathtub. I immediately called nine-one-one and held a damp cloth against the wound, but Ariana died before paramedics reached our home.' His voice cracked, giving away emotion that would be hard to fake.

Hunter pushed to his feet, his face a contortion of pain. 'As a husband, I can't imagine a crueler fate than what you endured, Mr Frazier. If you don't wish to continue—'

Nicki gently pulled Hunter back down. 'Please, sir, as painful as this is, these details may help find who killed her.'

Frazier nodded his head. 'According to the police report, of which I will provide a copy, the crime was a random break-in, not a home invasion. The thugs had been expecting to ransack an empty house. They gained entry through the garage, where one of them picked up a wrench from my workbench. Then they headed upstairs in search of cash and jewelry. Surprised to find us home, one knocked me out cold and the other must have heard Ariana in the bathroom. Afterwards they finished robbing the place. According to the police, the thug hadn't meant to kill my wife, but the blow fractured her skull.'

'It's still murder, either way,' said Michael.

'Yes, Mr Preston. I know the law. From the start, I felt the murder had been premeditated and the break-in merely a cover-up. The only thing the thieves took was some jewelry from a box on Ariana's dresser. No one touched her purse which had been on the hall table or my wallet on the nightstand.'

'Few people carry large wads of cash these days,' Beth commented.

'That evening my wallet contained six hundred dollars. Wouldn't that be sufficient to warrant a quick look?' Frazier's tone stifled Beth in a hurry.

'In the city where we live, people have died for far less. What was the homicide detective's conclusion?' Nicki asked.

'The *detective* assigned to my wife's case was a lazy, drunken sot. He should have been fired the last time he messed up. But because Atlanta has a strong police union and he was months away from retirement, he got away with his negligence. The detective concluded the thieves had been looking for gold jewelry and had missed the wallet when they left in a hurry.'

There was a buzz around the table as everyone spoke at once. Nate silenced them quickly. 'What in *particular* about their assessment of a random break-in do you disagree with? Why do you feel this crime was part of a larger conspiracy to kill one or both of you?'

'A good question, Mr Price. And we shall come back to that later. Allow me to finish giving details of the crime.' Frazier sipped from his water goblet. 'Using fingerprints left in the bathroom and on the murder weapon, police identified one thief as Mack Fallon, who had a long criminal history, as did his younger brother, Reuben. Both of their prints were on the wrench which the police found in the bushes down the street.'

'Sounds like an open-and-shut case,' said Beth.

'Indeed, Mrs Preston, it should have been. But the detective who showed up at the crime scene didn't do his job. Consequently, the assistant prosecutor had the case dismissed for insufficient evidence.'

'Were any of the thugs' fingerprints found in the bathroom?' Nate asked. 'With those and the murder weapon, the DA had plenty of evidence to convict.'

'One would certainly assume. But there was no mention in the report of bathroom fingerprints, only in the bedroom, and those belonged to Mack Fallon. After Mack died of a drug overdose while being held in county lockout, the case was dismissed for insufficient evidence. Reuben Fallon was released the next day. The detective simply closed the file on my wife's murder without tracking down the jewelry or seeking proof of Reuben's involvement.'

No one spoke for several seconds. Then Nate broke the silence. 'You are certain Reuben was one of your assailants?'

'Yes, I'm certain that Mack wielded the wrench that split my scalp, so his death in jail brought me great joy. But I'm just as certain Reuben was not only there, but the one who killed my wife. And he has lived as a free man all these years. What's more, someone paid the Fallons to enter our home that night.'

Frazier took another sip of bourbon. 'I told the detective that night the thugs surprised me from behind because my hearing aids were on the nightstand. Someone hit me hard on the back of the head and I went down. When I regained consciousness, I heard one creep say, "OK, we got the stuff from the dresser and inside the jewelry box. That guy's wife is probably in the bathroom and can't identify us, so let's get out of here while that guy is out cold." Then I heard a second voice say, "No, we ain't being paid to get a bunch of gold jewelry. Go take care of the wife. This guy's already dead." Then the first creep said, "No way, I don't want no part of that stuff." Then I felt a sharp pain behind my eyes and blacked out again. When I awoke I saw Detective Sanborn and the cops crawling around my bedroom. I told all this to him.'

Frazier splayed his hands on the tabletop and pushed to his feet. 'I invited your team here, Mr Price, to determine their accomplices and discover who paid the brothers to break into our home.'

'We're stuck out here on an island without internet access. How could we possibly help you?' Hunter Galen didn't mask the skepticism in his voice.

'You will start by interviewing the suspects you met last night, including Sanborn. Every one of them knows more than they told the police.'

Izzy pressed her fingers to her lips, her eyes flashing. 'Why did you lie to us? Why did you say they were staff members instead of the real suspects right from the start?'

'Forgive me, Isabelle, but I told a white lie to build suspense for my game.' Frazier's smile held no warmth. 'I invited to the island this week the Atlanta homicide detective, the assistant district attorney who had the case dismissed in court, the reporter who impugned my wife's reputation in the media, Reuben Fallon, and Mack's court-appointed attorney.'

Michael Preston shot to his feet. 'Those people know exactly who you are, Frazier. They never would have come willingly to this island.'

'Oh, they came willingly all right, at least three of them did. A one million-dollar cashier check provided plenty of incentive for them. Yes, they remembered me, but each one thought they had nothing to lose since the case was closed a long time ago. And they all desperately needed the money.'

Nicki looked confused. 'You offered a million bucks to Reuben Fallon? There's no statute of limitations if someone died during the commission of a robbery.'

'No, Reuben needed a bit of *physical* coercion to participate in my game. But now he's here.' Frazier's face glowed with excitement.

Nate cleared his throat. 'If you strong-armed or drugged Fallon to get him on your boat, the police will consider that kidnapping. Wherever the truth lies, charges against the brother were dropped. You will be the one in trouble with the law.'

Frazier's laughter was an unexpected response. 'Don't worry about *me* going left of the law. That's the least of your worries. You're here to find out who paid the Fallon brothers to kill my wife. If there are no more questions, I would like—'

'Wait a minute!' Beth interrupted. 'You said you paid three people, and strong-armed Fallon. I counted five suspects during dinner last night.'

'Quite right, my rude little Georgian.' Frazier turned toward Hunter. 'Our fifth invited guest is a former public defender, hired by the county to defend Mack Fallon at trial. That ne'er-do-well needed no million-dollar bribe or an armed guard to lure him here. Mr Kurt Ensley came willingly because he believed he was meeting a corporate client, Hunter Galen, for a few days of duck hunting. A bit of male bonding between client and attorney.'

As all eyes turned to Hunter for confirmation, Mr Creery opened the dining room's double doors. In stepped two guards with assault rifles. Frazier clucked his tongue. 'If your hotshot lawyer had done his homework, Mr Galen, Kurt Ensley would have learned waterfowl are protected on Elysian Island.'

'Why would you invite my attorney here? You can't possibly hold a public defender responsible for your wife's death.' Hunter took a step toward Frazier.

'But I do, and you're here to find out why!' Frazier shouted. Then the pendulum of his demeanor pivoted back. 'But I don't wish to ruin the fun for the *Price team of experienced investigators.*' He imbued his words with scorn. 'For the rest of the morning, we'll break into two teams. Team one will be given one clue to study in the library. Once you've learned all that you can, you'll be escorted to your rooms to rest until dinner.

Team two will be given free rein to explore the island, where hopefully you'll encounter clues and one or more suspects to interview. They were released first thing this morning. Be sure to grab notebooks and pens when you change into your warm outerwear and hiking boots. When you return to the mansion you'll find refreshments waiting in your rooms. Then we'll reconvene at dinner to compare notes on what we've learned today.'

'And if we refuse to play along with your game?' asked Hunter in a low growl.

'I'll handcuff and drag you away from your charming wife so fast your aristocratic head will spin.' Evil glinted in their host's dark eyes. 'If there are no other questions . . .' He waited until Hunter shook his head. 'Team one will be Nicki Galen, Michael Preston, and Nate Price. That leaves Hunter Galen, Beth Preston, and Isabelle Price on team two. I believe it's more fun to separate married couples, just like in a game of charades. Now, if team two would be kind enough to follow me?'

'Can't we at least speak with our spouses first?' asked Nate, not bothering to conceal his irritation.

'For heaven's sake,' Frazier barked in exasperation, the pendulum swinging back. 'You'll be separated for a few hours at the most. I have no ill-will toward any of you. You're here to find a murderer!'

Izzy stepped forward, breaking the tension. 'I'm ready to do my best.'

But Beth jumped up and beat her to the door. 'We'll play by your rules, Mr Frazier. But I'm captain of team two since Isabelle and Hunter aren't PIs.'

'Very well, Mrs Preston, whatever you say.' Frazier grinned as he followed them through the doorway.

And Nate's breakfast turned sour in his gut.

When the door closed behind Frazier, Nate looked at his two employees who were both waiting for his direction, and exhaled a sigh.

'What *exactly* are we supposed to do in here?' Nicki strode toward the window as though on a mission.

Nate shrugged. 'We're supposed to study one of the clues which hasn't been given to us yet.'

'I need more caffeine,' said Michael. 'No offense, boss, this retreat has gone from bad to worse.'

'None taken. Unfortunately, I don't think we're even close to hitting bottom.' Nate spoke softly in case Frazier's guards lurked nearby.

Michael filled three mugs with coffee. 'Drink up, members of team one. We may soon be asked to make sense out of nonsense.' He drank a hearty swallow.

Suddenly the door opened and Frazier entered with two guards at his heels. 'I hope you won't think *everything* in this file is nonsense, Mr Preston, because I'm depending on you to solve the mystery.'

Heedless of the guards' weapons, Nate grabbed the lapels of Frazier's jacket. 'If you harm one hair on my wife's head or any of my employees . . .'

Quickly, one guard knocked Nate back with the butt of his assault rifle.

'Relax, Mr Price,' said Frazier. 'I'm not referring to the lives of Price employees. So stop wasting time with unnecessary, macho theatrics. I give my assurance that all of you will be released, unharmed, once you figure out who paid the killers.' He tossed a thin manila folder on the dining-room table.

Michael reached for the papers that had scattered across the surface. 'Is this the detective's case file on the robbery-homicide?'

'It is, Mr Preston. Good to know you have a more level head than your fearless leader.' Tugging down his lapels, Frazier glared at Nate. 'Inside you'll find Detective Charles Sanborn's crime scene report. I trust an ex-forensic accountant will find more holes than the proverbial Swiss cheese, plus several glaring inconsistencies from my recount of what happened that night.' Their host looked from one to the other. 'On my life, I told you the truth. At this late stage of my life, I have no reason to lie. Good luck. Should you need snacks or more coffee, press the button on my chair to summon my housekeeper.'

When Frazier turned to leave, Nicki spoke. 'Please, sir, may I use the ladies' room?' Her accent couldn't get any thicker or more charming.

Frazier's benign expression turned curious. 'Of course,

Mrs Galen, but don't even think of trying to manipulate one of my employees. My housekeeper, Mrs Norville, will accompany you and watch your every move.'

Nicki's smile faded as she waited for her escort, while Nate and Michael carried their coffees to the table and sat down.

A middle-aged woman soon appeared to take Nicki away. Despite her age, the housekeeper looked like she could mud-wrestle alligators for a living.

'What have I gotten the team into?' Nate muttered.

'Don't beat yourself up, boss. It sounded like a good idea at the time. Let's just concentrate on the task before us.' Michael separated the papers in the folder into two piles.

'Not much of a case file.' Nate pulled the crime scene report to the top of the stack. For several minutes, he read and re-read the detective's summation, while Michael sipped coffee and mulled over the forensic reports of blood spatter and fingerprints. 'All right,' Nate said when Michael leaned back in his chair. 'What have you learned so far?'

Then Nicki re-entered the room, her complexion pale as a shade of skim milk.

'Are you all right?' Nate asked. 'You were gone a long time.'

'I'm fine.' Nicki sat down on the other side of the table. 'Nurse Ratchet *locked* me in the bathroom and then took her sweet time coming back for me.'

'Just relax for now while Michael tells us what's in the lab report.'

Michael laced his fingers behind his head. 'I agree with Frazier that Sanborn wasn't the best detective in the world. Not much forensic evidence in here, other than the fingerprints found in the master suite belonged to Frazier, his wife Ariana, and the chief murder suspect . . . Mack Fallon. The blood spatter on the bathroom walls and mirror belonged to Ariana Frazier, and finally skin cells found under Mrs Frazier's nails matched the DNA sample in the police databank for Mack Fallon, not Reuben. Frazier's wife apparently put up a fight and scratched her assailant. Photos taken after Fallon's arrest showed several long scratches on his face. Either no one dusted for prints in the bathroom, or none they found were any good. So none of the evidence in the file directly tied the younger brother to the crime.' Michael pushed his half of the file across the desk to Nate. 'Anything of interest in Sanborn's report?'

Nate slurped the last of his cold coffee. 'Two discrepancies stand out in the official report of the Frazier murder-homicide. First of all, the officers arriving on the scene reported no signs of forced entry, not at the windows or at the doors. Yet Frazier insisted he set the alarm before going upstairs. So either the assailants knew the code, which is unlikely in the case of the Fallons, or Frazier was mistaken about arming the security system.'

'Even if he forgot to arm the system, he still would've had to leave a door or window unlocked,' Michael observed. 'That doesn't sound like our illustrious host.'

Nate nodded. 'I agree. Sanborn's report states "one or more perps entered the residence without force." Sanborn's report describes the crime as a "random neighborhood break-in" and that "assailants had been unaware that the residents were home."'

'That guy sure made up his mind in a hurry.' Michael stacked his sheets into a pile.

'I agree. There's absolutely no indication that this break-in was part of a larger conspiracy or paid for by a third party.'

Nicki popped to attention. 'Frazier said he would come back to that part of the story, but he never did.'

'That's right. In the meantime, let's make sure we learn what we can from this case file. We'll switch piles and go over everything again.'

Nicki picked up each sheet they discarded to read. Within the hour, Nate pressed the button on the chair.

Jonah Creery stuck his head into the dining room. 'Need more coffee, Mr Price, or bottled water?' he asked.

'No, thanks. What we need is to interview the detective, Charles Sanborn. We've got plenty of unanswered questions based on this case file.'

A grin spread across the assistant's face. 'And so you shall. I'll have the detective join the entire team at dinner tonight. In the meantime, a guard will escort you to your rooms. You can rest until the other team returns. Then Mr Frazier and I will see everyone back here at eight o'clock.'

Creery was soon replaced by several armed guards who

marched the three back to their rooms. Not one of them uttered a single word, even though Nicki did her best to stimulate conversation.

When Beth left with her teammates after breakfast, she hadn't expected to be escorted by armed guards. 'What's going on, Mr Frazier?' she asked. 'Is this your private militia? I thought you brought the Price team here to solve a cold-case murder.'

'Exactly right, Mrs Preston, I don't know whom to trust since I have all five suspects on the island.' Frazier gestured toward the guards. 'These men are well-paid mercenaries – hired guns, if you will. You and your co-workers are here to find my wife's killer. Then you will return home well-compensated for your time and trouble.' His lips drew into a thin line. 'But I know you were trained as a Natchez police detective, despite having left the force in disgrace. So I want to make sure you and the others don't try to leave the island before your job is done.'

Beth blinked. 'You've done your research on our backgrounds. But wouldn't our ability to research help us solve this case?'

'You'll be provided every tool necessary to succeed, including the internet, should I deem it necessary. Right now, you'll be escorted to your quarters to change into appropriate clothing. Then you'll be released outdoors to search for suspects. Don't forget your pens and tablets.'

Frazier nodded and re-entered the dining room, leaving the team captain with plenty of questions.

'Follow me, Mrs Preston,' said one guard. 'Mrs Price, Mr Galen, if you would be kind enough to follow your respective guards.'

'Team two, we'll reconvene outdoors as soon as possible. Follow each instruction as given.' Then Beth followed a rather nasty-looking guard to her room, feeling like a total idiot. *Really? This creep would shoot me if I didn't follow orders?* But, for the moment, the man with a very real assault weapon was hard to argue with.

Beth followed him to the room she'd shared with Michael last night. The guard unlocked her door and motioned her inside. Once in her room she pulled out her cell phone, punched in

9-1-1, and received an immediate recorded message saying her call could not be completed as dialed. Next she tried the landline that the host had promised would be working this morning. That proved to be as worthless as her cell and her windows remained nailed shut. So, pursuing her only available option, Beth changed into warm sweats, a thick sweater and hiking boots. Yet when she tried the door, it wouldn't budge.

'Hey, I can't get out of here,' she shouted and beat her fist against the thick wood panel.

The heavy door swung open. 'No need to cause a ruckus, Mrs Preston. We're right here,' said the sweet voice of one of her two armed guards.

'Now there's two of you to watch little ole me?' she drawled.

'Mr Frazier seems to think you're a force to reckon with,' said the second guard. 'But I've dealt with women like you my whole life. Bring on your best.' Then he called Beth a name her mother wouldn't approve of.

'Hey, no need to get vulgar. I just wanted to tell you my door was stuck.'

While one guard scowled, the other nudged her down the hallway toward the stairs. After a circuitous route through several hallways, the guard pushed Beth out a door at the back of the house. She landed in a heap at the bottom of the steps.

'Are you all right?' Hunter hauled her unceremoniously to her feet.

'What took you so long?' Izzy brushed dirt and dead leaves off Beth's clothes. 'We were starting to worry about you.'

'I'm fine,' she muttered, yanking down her sweatshirt. 'I tried to get an outside phone line, that's all.'

Izzy glanced left and right. 'At least it doesn't look like any guards are out here.'

'Good.' Hunter's face held a tight, unreadable expression. 'So what's the plan, team leader?'

Beth knew they had few options. 'We'll scout the island to see exactly what we're up against and if there's a way off this rock, like a boat somewhere. Maybe we'll find a caretaker's cottage with a landline that Frazier forgot about. At the very least, if we find a beach we'll write "send help" in the sand for a low-flying aircraft to see.'

Hunter tilted his head back to study the windows on the
second and third floors. 'Our host might be a madman, but
Frazier has put serious thought into his game. I doubt he would
leave a sailboat hidden in the weeds or easy access to a phone.'

'So what do you suggest?' Beth pulled up her hood as a light
rain began to fall.

Hunter frowned. 'I hate leaving Nicki here in the company
of trained mercenaries. Maybe we should find another way in
and try to free team one from the dining room.'

Beth arched up on tiptoes to get face-to-face with Hunter.
'Nicki isn't *alone*. Nate and Michael are with her, and they
would die before letting one of those creeps touch her.'

But Hunter wouldn't back down. 'So all three end up dead
while we're hiking the trails, looking for one of Frazier's stupid
suspects to question.'

Isabelle wedged herself in between them. 'Hey, we're a team,
remember? We have no reason to believe Frazier means to harm
us. Let's just play along with his game. The sooner we solve
his mystery, the sooner he'll let us leave. Agreed?' Izzy looked
from one to the other.

'Agreed. Sorry, Beth,' Hunter added.

'No problem. I'll take the lead. Hunter, you bring up the rear.
Izzy, you keep your eyes peeled for clues along the way.'

Thus, the threesome set out across the lawn toward a stable
that looked much better from far than up close. The old horse
barn was so deteriorated that Beth feared the floorboards might
not hold their weight. Following a twenty-minute perusal of
every cobwebby nook and cranny, their team discovered only
a rotted harness, moldy straw, and one dead mouse. After they
left the stable, they spotted a path into the woods beyond the
pasture. For the next hour, the team members swatted black
flies, tripped over hidden roots, and got scratched by every type
of thorn and bramble. Beth suffered a gash on her cheek from
a low branch; Hunter tore his cashmere sweater, and Izzy limped
from her new fashionable boots.

'Those are not hiking boots, Izzy,' said Beth, stating the
obvious.

'I wasn't expecting Survivor Elysian,' Izzy shot back.

'*Shhh,* both of you,' said Hunter. 'Do you hear that?'

'Hear what?' Beth swatted a buzzing insect by her ear.

'The sound of waves hitting a shore.' Hunter passed them both up on the path and didn't stop running until he reached a wide-open expanse of sand, sea, and clear blue sky. 'It's the beach!'

Beth caught up to Hunter first. 'At least we're out of the jungle!'

'Can you see St Simons Island?' asked Izzy, panting like a dog.

Beth shielded her eyes to study the horizon. 'Nope, nothing but water for as far as the eye can see.'

Hunter wiped sweat from his face and neck. 'If my sense of direction is any good, we've reached the opposite side of the island from St Simons.'

'Who will see writing in the sand way out here?' wailed Izzy.

'Maybe no one, but I'm writing a message anyway.' Beth picked up a piece of driftwood. 'Then we'll search the beach in that direction – south, judging by the sun's position. We'll look for clues, along with a better path through the woods to the house.'

Surprisingly, no one argued with her. Izzy plopped down on a log to rest, while Hunter found her a better writing stick and searched the dunes for anything out of place. Once Beth had etched her message as deeply in the windswept sand as she could, she led her teammates down the beach. She and Hunter took turns plodding through the sawgrass where the deeper sand tired their legs.

Izzy, less accustomed to exercise, kept to the hard-packed beach at water's edge, hoping to flag down a passing boat. 'Oh, no,' Izzy moaned. 'What's that up ahead?'

Looking in the direction of Izzy's finger, Beth tasted stomach acid surge into her mouth. During her years on the Natchez police force, she'd seen her share of dead bodies. She broke into a run, shouting over her shoulder, 'Wait here, you two.'

Of course, neither listened. Hunter almost beat her to the body and Izzy arrived close on his heels. 'Oh, my goodness, is that—'

Hunter finished Izzy's sentence. 'Suspect number one, I presume.'

'Reuben Fallon, Mack's accomplice at the murder of Mrs Frazier.' Beth dropped her voice to a whisper, more out of respect for Ariana Frazier than the recently deceased. Since Reuben's eyes were still open and his hand had frozen in an outstretched pose, no one bothered to check for a pulse.

'Look.' Izzy pointed at a piece of metal, partially buried in the sand. 'Is that the . . .'

Beth completed her sentence. 'The wrench that Mr Frazier had in the dining room last night. Looks like it was used to kill Reuben.'

'If that really is Reuben Fallon.' Hunter apparently decided to be the voice of reason. 'And that wrench may or may not be the actual murder weapon used eight years ago.'

'True,' Beth agreed. 'But one thing is clear – Mr Frazier's ploy to have us solve Ariana's cold case is no longer a parlor game. Whoever that man is, he's dead. And we need to get back to the house.'

Without warning, Jonah Creery, Mr Frazier's assistant, stepped out from behind the dunes. And he wasn't alone. Several armed guards were with him. 'Well done, ace detectives on team two. You have not only found clue number one, you've eliminated a suspect. And yes, that miscreant indeed is Reuben Fallon.'

'What's wrong with you people? Frazier can't go around killing people like this!' Beth rushed toward Creery, but Hunter's grip on her arm stopped her progress.

'Well done, Galen. I'd hate to see the fireball, Mrs Preston, accidentally shot so early in the game.' Creery glared down his long nose.

'I want to go back to Mr Frazier's house,' Izzy whimpered.

'Of course, Mrs Price. Your host has no animosity toward you, only those culpable in his wife's death.'

Beth fought against Hunter's restraining arms. 'Frazier has his other killer now. He should let the rest of us go home.'

Flanked by his protectors, Creery glared down his nose at Beth. 'Allow me to rephrase. Mr Frazier also wishes to hold responsible those who withheld evidence from the police. After that, you'll be free to return to your mundane, mediocre lives.' Creery turned on his heel and strode down the beach. 'Accompany members of team two back to their rooms. Make sure no one goes astray. Shoot anyone who wanders off.' After a few steps, Creery looked back at them. 'If your team members manage to return, you'll be reunited with your spouses at dinner. And you're in luck – I believe there'll be a standing rib roast tonight.'

As Creery headed down the beach, they plodded along slowly behind him. Beth came to the frightening realization that Mr Frazier wasn't the only madman on the island.

FIVE

Charleston, Sunday p.m.

With a feeling of supreme satisfaction on many levels, Kate pushed back from the table. Sunday dinner with the Manfredis never failed to boost her spirits. The quirky, highly opinionated, and often boisterous group of people had welcomed her almost from the day she moved upstairs. Having lived alone for so long, Kate had been overwhelmed and offended by the family's intrusiveness. But that's just how the Manfredis showed their love – by sticking their noses into each other's business. Everything was fair game, including her and Eric's fledgling relationship.

Kate locked gazes with the patriarch, a man she helped free from jail by tracking down the true killer. 'Thank you, Mr Manfredi. That was the best lasagna I've ever tasted.'

Her declaration created a minor uproar since everyone at the table took *cooking* seriously, including Eric, who pressed a palm to his chest and feigned a heart attack.

With a raised hand, the patriarch commanded silence. 'Then you should eat more, young lady. That's how Italians show appreciation. And why do you keep calling me Mister? Alfonzo is the name my mother gave me, or you could call me Papa.'

Kate squeezed Nonni's hand. 'Someday, when you least expect it, I'll call you Alfonzo. It just won't be today. And if I ate another bite I would explode.' She placed both hands on her midsection.

Alfonzo wagged a finger in her direction. 'Son, that woman knows her mind. You're in for a run for your money. I'm glad my wife only knows how to say "yes, dear" and "no, dear."'

With an undignified snort, Irena smacked her husband's arm. 'Don't say things like that. People might think you're serious.'

'No one in this kitchen will.' Eric winked at Kate across the table as she pushed to her feet.

'Since Eric and I didn't lift a finger for this meal, why don't we clean up while everyone relaxes in the front room?' The rambling stone structure, reminiscent of Tuscan farmhouses, had once been the Manfredi home, and the family maintained a private room off the foyer for watching Sunday football or sipping espresso by the fire.

'Nothing doing,' cried Bernadette. 'You two are supposed to be on a company retreat. You're only here because I wasn't paying attention in a dark parking lot.' Bernadette grabbed hold of her daughter's arm with one hand and her husband's arm with the other. 'The Conrads have kitchen duty today and I will supervise. If you leave now, you should be able to get to St Simons by seven.'

'Mom's right,' said Danielle. 'You're supposed to be on a romantic getaway.'

Kate laughed. 'You think talking shop with your boss and the rest of your co-workers will be romantic?'

'Everything is what you make it.' The seventeen-year-old wiggled her brows comically.

Eric pulled Kate toward the back staircase. 'If you're sure you and Mike can handle Bella for another five days, then I intend to give romance my best shot.'

Alfonzo scowled. 'What's the matter with you, Enrique? Your mother and I were managing this trattoria while you were still eating Spaghetti-o's out of a can.'

As the family howled with laughter, Eric and Kate ran upstairs for their luggage. Three hours later, they exited I-95 onto Highway 17, a scenic two-lane road that crossed countless creeks and rivers, ran along tidal flats and great expanses of salt marsh, and offered a few glimpses of the mighty Atlantic Ocean.

'Have you ever visited Georgia's Golden Isles before?' Kate asked, switching off the radio. 'I read that slogan on a billboard.'

'Hmm, let's see.' Eric joined the queue turning left onto the F. J. Torras Causeway to St Simons. 'We went camping at Jekyll Island State Park when Bernie and I were kids. And once I went to Sea Island with my dad to visit his friend. If I remember correctly, we drove through St Simons to get to Sea Island, but I don't remember more than that.'

She pivoted to face him. 'Hopefully you and I will make plenty of memories on this trip.'

'Count on it, baby.' Eric's leer was downright obscene.

As they reached the island, Eric had to drive around a rotary three times before Kate punched the address into GPS. 'Sorry,' she murmured. 'I should've done that before now. Now we're really going to be late.'

'Not to worry – at least we won't get lost.'

But being late or getting lost was the least of their problems.

When they reached the location of Nate's retreat, no lights were on and no one answered their knock at the door.

Eric stepped back to check the second floor. 'There are no lights on anywhere. Could you possibly have the wrong weekend or maybe copied the address incorrectly?'

Kate pounded harder on the door. 'No way. See that red Charger parked down the street? It belongs to Michael and Beth. And how many people own a dark green Maserati like Hunter Galen?' She pointed at two very distinctive cars. 'Let's find a way into the backyard. Maybe everyone is outside around the pool.'

After a minor amount of trespassing and wall-scaling, status quo for any PI, Kate and Eric found their way into the correct courtyard. Empty and dark, just like the rooms in the back of the house. A few empty beer bottles sat between lounge chairs while a forlorn volleyball floated on the pool's surface.

Irritation crawled up Kate's spine like a spider. 'So they went ahead and left without us. I was hoping they would wait. How are we supposed to get to Elysian Island if that boat doesn't come back?'

'Nate told us to call as soon as we arrived. But first, why not check your messages? Maybe your boss left more instructions.'

Kate inhaled a deep breath and punched in voicemail. First she listened to Nate's original message that told them to come as soon as possible and they would leave the lights on. 'Oh, good, there are two new messages.' She held up one finger and pressed the speaker button.

'Kate and Eric, the owner of the island didn't want us to wait. So we caught a ride to paradise on Saturday.' The exuberance

in Nate's voice bubbled from the phone. After a short hesitation, he added, '*Just call me when you can and we'll make arrangements to get you to Elysian Island. The Price team sticks together.*'

She gazed up into Eric's dark eyes.

'See? No need to worry.' Eric put both his hands on her shoulders. 'Let's listen to the second message.'

Kate nodded, feeling a little foolish. When she pressed the play button, they heard Nate chuckle as the message began:

'*In the meantime, let yourself into my friend's condo and get comfortable. My friend's in Europe so you two will have the place to yourselves until you can join us on Elysian. Here's the code for the front door.*'

After a series of numbers, Kate heard the inevitable click of Nate hanging up for a second time. 'We'd better call him.' She scanned through her contacts for the boss's number.

But Eric stopped her. 'No, let's backtrack to the front door before someone calls the cops on two suspicious peeping Toms.'

'Only one of us looks suspicious and that's you,' she teased. 'I'll race you to the front.' Kate boosted herself over the wall and ran as fast as she could through the neighbors' yards.

But with his long legs, Eric had no trouble catching up and passing her. When she reached the stoop, he was already punching in the security code from memory. Like magic, the door opened, and they entered a living room that reeked of perfume and garlicky tomato sauce.

Eric sniffed the air like a bloodhound. 'Smells like the old gang ordered pizza before they left for the new world.'

'And I can tell Nicki Galen was here. She's the only one who sprays on Dior like five-dollar body mist.' Kate picked up an empty soda can from the coffee table. 'Now can we call Nate?'

'Nope, sit for a minute.' Eric pointed at an expensive leather sofa. 'I'll see what your pals left us to drink.'

Kate readily complied. It'd been a long day, between dinner with the Manfredis, the drive from Charleston to St Simons, and sprinting across several yards.

A few minutes later, Eric returned with the remnants of a party tray, an opened bottle of champagne and two flutes. 'First, we'll toast to our good fortune – this champagne is Veuve Clicquot with only one glassful missing. We can't let it go flat.' He filled both flutes.

'Let's toast the Galens bringing the good stuff. And let's drink to a successful retreat with our friends.'

'And let's toast to one night alone for our own retreat.' Eric tapped the rim of his flute to hers. 'After all, my niece, Danielle, gave us strict orders.'

Kate sipped her champagne and punched in Nate's number. Unfortunately, the call went straight to voicemail. 'Uh-oh, his phone didn't even ring. Where *is* this Elysian Island?'

Eric tapped on his phone's Google app. 'Only twenty-two miles out in the Atlantic Ocean. St Simons is the nearest body of land. Let's have a sandwich now and try the call later.'

'How could you possibly be hungry?' she muttered. Nevertheless, Kate rolled up a slice of ham and cheese and grabbed a handful of olives.

Two hours later, with the tray picked over and the champagne gone, Kate tried Nate's number again and received the same result. Although she had every intention of calling him later, fatigue finally caught up with them.

They both fell asleep, fully dressed, on the couch.

Elysian Island, Sunday p.m.

After the unfriendly guards escorted members of team one back to their rooms, Nate wasn't able to rest or enjoy the plate of cheese and crackers on the coffee table. Members of team two still hadn't returned from their trek around the island in search of clues or one of the suspects. From his window, Nate watched the fog creep from the forest across the lawn like bony fingers. Pacing the room did him little good. Trying for a cell connection did even less. Not until he heard a key in the lock and saw Izzy walk into the suite did he relax.

'What took your team so long?' he barked. 'How *big* is this island?'

Izzy, cold, wet, and dirty, limped across the room into his arms. 'Oh, Nate,' she sobbed. 'This is far worse than we could've imagined.'

'What is . . . the island?'

She nodded. 'Yes, plenty of thorny briars and lots of low marshy . . . spots.' Tears streamed down her face as her words broke into a staccato. 'That's not the worst . . . of . . . it.'

Nate helped her to the chair by the fireplace and draped an afghan around her shoulders. 'Now tell me what happened. Are you hurt?'

'No, but my feet hurt from wearing these new boots.' She shivered uncontrollably.

'Is that why you're upset?' He tightened the afghan around her.

'No,' she cried. 'We found a dead body on the beach. It was that skinny guy who fought against his restraints during introductions.' She drew in a breath. 'We think it was Reuben Fallon.'

'Are you sure he was dead?'

Izzy's head bobbed up and down. 'No doubt in my mind. There was a big gash here and a lot of blood on his clothes and in the sand.' She touched a spot where her forehead met her scalp. 'Remember that we were supposed to find a clue and a suspect on Frazier's wild-goose chase?' She laced the question with plenty of scorn. 'We found the wrench that was on the table. It was lying in the sand next to the body with blood all over the heavy end.'

'I hope no one touched it,' Nate murmured.

'What difference does it make?' she cried. 'This whole thing has been *staged* for our benefit. Frazier killed someone as part of his stupid mystery game.'

'Why would Frazier wait until now to kill Reuben Fallon, if that really was him? He could have had him whacked at any time during the last eight years.'

'I don't know.' Izzy dropped her face into her hands. 'But as soon as we found the body on the beach, out pops that head of security, Jonah Creery, along with several guards. Creery even made a joke of Fallon's death.' She mimicked a singsong-y accent. 'Look at you, ace detectives, you not only found a clue, but eliminated one of the suspects! Well done. Time to head back to the house and get ready for dinner.'

Nate walked to the sideboard and considered pouring a drink.

But having anything less than a clear head wouldn't help him tonight. He drank cold coffee left over from breakfast instead. 'Stretch out on the bed, Izzy, and get some rest. Let me think about how I want to handle this.'

'What's to handle?' she moaned, shrugging off her outerwear. 'We're trapped on an island and at Frazier's mercy.'

Although Izzy had lain down on the king-size bed, Nate knew she wouldn't sleep. Nate settled in an upholstered chair to think, but he found neither rest nor much of a solution when it was time to get ready.

Izzy swung her feet off the bed. 'I'm just wearing what I have on. I refuse to get dressed up for a murderer's standing rib roast dinner.'

'Right now, we don't know if Frazier's the murderer or one of the other suspects he let roam free on the island.' Nate pulled a clean shirt from his suitcase. 'It's in the team's best interest not to overreact.'

'How are we supposed to act when we find someone with their head bashed in?' She rested one hand on her hip.

'For now, we'll assume that Frazier was just as shocked as you were and has already called the police or whoever has jurisdiction over this island. Let's give him the benefit of the doubt and play our roles. Please change out of those dirty clothes.'

'Fine,' she said after a moment's consideration. 'I'll put on a dress and heels, but this is the hairdo that crazy man is going to get.' Izzy pointed at her tangled mess of curls.

Nate knew better than to press his luck. Ten minutes later, an armed guard released them from their comfortable bedroom, which was feeling more and more like a prison cell.

'Ready to go, Mr and Mrs Price?' he asked. At least his rifle was on his shoulder instead of pointing at their chests.

'We are.' Nate took his wife's arm and walked slowly to the grand foyer, trying to memorize every stairwell and hallway they passed. When the butler opened the dining-room door, they discovered Frazier at the sideboard with his head of security, Jonah Creery.

Both men turned around with glasses of amber liquid in hand. 'Nate, Isabelle,' greeted Frazier. 'I'm so glad you're the first couple to dinner.' He set down his glass and rushed to Izzy's side. 'I'm so sorry, Isabelle. What an awful shock that must have been for you.'

'I suppose more so for me than for you, considering Fallon was the other assailant. Now that Reuben is dead, justice – or rather your retribution – has been served.' She gently pulled her fingers from his grasp. 'This ties up your mystery with a bow, no?'

So much for not overreacting, Nate thought. 'Come, Izzy. Let's sit down.'

Frazier's head reared back as though she'd slapped him. 'I didn't kill Reuben Fallon! I brought him here to find out the truth. One of the brothers took money to kill my wife. And I want to know who paid them.' He took his usual place at the head of the table, his hand shaking as he sipped his drink.

'Are the police on their way to examine the crime scene and interview those who discovered the body?' Nate asked.

Suddenly, Compton ushered the Galens and Prestons into the dining room without the formal announcement of names.

Hunter rushed toward the head of the table. 'What kind of sick game are you playing?' Hunter would have pulled Frazier from his chair if not intercepted by two heavily armed guards. One guard threw Hunter into a chair and the other pressed a gun to his neck, while Nicki screamed like a banshee.

Beth probably would have joined Hunter's assault if Michael hadn't picked her up by her waist. 'Put me down!' Beth screeched.

'Would everyone sit down,' Creery demanded. 'And quiet down so we can sort this out!' he added when everyone continued to talk.

Although it took several minutes, everyone finally took their seats, stopped talking and directed their attention to the head of the table. Compton began filling glasses with wine as though it would be dinner as usual.

'Isabelle, Hunter, Beth, I know exactly how you felt when you found Mr Fallon this afternoon.' Although he addressed all three, Frazier kept his focus on Izzy. 'And I swear, I had nothing to do with his death.'

When shouting erupted around the table again, Creery fired his handgun into the ceiling.

That got the guests' attention. 'I hope there are no guests in that room,' Nate said quietly.

'That room belongs to the Galens, so no.' Creery gestured toward Nicki and Hunter. 'For now everyone is fine. Listen to Mr Frazier.'

Their host took another swallow of bourbon. 'When Jonah reported the gruesome discovery on the beach, I immediately tried calling the Glynn County Sheriff's Office from the phone in my office. But the landline is dead. That service has never gone out since I've lived here.'

'How convenient!' Beth muttered.

'There must be another way to reach St Simons or the mainland,' said Nate.

'Tomorrow I'm expecting Captain Burke to pick up Kate Weller and Eric Manfredi and bring them to the island. He sent them a text to be at the village fishing pier at noon. When the *Slippery Eel* arrives, we can use the boat's radio to contact the coastguard. They can get ahold of the correct branch of law enforcement.'

'You have no other boats on the island?' Nate asked.

'I do not, and I'm not expecting any deliveries until later in the week.'

'A rich man like you with only one boat? I find that hard to believe,' Beth snapped.

'There are small skiffs and kayaks used for exploring, but they neither have radios, nor can they reach the mainland with the strong currents around the island. And I resent your snide tone, Mrs Preston. If you can't be civil at my dinner table, then keep your mouth shut.' Frazier's face flushed to a shade of scarlet.

Michael whispered something to Beth, before addressing Frazier. 'Team one was in the library, studying the detective's case file. Could you tell us everything you know about what happened on the beach?'

Frazier nodded at Jonah Creery who took over the explanation. 'The surviving Fallon brother, Reuben, was found with his head caved in, apparently with the same weapon that had been used to kill my wife.'

'That weapon should still be locked up in police evidence,' said Nicki.

'Yes, Mrs Galen,' said Frazier. 'But since the police no longer had any use for evidence, I had it retrieved and brought to the island, along with the case file. The wrench and other clues were locked in my office. Someone broke into my office, disabled the phone and stole the weapon used to kill Reuben Fallon. I remained inside this house all day.' Frazier's voice lifted a decibel.

'But you could have—'

'Enough.' Nate interrupted Michael. 'We were brought here to solve Ariana's murder, not throw around accusations. Members of team two, did you see anyone else today on the island? Izzy didn't mention seeing anyone, how about you, Hunter?' Nate thought it best to leave Beth out of the conversation for now.

Hunter set down his glass. 'We searched the stable behind the house and then found a path through the interior to the beach. We saw no signs of anyone until we found Reuben Fallon, except of course Mr Creery and four of the guards here in this room.' Hunter stood and pointed out four of the seven armed men in the dining room.

'If one of the hired security force wanted to kill Fallon, he would have used a bullet, not a wrench.' Creery scoffed at the idea.

'This morning,' said Frazier, 'I released all suspects to see what they would do. They were made aware of the rules of the game when they first arrived. They were told they couldn't leave until you solved the mystery, but two found an old rowboat on the other side of the island and tried to get off the island. Since the boat had holes drilled in the bottom, the escapees had to swim back to shore and were soon apprehended. We found the other two suspects on the dock, trying to flag down passing fisherman. Local fishermen know better than to set their nets too close to Elysian. All five suspects were found, but any of them had time to kill Fallon before the guards recaptured them.'

'I doubt they had enough time to break into your office?' Nate said.

Creery cleared this throat. 'Actually, when I questioned the housekeeper, Mrs Norville admitted she might not have locked the door after cleaning the room. So, yes, one of the suspects might have sneaked in.'

Frazier glared at his assistant. 'All right, if team two has nothing else to add, then let's hear what team one learned from the detective's report.'

Nate glanced around the room, then pulled a folded sheet from his pocket. 'As Mr Frazier described, the detective's case file on the murder was woefully incomplete. In addition, one major inaccuracy stood out.'

'Finally, we're getting somewhere.' Frazier banged his fist on the table. 'Let me allow the staff to serve dinner, so they can be dismissed for the evening. If you don't mind, we're dining less formally tonight.' He pressed the button on his chair.

Nate was forced to wait until Compton sliced the roast and maids delivered side dishes to the center of the table. Once they left the room, he continued, 'Detective Sanborn concluded the thieves entered the house through an unlocked garage door or back window, because there were no signs of forced entry. Nowhere in his report is Mr Frazier's insistence that he locked up and armed the security system.'

'With all due respect, sir,' said Michael, 'you said we could question the suspects. Wouldn't now be a good time for Detective Sanborn to join us?'

'A splendid idea. I'll see what's keeping him.' Frazier refilled his glass from the decanter and passed the bottle to Nate. 'Mr Creery, would you be kind enough to fetch the retired cop? More wine, Isabelle?' he asked when his assistant left the room.

'No, thank you. I'm not getting tipsy tonight.' Izzy took a dinner roll and passed around the basket.

In a few minutes, Creery prodded Sanborn into the room and pointed at the chair next to Michael. 'Sit next to him.'

Nate instantly recognized the suspect's telltale signs of alcohol abuse. In fact, judging by his glassy eyes and unsteady gait, Sanborn appeared to be drunk right now. He practically fell into his chair.

'Have you been drinking, Detective? Because we have a few questions to ask you.'

Sanborn shook an accusing finger at their host. 'I told that crazy rich guy I was on the wagon when he offered me a million bucks to come here. Frazier said "no problem" but he made sure I got plenty to drink on the boat ride here and then left full bottles of Scotch in my room. He knew I'd be tempted.'

Izzy nudged Nate under the table, remembering their own boat ride.

'What did Mr Frazier say you had to do for the one million dollars?' Nate asked.

Sanborn continued to point his finger. 'He said some PIs were going to ask me some questions and that I had to tell the truth. So far he's kept me locked up with only stale sandwiches to eat and water to drink. Until today, when he let me out knowing there's no way off this hunk of jungle.'

Frazier took a slice of roast from the platter. 'You ate what you would have eaten in jail. After all, obstruction of justice is a serious crime.'

'I didn't obstruct nothing.' Sanborn slurred the words. 'I did my job, better than lots of 'em on the Atlanta force.' Suddenly the detective lurched forward and stabbed two pieces of beef from the platter with his fork. After he gobbled the meat almost without chewing, Izzy passed him the bowls of glazed carrots, asparagus, and sweet potato casserole.

'Could we continue while you eat?' Nate tapped his knife on his glass to get Sanborn's attention. 'Why did you state in your report that thieves entered through an unlocked door or window?'

'Because there were no signs of forced entry. There had been plenty of break-ins in the neighborhood – dopers looking for stuff they could fence to feed their habit. How would punks like the Fallon brothers know the security code to Frazier's big fancy house?' Sanborn glared at him as he scooped more carrots.

'But when you initially assessed the crime scene, you had no idea who the fingerprints would match up to,' Nate reminded the detective. 'Why didn't the victim's statement appear in your report?'

Sanborn stopped gobbling food long enough to glare around the table. 'Yeah, but take a good look at the victim. He's an old man. Plus he was acting all crazy-like, so I thought he had Alzheimer's or maybe a concussion from the crack on his head.'

'Maybe the fact his wife was dead had something to do with his behavior,' Izzy suggested.

'Your personal assumptions shouldn't matter in a police investigation,' Nate said through gritted teeth. 'You had an obligation to take an accurate statement and let any extenuating circumstances like a medical condition come out at trial.'

Sanborn pointed his fork at Nate. 'Listen to you talk, Mr PI to the rich-and-famous. You have no idea what it's like to work robbery-homicide in Atlanta.'

Beth responded before Nate had a chance. 'I worked robbery-homicide for the Natchez PD, so I know exactly how difficult the job can be. But you still take down everything the victim says at a crime scene. So don't make excuses for yourself.'

When Sanborn looked confused, Nate clarified. 'Mr Frazier told you he overheard the thieves mention getting paid by someone else.'

Sanborn stared at Frazier with his mouth full of food. 'Look, you were bleeding from a head wound when I arrived on the scene. I told you to tell all that to the officer who would interview you at the hospital.' Sanborn shifted his focus back to Nate. 'I didn't know if he was dying of a brain bleed or not. The next day the cop made an audio recording of Frazier's statement. It should have been in the case file.'

'Well, there was no audio recording in the file,' Nate said.

'I thought the next day at the hospital would be a better time to give your statement!' Spittle flew from Sanborn's mouth as he shouted.

'Why?' Frazier demanded. 'Because you were too inebriated that night to take down a coherent statement?' Frazier pushed away the bowl Izzy passed him. 'You were a worthless drunk then and still are now. Just look at you!' Frazier was shaking with rage as he stood up. 'I won't dine in that man's company. But please, Mr Price, your team can ask him anything they wish.'

'One more question before you go, sir.' Beth rose to her feet. 'Do you have any idea who paid the Fallon brothers to invade your home?'

'If I knew, I would have taken care of them long ago. But Sanborn or one of the other suspects knows who they are. And that's why you're here.' Frazier leaned heavily on the table. 'Let me make this very clear – there's no way off this island, no way to communicate with the mainland, and none of my staff will help you, so the faster you solve my mystery the faster you can resume your lives.' Frazier stormed from the room with Jonah Creery at his heels. The guards, however, held their places by the wall.

'That guy is crazy!' Sanborn muttered the moment the door closed. 'Why doesn't somebody ask Reuben Fallon who paid them? He's here on the island someplace because I saw him last night when Frazier trotted us out for you PIs.' Sanborn tried to stab more beef roast, but Michael pulled the platter beyond his reach.

'You've had enough meat. Eat your vegetables if you're still hungry.' Michael took one slice and handed the platter to his wife.

Beth took one slice and passed the platter on. 'We would love to ask Reuben. We set out today with the intention of questioning him, but unfortunately we found him dead instead. What were you doing this afternoon?'

Sanborn choked on his carrots. 'Trying to find my way back to the dock. I thought the boat that brought me here might still be there.'

'But no such luck?' Hunter took a small portion of food, then dished some onto Nicki's plate since she refused every bowl passed to her. 'Who was on the boat dock with you, trying to flag down a fisherman?'

Sanborn blinked at Hunter. 'It was that lawyer, the guy who got assigned to be Fallon's public defender. I never saw Fallon on my way to the dock and I had no reason to kill him.' Sanborn scanned the table with his bloodshot eyes. 'OK, I admit to being drunk the night Mrs Frazier died. I'd been home from work for hours and didn't think I'd get called out again. I don't remember what Frazier told me that night and I don't know anything about someone paying the Fallons for a hit. Like I wrote down in my report, I thought the robbery had been a random break-in.'

SIX

K ate awoke Monday morning as the first rays of dawn
filtered through the living-room curtains. 'Ouch,' she
moaned. 'What happened to my back and neck?'

Eric stretched his arms over his head, equally stiff. 'And what
happened to our plans for a night of romance?'

Kate shot to her feet. 'I forgot to call Nate again. Let's try
him now.' But before pressing the redial button, she noticed a
blinking icon. 'There's a message from Nate!' She tapped on
the message and pressed the speaker button:

'I hope you're enjoying my friend's condo.' The upbeat voice
of her boss filled the room. 'Don't worry – we'll all come back
to clean the place before leaving St Simons. In the meantime,
the boat to take you to Elysian Island will be at the village
fishing pier at noon on Monday. The ride is only thirty minutes.
We'll catch you up on anything you've missed when you get
here.'

Eric glanced at his watch. 'See, what did I tell you? Nothing
to worry about. We have plenty of time.' He leaned in for a
kiss.

'Get serious, Manfredi! No kisses until I brush my teeth.
Plus we both need showers. Then we'll have just enough time
to grab breakfast somewhere before heading to the dock.
Unfortunately, your niece's delightful idea will have to wait for
the next island.' Kate headed to the kitchen to make coffee,
while Eric muttered about falling asleep at the worst possible
time.

The village of St Simons could be described as the dictionary
definition of charming. It had one main thoroughfare leading
straight to the water's edge, lined with everything a resident or
tourist needed – restaurants, bars, boutiques, salons, and places
to rent anything from a sailboat to a beach umbrella. On streets

shaded by giant live oaks were homes ranging in size from quaint cottages to classic southern-style mansions, along with luxury condo and apartment units. The village was simple and straightforward, a hard place to get lost even for someone navigationally challenged like Kate Weller.

An hour later she and Eric were eating pancakes and country ham in a local eatery within walking distance of the pier. 'What do you know about this Elysian Island? I know you Googled it while I was in the shower.'

Eric sipped his coffee. 'Not much information is available. Only that the island is privately owned – boats are forbidden to dock without express, written permission by the owner. The place is also a protected habitat for rare plants and a rest stop for migratory birds and butterflies. According to Google, it once had a thriving settlement in colonial days, but I doubt any of that is left. According to Google maps, there's one large mansion, what looks like a barn, and a few small outbuildings.'

'I can picture hiking trails and a long gorgeous beach. Do you think there'll be water sports?' Kate swabbed her last bite of pancake with maple syrup.

'If there are, they're only for the invited guests.'

She dabbed her lips. 'And the Price team got an invitation. Ain't that cool?'

Eric didn't look so sure. 'I don't think there'll be any restaurants or shops.'

Kate thought for a moment. 'We can find bars and T-shirt shops everywhere. This island sounds unique. We'll probably have a couple days of employee bonding and then come back here.' She glanced at her watch. 'Let's pay the check and head to the dock. We're not missing the boat this time around.'

Eric parked the car in a well-lit public lot and hefted their bags from the trunk. 'At least we can be reasonably sure the car will still be here when we get back. I wonder how well Nate knows the owner of this island.'

'I have no idea. And why are you so worried?' Kate tugged her duffle from his grip and hefted it to her shoulder.

'Nothing, but this change in plans came up spur of the moment.' Eric dodged a pair of teenagers on skateboards.

'Maybe the owner had a cancellation and Nate jumped at

the opportunity.' Kate hooked her arm through his elbow as they started down the long pier. 'Relax. All our questions will soon be answered.'

Yet the appointed meeting time, noon, according to the text, came and went with no sign of a private yacht from Elysian. Kate and Eric sat on a wooden bench for almost an hour, watching children throw bread to the ducks and fish. She had tried calling and texting Nate, Beth, and Michael with no luck. Just when they were ready to give up, Kate's phone dinged with an incoming text message. 'Finally,' she declared, clicking on the message.

'*Hello, Miss Weller and Mr Manfredi,*' she read aloud. '*I am Captain Mike Burke, in the employ of Mr Julian Frazier of Elysian Island. I've been instructed by Nate Price to arrange your transportation here. Unfortunately, today's high tide and strong currents make a safe crossing from St Simons impossible. Thus we must postpone your joining the company retreat until tomorrow – same time and same location for pickup. We'll hope for better sea conditions. Respectfully yours, Captain Burke.*'

Eric leaned over her shoulder. 'Wow, I've never heard a text sound like a letter written longhand with a fountain pen.'

'Me neither, but what do you make of this? The ocean doesn't look very choppy to me.' Kate pointed at the gentle waves lapping at the posts.

Eric focused his gaze out to sea. 'I agree, but that means nothing in terms of currents at high tide. Haven't you heard about the strong currents surrounding Alcatraz? Lots of prisoners drowned while trying to escape.'

'No, I haven't. But I don't like not being able to join the group.'

'And we will, as soon as Captain Mike says it's safe to cross. In the meantime, how 'bout we take in the sights of St Simons? This island looks pretty cool.' Eric lifted her chin with one finger. 'By the way, I recently brushed and even flossed my teeth.'

Kate planted a kiss on his lips. 'Thank you for that. And thanks for putting up with my worrying.' She kissed him a second time.

'I see a lighthouse over your shoulder. Why don't we check it out? If it's open, I'll race you to the top.'

'It's deal, Manfredi. The loser cooks dinner tonight.'

If there ever was an incentive for Eric not to do his best, this was it. The only thing she knew how to cook was ramen noodles and canned soup.

When Nate and Izzy arrived at breakfast Monday morning, Hunter and Nicki and Michael and Beth were already seated at the table, coffee cups in hand. Mr Frazier and Jonah Creery were standing by the coffee urn. 'I don't see Mr Sanborn,' Nate said upon joining their host. 'Won't he be coming to breakfast?' Nate filled his cup to the brim.

'I'm afraid not,' Frazier replied without an ounce of the cordiality displayed on previous mornings. 'Sanborn is sleeping off a nasty hangover, so I doubt he'll have much taste for food.' Frazier walked to the head of the table. 'If everyone has their beverage, I'll signal the butler to bring in the food. You'll have to serve yourselves today. I told the maids to remain in their quarters until the boat takes them back to the mainland. They will be paid, of course, but I can't risk their safety with a killer loose on this island or perhaps inside this house right now.'

Hunter snorted with contempt. 'Yet you're more than willing to subject Isabelle, Beth and Nicki to danger without a second thought.'

Frazier's dark eyes could have bored a hole through him. 'Your wife, along with Beth, Michael and Nate are trained investigators. The Price agency was touted as the best in the business, according to my friend, Mrs Baer. And don't forget, these aren't the parameters I created for my game. No one was supposed to die. I simply want to know who paid the Fallons to attack us.'

Hunter sneered at their host. 'That's getting hard to believe, since you're the one pulling all the strings. I want to talk to my lawyer, Kurt Ensley.'

'I don't care what you believe, Mr Galen, or what you want.' Frazier sneered back with equal venom. 'You're a long way from Orleans Parish, so I warn you to keep a civil tongue in your head.'

'What exactly does that mean?'

'You can't use old family money or your connections to buy your way out of trouble.'

Nicki silenced Hunter's retort with her hand to his lips. 'Bickering won't get us anywhere. What are your plans for the teams today, sir?' Her drawl was sweeter than honey.

Frazier's expression softened. 'Thank you, Nicki, for the voice of reason. After breakfast, team one – you, Nate, and Michael – will search the island for the suspects to interview, while team two – Isabelle, Beth, and Hunter – will spend time in the library studying a new clue.'

'Are you releasing the suspects to roam the island again?' Nate asked.

'Yes, in fact I'm giving them a head start before your team sets out.'

'Wouldn't it be easier if we interviewed the suspects one at a time right here?' Michael flourished his hand around the room.

'I have no desire to make it *easy* for you, Mr Preston. This is my game and you'll play by my rules. Prove that you're worth the money I've spent to wine and dine you.'

Nate spotted a nervous tic in Frazier's cheek he hadn't noticed before. It would do them no good to inflame their host. This guy might go off the deep end.

They heard a knock; Compton opened the door and an older woman with a teenaged boy carried in trays of food.

'Ah, here's your breakfast,' Frazier said. 'Some of you haven't met my cook yet. This is Mrs Eliza Norville and her son, Paul. Just leave the trays on the hutch, Mrs Norville. My guests will help themselves.'

Mrs Norville bobbed her head at the guests and followed the instructions. But on her way, she shot a loathsome glare at Nicki.

Was everyone in this household bat-crazy? 'Aren't you dining with us, sir?' Nate asked Frazier.

'No, but I'll see you at dinner. When you all finish breakfast, team one will be escorted to their rooms to get outerwear, while team two will be taken to the library. I wish you all an enlightening morning and afternoon.'

Once the door closed behind Frazier, Nate's wife and

employees were left alone, except for the two armed guards at the door.

'I don't think the cook likes me,' murmured Nicki. 'I shouldn't have called her a name when she locked me in the bathroom.'

'And I don't like you roaming the island with a killer loose,' said Hunter.

'Nate and I will take good care of her,' said Michael, on his way to the hutch with his plate.

Hunter slid back his chair. 'With what – a big stick or maybe a butter knife? Frazier's henchmen have assault weapons.'

Nicki stood too. 'And *you* getting under Mr Frazier's skin isn't helping, dear husband. Like our host pointed out, I'm a trained PI, so let's just play along for now.' Nicki spooned some sticky oatmeal onto her plate along with some sliced fruit.

'Don't eat anything cooked by Mrs Norville.' Hunter tried to pull the bowl away from her.

Nicki refused to relinquish her grip. 'Eat or don't eat, Hunter. But I'm not stomping across this island on an empty stomach.'

And so went breakfast for the Price team: the Galens argued; Michael Preston attempted to engage the guards in conversation; Beth studied the locks on the windows, and Izzy appeared to be praying while picking at her food.

And him? Nate needed to find the closet where their guns were stored. Someone other than the bad guys should have a weapon. Unfortunately, on the way to his room or through the maze of hallways to the back door, the guards gave him no opportunity to press on any panels in the foyer. When his fellow team members joined him outdoors fifteen minutes later, Nate wasn't in a particularly good mood.

'I looked for my cell phone,' said Nicki. 'I thought it might work on the other side of the island, but it's gone.'

Michael nodded. 'Mine's gone too. I thought of the same thing.'

'Mine also disappeared, along with my laptop. Our best hope is to intercept Kate and Eric when they step off the *Slippery Eel* today, *before* Compton has a chance to strip them of their weapons and phones,' said Nate.

'Good idea, boss.'

'Thanks, Nick. Now while I'll lead this entourage, you stay right behind me. I've seen Hunter mad and I have no wish to incite his wrath. Michael will make sure nobody sneaks up from behind.'

Nicki stood on tiptoes to reach his eye level. 'Fine, but if you recall, I handled myself well on that case we worked together in New Orleans.'

'Yeah, but this ain't New Orleans. Just keep watching for clues along the way or something that can be used as a weapon.' Nate headed around to the front of the house, staying close to the foundation. 'There's that fountain and fancy pergola on the terrace.' Nate pointed in the direction they needed to go. 'Let's cross the lawn and find the path to the dock.'

'Forge on, boss,' said Michael. 'I'll make sure nobody's following us.'

The path leading to Frazier's dock was easy enough to find. But after an hour of beating through tall weeds and checking under bushes, they reached the water between Elysian Island and the Georgia coast without finding a single clue. Along the way, they neither spotted another human being nor heard as much as the rustle of leaves behind them. And at Frazier's dock, they saw no yacht tied up or approaching from the west. There was nothing but calm water and blue skies in three directions.

Nicki shielded her eyes from the sun. 'No boat, no Kate, no Eric. What now, cousin?'

Nate voiced the first idea which came to mind. 'Find a rock or log to sit on where you'll be hidden from the path and any approaching boat. In case the *Slippery Eel* is arriving later, we don't want to alert anyone until we see Kate and Eric.'

Members of team one sat and waited until their hands grew cold and their legs numb. Finally, Nate stretched to his feet. 'I guess couple number four isn't coming, at least not today.'

'You don't think maybe . . .' Nicki began.

'What, Nicki? That Frazier chained them up in John's condo without food or water?' Nate shook his head. 'Don't let your imagination run away with you. There are plenty of reasons why Eric and Kate haven't shown up yet. Maybe Eric couldn't be spared at Bella Trattoria.'

'Don't you think Kate would have come by herself?' Michael leaned one shoulder against a tree.

'Oh, not you too, Preston. Both of you need to keep level

heads. Don't start imagining Julian Frazier as a reincarnated Freddie Krueger.'

Michael nodded. 'You got it. I'm just voicing an opinion to my team.'

'I'm with ya, boss.' Nicki saluted as though Nate was her commanding officer. 'What's the plan?'

Nate took another glance at the water between them and the speck that was St Simons. 'Let's find a different way back to the house. Maybe we can find where the suspects hide when they're released by Frazier.'

But after walking the shoreline for an hour in one direction and an hour in the other, the team found no other way back other than their original path. Armed with heavy clubs found as driftwood, Nate, Nicki and Michael moved slowly along the path, checking the undergrowth for hidden clues while vigilant for suspects or killers out for blood. Yet once again, they fended off no surprise attacks and found nothing until one hundred yards from the rambling Frazier mansion.

There, hanging from a stout limb of an ancient, moss-covered tree, was the body of Charles Sanborn, retired detective from the Atlanta Police Department. Nate and his team stared at the macabre scene for a long moment. A heavy noose had been draped around his neck and then Sanborn had been hauled up until his feet dangled several feet from the ground.

'Oh, Nate, what a horrible way to die.' Nicki grabbed his arm with both hands.

'You're not kidding.' Nate swallowed down the bile surging up his throat. 'Sanborn didn't deserve this. I don't care how drunk he'd been the night Mrs Frazier died. He couldn't have prevented the break-in.'

'Look over there.' Michael slipped on latex gloves and carefully plucked an empty whisky bottle from the leaves and pine needles. 'Looks like the one we saw at Frazier's first dinner.'

Nate walked to the tree where the hanging rope had been tied off. 'Sanborn certainly didn't get drunk and hang himself.'

'Shouldn't we let the cops photograph and gather evidence at the crime scene?' Nicki asked in a whisper.

'What cops?' Nate felt his heart pounding in his chest. 'You really think Frazier wants law enforcement on this island? I'm not leaving Sanborn hanging from this tree.' Untying the knot, Nate released the rope and lowered Sanborn slowly to the ground. 'Preston, you bring a bag with you today?'

'Yep, I did.' Holding the bottle by the base, Michael dropped it into a plastic bag.

'Should I remove the rope from Mr Sanborn, boss?' Nicki pulled gloves from her jacket pocket.

'No, leave the rope on. Let's take the evidence back to the house before it gets dark. Stay right behind me, Nicki. We don't want any other surprises.'

As the three crossed the front lawn toward the terrace, they were greeted by a welcoming party – Jonah Creery and four guards.

'There you are, Mr Price,' Creery said. 'Mr Frazier had begun to worry about team one.' The guards quickly surrounded them. 'How was everything on the island today?'

Nate gazed into the cold eyes of Frazier's assistant. 'We're fine, but Detective Sanborn is not. You'll find him dead about fifty feet into the woods. But you probably knew that already.' Ignoring the guards, Nate stepped around Creery with Nicki and Michael close on his heels.

'Dear me, Julian will be brokenhearted to hear that.' Creery's words dripped with sarcasm as the guards chortled with laughter.

Nate and his team stomped up the front steps and pounded on the door until Compton finally admitted them.

'What's wrong with you, Mr Price?' the butler demanded. 'I came as fast as I could.'

'There are plenty of things wrong, Compton, but right now I want to get to my room and see my wife. See that Mrs Galen gets safely to her room. Michael, I'll see you at dinner,' Nate said over his shoulder as the guards caught up with them.

'Slow down, Mr Price,' said a guard. 'None of you can get in your rooms until one of us unlocks the door.'

Without thinking, Nate drew back his fist and socked the guard in the jaw with everything he had. The guard's head bounced off the wall before he slid to the floor.

Suddenly, someone pressed a gun to the back of his skull. 'That was a bad idea, Mr Price, unless you're eager to end up swinging from a rope just like Sanborn.'

Nate unclenched his fists while the guard rubbed his jaw, picked himself up, and retaliated with a right hook that sent Nate flying. 'You try that again, Price, you're a dead man. I don't care about Frazier's orders. I got nothing to lose in this country.'

Before Nate could get to his feet, he heard a click of the lock opening. Then he was half pushed, half kicked into his suite.

Following his undignified entry, Izzy screamed. And Nate realized he'd just made a bad situation worse.

The first thing Beth noticed after being locked in the library was a sheaf of papers on the desk. The second thing she noticed was a smile on Hunter's face. 'What do you know that we don't, Galen?' Beth asked.

Pressing his ear to the door to the hall, Hunter held up his index finger. 'Shhh,' he cautioned. 'The guards are still right outside.'

Izzy slumped into one of the two chairs at the desk. 'That's probably where they'll stay until we're finished.'

'I'm betting they'll get hungry and head to the kitchen or wherever they feed hired mercenaries.' Hunter leaned a shoulder against the door for support.

Beth took the leather-upholstered chair usually reserved for the master of the mansion. 'What are you up to?' she whispered.

Hunter stepped away so he wouldn't be overheard. 'An old trick I learned in my grandmother's house in the Garden District. Granny used to lock me in my room until my homework was done. I don't believe Frazier's landline is down. If I can get to his office, I might be able to call nine-one-one or send out an SOS. In the meantime, you two study whatever clues are in that folder.'

Izzy shook her head. 'Maybe I should go instead. Frazier already doesn't like you.'

'No way. This is my idea. And if it works, I think I know where the office might be.'

'Nobody's going anywhere. Let's just do what we were told.' Beth dumped the folder of papers onto the desk. 'Those guards won't leave their post while we're in here.'

Nevertheless, Hunter returned to his listening position at the door.

Despite being captain of their team, Beth couldn't exactly order Hunter Galen around. She picked up the top sheet. 'This appears to be the official court transcript for the State of Georgia versus Mack Fallon. The prosecutor on the case was Assistant District Attorney Jennifer Jacobs. After I read a page, I'll hand it to you, Izzy. Two pairs of eyes are better than one.'

'I agree,' Izzy said, but still slid nervous glances at Hunter.

By the time Beth and Izzy were halfway through the proceedings, they'd all but forgotten about Hunter. The case against Mack Fallon had been destroyed by two factors: first, because Mack died from a drug overdose before the trial. And secondly, the wrench which had been bagged and tagged as the murder weapon was ruled inadmissible in court due to Detective Sanborn's mishandling. Instead of logging in the evidence immediately after leaving the crime scene, Sanborn had left the murder weapon in his unlocked car overnight. According to the transcript, Sanborn had stopped at a bar on his way home and had then forgot about the evidence when he went inside his house.

'So he was drunk at the crime scene, then he continued to drink on his way home. Could he have messed this case up any worse?' Izzy asked after reading the same page.

'I doubt it, and that wrench was the only proof Reuben Fallon was inside the house that night. He must have picked it up in the garage and handed it to Mack at some point. And that's why the ADA dropped the charges and let Reuben go after Mack died in lockup. She had probably hoped one brother would turn on the other, but with Mack dead she had nothing on Reuben without the wrench.' Beth dropped the sheet on the pile.

'Jennifer Jacobs,' murmured Izzy. 'She must have been the female in the lineup of suspects. I understand why Frazier has hated Sanborn all these years, but it's not fair to blame Jacobs. You can't prosecute without sufficient evidence.'

'Seems like Mr Frazier holds anyone connected with the case responsible.' Beth stretched her arms over her head and then moved to the window. 'I wonder where the other team is,' she said absently.

'Someplace not as warm and dry as this.' Izzy joined her at

the window. 'Hunter, give it a rest and take a look at this transcript.'

He again put his finger to his lips. Then, with the quick movement of a cat, Hunter opened the door and slipped from the library.

They stared with mouths agape. 'How did he do that?' Izzy whispered.

Quietly they both padded across the room. Listening at the door as Hunter had, Beth heard no sounds in the hallway. 'I have no idea,' she whispered back. 'But I wish him luck with whatever he's up to.'

As they waited for Hunter to return, Beth and Izzy re-read portions of the court documents. Twenty minutes later, Jonah Creery entered the library with his guards, destroying the room's quiet serenity. One guard paused at the doorjamb to pry something out of the strike-plate. He carried it to Creery on the tip of his knife.

'A wad of gum?' Creery asked. 'What a clever group of detectives you are. But not quite clever enough. Poor little Nicki won't be seeing her overly protective husband for a while.'

Beth rushed toward the head of security. 'What did you do to Hunter? Mr Frazier gave his assurance none of us would be harmed.'

'As long as you played by his rules. Trying to sneak into Frazier's office wasn't part of your directions.' Creery glared down his nose at her. 'You have been ordered back to your quarters. If you're *good girls*, maybe you'll find out what happened to Hunter at dinner.'

One guard grabbed Beth's forearm while another took hold of Izzy. Then they were dragged back to their rooms with far more force than necessary. Once locked in her room, without a way to call for help, Beth reached down to pat her ace-up-the-sleeve – a small, twenty-five caliber Ruger, hidden in a holster at her shin. Those five bullets might just save their lives.

SEVEN

Monday p.m.

When Nate and Izzy were escorted to dinner that night, they found Michael and Beth already at the table, but neither was smiling.

Frazier, in his usual chair, studied them over the rim of his glass. 'There you are, Mr and Mrs Price. I was sorry to hear about your altercation with one of the guards. No one likes to be sucker-punched, highly skilled mercenaries least of all. Looks like you'll have quite a shiner.'

Nate gingerly touched the swollen skin around his eye. 'I'll be fine, unlike Mr Charles Sanborn, who's quite dead.'

Beth pivoted around to face Michael. 'The detective is dead? Why didn't you tell me?'

Michael answered his wife without taking his eyes off Frazier. 'Because by the time we got back, I barely had time to jump in the shower before our escorts were expected to arrive.'

'Don't glare at me, Mr Preston,' Frazier snapped. 'I didn't hang that drunkard from a tree. But now that's he's dead, I can't say I'll mourn his passing.'

'If you didn't give the order, maybe your guards are working on their own.' Nate pointed at the cluster by the door. 'It would've taken more than one person to kill an oversized ex-cop.'

'And why would they? I'm the one paying a king's ransom for their services, with the promise of a bonus at the end.' Frazier thumped his chest. 'Maybe two of the suspects decided to work together, because they were afraid what Sanborn might say if pushed hard enough.'

But Nate had no chance to argue. When the door opened, Nicki stomped into the room, picked up a butter knife, and stopped at their host's chair. 'What did you do with my husband, Mr Frazier? Hunter wasn't in our room when I returned and he's still not back yet.'

Two guards closed in on the agency's skinniest agent, but Frazier waved them off. 'Sit down, Mrs Galen, and let me pour you something to drink.' Frazier poured a second glass.

'Not until you tell me where he is.' Nicki waved the butter knife menacingly.

Creery pushed away from the wall. 'Sit down and act like a lady,' he roared. 'Then you'll find out.'

Nate pulled the weapon from his cousin's hand and maneuvered her into a chair.

Blushing as red as a tomato, Nicki folded her hands in front of her.

'That's a little better.' Frazier passed her the glass of bourbon. 'As Beth and Isabelle will attest, Hunter refused to do what I asked of team two. Instead, he inserted a piece of gum into the lock on the door and sneaked out while my guards were getting a sandwich.' Frazier shot a malevolent glare at the two guards who had let hunger get the better of them. 'Then he tried to break into my office to use the phone. If not for my house-keeper's watchful eye, Hunter might have damaged the hand-carved cherry woodwork that dates back to the mansion's original construction.' Frazier refocused on Nicki. 'Apparently, your husband didn't believe me when I said the landline is out of order. Like you, I don't have any way to contact the mainland.'

'Is that true?' Nicki looked from Izzy to Beth, who nodded affirmatively. 'In that case, I apologize for the butter knife and for any damage done by my husband. But I would greatly appreciate knowing where Hunter is.' Nicki's tone and demeanor had changed on a dime.

Frazier's smile took a long time coming. 'I'm sure you would, but the exact location is immaterial. For now, Hunter has been incarcerated somewhere on the island where he'll receive food, water and air to breathe, but nothing else. Regardless of how you sweet-talk or bat your long eyelashes, you'll get no more information than that. So I suggest you compare notes with the others regarding what you learned today. The sooner you solve my wife's murder, the sooner Hunter will be released and you can go home.'

Nicki took a swallow of the drink. 'All right, why don't I

summarize what we found on the island today?' She directed
her question to Nate.

'That'll be fine. I'll take over where you leave off.'

Nicki took another sip. 'Team one hiked to the same dock
where that boat dropped us off on Saturday. We waited there
for Kate and Eric a long time, but they never showed up. In
fact, no boats of any kind came near Elysian.'

Frazier turned in his chair toward Creery. 'Didn't you instruct
Captain Burke to pick up the fourth couple on Monday at noon?'

Creery nodded deferentially. 'I did indeed, sir. But Captain
Burke mentioned that if the currents were too strong, he would
text Mr Manfredi and Miss Weller, and then try to pick them
up Tuesday.'

'That must have been what happened.' Frazier turned back
to his guests. 'You'll see your friends tomorrow afternoon.
Hopefully, they'll add an additional layer of talent. Continue,
Mrs Galen.'

'When we finally figured out the boat wasn't coming, we
tried to find a different way back because we hadn't found any
clues.'

'Did you find another path?' Frazier asked.

'No, your island is an overgrown jungle,' Nicki muttered as
her ladylike tone slipped a tad.

'My island is a natural maritime preserve. Your use of the
term "jungle" implies you know nothing about Eastern Seaboard
indigenous plants.'

'Guilty as charged.' Nicki filled her glass with white wine.
'But we did find something interesting on the way back. We
found Detective Sanborn hanging from a tree. Dead. Know
anything about that, Mr Frazier?'

His brow pulled into a frown and his lips turned downward.
'As I told your boss, I knew nothing about Sanborn's death
until Mr Creery reported it late this afternoon. I only hope
whoever killed him learned something pertinent before he died.
Did you find any clues, Mrs Galen?'

'Are you referring to the empty bottle of whisky as a clue?'
Nicki arched an eyebrow. 'Yes, Chuck Sanborn was an alcoholic.
And due to his drinking he didn't do a good job investigating
your wife's death, or maybe at any point in his career. But an

empty whisky bottle isn't much of a *clue*. Sanborn didn't drink himself to death.' Before Nate or Michael could stop her, Nicki rose to her feet. 'You, Mr Frazier, are a reclusive wacko with nothing but revenge on the mind. And I won't play your little game anymore.'

Frazier studied Nicki like a bug under the microscope. 'Such a shame you still have so little class after years of rubbing elbows with New Orleans's elite.' He clucked his tongue. 'Mr Creery, take Mrs Galen to her quarters. Rude behavior warrants no supper under my roof.'

While Nate and his employees watched helplessly, two guards lifted Nicki up and carried her from the room. 'Is that really necessary?' Nate demanded.

'Yes, I'm afraid it is. I refused to be disrespected in my own home. Now, team two, are you ready to share your findings?' Frazier's gaze fell on Izzy and Beth.

After the two women whispered between themselves, Izzy lifted her hand. 'Yes, sir, we are. In the library Beth and I studied the official court transcript of The State of Georgia vs Mack Fallon. Assistant Prosecutor, Jennifer Jacobs, asked the judge to dismiss the case because there was insufficient evidence to proceed to trial.'

Frazier nodded his head sagely. 'Please tell members of the other team the reason for insufficient evidence.'

'Because Mack Fallon, believed to be the ringleader of the brothers, and also the one who wielded the fatal blows against Mrs Frazier, died of an overdose of heroin before the trial, even though both brothers were being held without bail.' Izzy inhaled a deep breath.

'Hmmm,' intoned their host. 'How do you suppose that lifelong criminal got ahold of drugs?'

'With all due respect, sir,' Beth interjected, 'drugs are unfortunately available at most jails and prisons across the nation, despite law enforcement's desire to keep them out.'

'Such a shame for a thug to meet his Maker under such circumstances.' Frazier didn't show an ounce of compassion. 'But evidence collected at the crime scene placed the younger brother in my house too. Correct me if I'm wrong, but weren't Reuben Fallon's prints found on the murder weapon – the wrench taken from my workbench?' He stared at Isabelle, waiting for her response.

Izzy straightened in the chair. 'Yes, that's correct. However, the assistant district attorney had no choice but to drop the case against Reuben when the wrench was declared inadmissible as evidence.'

'You're doing very well, Isabelle – please continue.'

'Detective Sanborn didn't properly log the wrench in a timely manner at the police station. The murder weapon remained in his unlocked car while he drank at a local bar. Then the evidence stayed in his car overnight until Detective Sanborn went to work the next day.'

'Was the car at least inside his garage?' Frazier asked, already knowing the answer.

'No, his car was parked on the street.'

'Since the only place Reuben's fingerprints were found were on the wrench,' added Beth, 'when the wrench was thrown out, Jennifer Jacobs was forced to release the second suspect.'

'And Reuben Fallon has been free as a bird all these years because Sanborn was too drunk to do his job. Hence, whisky led to the retired cop's undoing,' Frazier concluded.

'All right, we understand why you left the bottle as a clue, but you had no right to take Sanborn's life,' said Izzy. 'Judgement belongs to the Lord.'

'Spoken like a true Sunday School teacher,' Frazier smirked. 'Thank you, Isabelle, but I didn't kill Sanborn. I merely had the clue left where team one would find it and make the connection.'

Everyone at the table started talking at once, with most of the chatter directed at their host.

'Simmer down,' Creery threatened, 'or you'll all go without dinner like Mrs Galen.'

'Where were you two all day, Mr Frazier?' Nate asked once the room grew quiet.

'Not that it's any of your business, but Mr Creery and I have other responsibilities besides hosting this disappointing soirée. Team two didn't need a babysitter while studying the evidence. If you need someone to vouch for the fact we remained indoors, you may check with my cook or with my butler. Mr Compton, Mrs Norville, and her simpleton son are all the staff I have left on the island.'

Beth studied the staff in the room. 'Where are your maids if that boat didn't come here to pick them up?'

'When Captain Burke brings Mr Manfredi and Miss Weller tomorrow, he will take my remaining staff back to St Simons. In the meantime, they are staying on the third floor for their own protection. If there are no more questions, I shall signal Mr Compton to bring in your supper.'

'I just have one more, sir. Why now?' Nate kept his voice so calm, he could've been asking about tomorrow's weather. 'Your wife was killed more than eight years ago. I'm curious why you waited so long to shake the truth from those you hold culpable. If you're not the one eliminating the suspects one by one, you're providing an opportunity for the killer to operate. Aren't you worried you will eventually be arrested?'

Frazier's laughter sounded almost cruel. 'I was wondering when someone would ask that. For years, I'd been biding my time, thinking I had all the time in the world. That was a mistake. According to the best doctors on the east coast, I have less than six months to exact my retribution. Even if law enforcement holds me blameworthy, our court system will never dispense justice in a timely enough fashion for me spend a single day in jail.'

'You're dying, Mr Frazier?' asked Izzy.

'I am, Mrs Price, but I refuse to face Ariana without knowing who was behind her murder. So I suggest both teams stop considering me the murderer and concentrate on Bob McDowell, a news reporter in Atlanta; Kurt Ensley, a former public defender, now a lawyer in private practice, and Miss Jennifer Jacobs, the former assistant district attorney for Fulton County. All three were roaming the island today, just like Detective Sanborn. One of them killed him to prevent him from telling what he knew. Just remember, esteemed Price investigators, none of you will go home until I find out who paid the Fallon brothers.'

'I assure you, we'll do everything in our power to find McDowell, Ensley and Jacobs tomorrow and find out what they know. We don't need your threats, Mr Frazier. We plan to find your wife's killer, along with Fallon's and Sanborn's, before we even consider going home.' The venom in Nate's voice made his intentions abundantly clear.

When Kate awoke on Tuesday and glanced around the austere bedroom, she had no clue where she was. Then the recent events came rushing back: arriving on St Simons to find her fellow employees already gone from the condo; getting a text that she should take a boat out to a private island; then getting a second text from a boat captain instructing her and Eric to wait another day due to rough seas, same time, same place. *Rough seas?*

She bolted upright in bed. 'Eric, where are you?' For one uncomfortable moment, Kate feared she might have been dreaming. Did you imagine climbing to the top of the lighthouse, looking out for miles in every direction, gathering shells on Massengale Beach and throwing several starfish back into the ocean? Last night they'd split a seafood platter and took dessert home to share during reruns of old movies. All in all, yesterday had been the most relaxing day they'd had in a long time. 'Eric?' she called again.

'I'm here, Sleeping Beauty.' Her handsome boyfriend carried a flimsy tray into the room. 'I went for a run and then cooked breakfast, but I didn't think you'd ever wake up.' Eric set the tray at the foot of the bed.

Kate slipped on a robe and sat down on the blanket chest. 'What did you make us?' She picked up a mug of coffee.

'In a manner of speaking, blueberry pancakes. The guy who owns this condo sure doesn't take cooking seriously. All he had in the pantry was bleached white flour, sugar in little packets, margarine instead of butter, and blueberry jam. No frozen fruit, no baking powder and no whipped cream.' Eric sipped from his own mug.

'It will be just fine.' Kate smiled at her personal chef as she tried the first bite. 'Mmmm, not bad; if only we had some whipped cream.'

Eric stabbed a pancake from the plate, folded it in half, and ate it like a sandwich. 'I like St Simons Island. I vote we stay here for the week. We found some great restaurants and a bar that plays live music until late at night. What do you say?' Eric licked jam from his fingertips.

'As intriguing as that sounds, I already promised Nate we'd come to the retreat. He must have had a good reason to change the location.' Kate continued to eat her pancake with knife and fork in a dignified fashion. 'I don't want the boss to think I'm not a *team player.*'

Eric rolled his eyes at her corporate jargon. 'OK, but don't think you'll get food this good on Elysian.' He grabbed the last pancake and headed back to the kitchen.

While Kate showered and dressed, she contemplated how Nate might react to their late arrival. Hopefully he hadn't planned any activities which required two teams of four people. But as usually is the case, she needn't have worried.

Same as yesterday, Kate and Eric arrived at the town pier promptly at eleven forty-five. And there they sat for a solid hour, watching fishermen feeding bait to the fish, children feeding bread to the fish, and the fish going about their lives in peace. But no yacht arrived to pick them up and take them anywhere, despite the fact barely a ripple broke the surface of the water.

Eric, whose head had been resting against a post, opened his eyes long enough to scan the horizon. 'Captain Burke doesn't seem to be coming for us,' he said.

'It would appear that way.' Kate stretched to her feet.

'Have you tried texting Nate or maybe calling that boat captain? You should have his number since the captain texted you.'

'Yes, Eric, that occurred to me too. I tried both of them while you were napping.' Unfortunately, Kate sounded a tad sarcastic.

Eric drew his sunglasses down with one finger. 'Don't get huffy with me, missy. I voted to forget this whole idea.'

Embarrassed, Kate dropped her chin to her chest. 'Sorry, feeling foolish makes me crabby. I keep thinking it's *me* who's getting the signals wrong.'

Eric wrapped both arms around her waist. 'I listened to the captain's message too. You're not getting anything wrong. Something's going on out on Elysian. We just don't know what.'

'You're such an amazing man. Why do you put up with me?' Kate kissed him softly on the cheek.

'I'm a sucker for a woman who eats whatever I put on her plate. What do you want to try next?'

Kate pondered a moment. 'I vote we go back to John's condo. We need to seriously research Elysian Island, especially the person who owns it now. I got a bad feeling someone's trying to keep us away.'

Once at the condo, Kate started a pot of coffee and pulled out her laptop. It wasn't easy gleaning more information than what Eric found on Google. And unfortunately the agency's internet expert, Michael, was on the island. But after an hour's search of real-estate transfers in the state of Georgia, Kate discovered the name of the current owner. Approximately ten years ago, Julian and Ariana Frazier purchased the island from a real-estate holding company, primarily as a nature preserve for tax purposes and as a private retreat for the rich and famous. *Not exactly an apt description for Nate Price and employees.*

Searching the database of Georgia business tycoons yielded how Julian Frazier had earned his millions. Frazier had begun the best-known manufacturer of auto parts in the state and had later taken his company public, generating billions. He retired as CEO right around the time he bought the island, but retained a majority ownership of the company's stock. Although Frazier shunned the public eye, Kate located several old photos of Ariana Frazier, a woman at least twenty years his junior, on Atlanta society pages. While Kate continued to research Nate's host for the week, Eric called the local phone company for information on reaching the island.

Just as Kate returned with fresh mugs of coffee, Eric hung up with a scowl. 'Guess what? I explained we've been trying to contact friends on Elysian Island for days and can't get through. The customer service tech said sometimes cell phones work and sometimes they don't. It depends on the service provider, the weather, and believe it or not the time of day, because sound waves travel better at night. When I said we tried at all times, she agreed to call the island's landline but refused to give me the number. She just called me back and said the phone line seems to be out of order. She put in a service request, but it could take weeks since the cable lies under the ocean. What century is this?'

Kate handed him a mug, then filled him in on what she'd learned about the reclusive billionaire. 'Who's to say this Frazier guy hasn't gone crazy from all the peace and quiet? I agree something's going on out there and it isn't good.' Kate shut her laptop. 'We need to find a marina on St Simons. How much money did you bring for our little getaway? If we pool our funds, maybe we can pay somebody with a boat to take us to Elysian.'

Eric pulled out his wallet with a smirk. 'How'd I know *your* company retreat was going to cost me? I got a few hundred, plus plastic.' He laid his money on the table.

Kate found less than eighty dollars in her purse which she added to his pile. 'I promise you, Nate will reimburse every penny . . . or I will. Now let's pack some sandwiches and grab a few bottles of water. We might need provisions on our way to the island.'

However, they ate those sandwiches and drank the water sitting at a marina, staring at the water. They asked every boat owner they could find on a Tuesday afternoon at both the large private marina off the causeway and a small public marina on Gascoigne's Bluff, but no one was willing to take two strangers out to Elysian Island. Everyone gave more or less the same reason.

'No, ma'am, that island is private and Mr Frazier expects his privacy to be respected. Good day to you.'

'Sorry, but boats ain't allowed to pull up to that private dock. They're not even allowed to drop anchor within five hundred yards.'

And two boat owners were less polite but more forthright.

'Nope, I don't need money that much to try to dock a boat on Elysian. The signs say "No trespassing" everywhere around that island and that guy means every word of it.'

And: *'No way. Our grandkids took jet skis around the island to the nature preserve where the turtles nest and birds roost on their way to South America. They meant no harm, just wanted to look around. An armed guard walked out of the brush and ordered the kids to get back on their jet skis or he'd make them swim back to Simons. My grandkids were just fifteen and sixteen at the time.'*

As Kate and Eric headed toward the car, Kate grew more discouraged by the minute. 'What are you thinking, Manfredi?' she asked.

'I think there's got to be a way to get out there.' Eric rubbed the back of his neck. 'The people we asked are well known in the marina and maybe all over the island. Someone must be willing to incur the wrath of the local billionaire for four-hundred-eighty dollars. Where could we find such a rebel?'

'If he's anywhere, he won't be at the fancy yacht club.' Kate climbed in behind the wheel. 'Let's drive around watching for homes with boat docks on rivers like the Little River or the Frederica.'

It was almost dark by the time Kate spotted a small house with a boat dock on the Crooked Creek, which fed into the Mackay River, then into St Simons Sound and the Atlantic Ocean beyond. They sprang from Eric's SUV and hurried toward the front door. But as they got closer they noticed the home's peeling paint and loose shingles on the roof. More importantly, the dock out back was sagging ominously to one side. But Kate focused mainly on the boat.

Eric grabbed her arm. 'Are you sure you want to ask this family? From the looks of things, their boat may not be seaworthy.'

Kate shook her head. 'Don't judge a book by its cover, Manfredi. Let's at least ask.' She knocked with confidence.

After a short wait, a long-haired, long-bearded man opened the door. 'Can I help ya? Are you folks lost?'

'No, sir, we're not. But we noticed you've got a powerboat at your dock and we're in desperate need of one. Could we come inside and talk?'

The aging hippie looked them over from head-to-toe. 'Neither of you appears to be dangerous . . .' He swung open the door. 'Come in and have a seat. Name's Greg Dotson.'

'Thanks. Kate Weller and Eric Manfredi.' She and Eric entered the clean but cluttered living room of a true bibliophile. Hundreds of books filled his built-in bookcases, while his coffee table was stacked with newspapers.

'Sorry, the place is a mess. I wasn't expectin' company.' Greg moved more books from a chair.

'Your home is fine,' said Kate. 'We're sorry to barge in.'

Eric cleared his throat. 'May I ask, sir, if that cabin cruiser out back is seaworthy?'

'My cabin cruiser has never been in better shape, *sir.*' He mimicked Eric's overly polite accent. 'And why would this be *your* business?'

Kate stepped in front of him. 'Don't pay any attention to my friend. Eric's not familiar with well-maintained classic Chris Crafts. My dad took me fishing on a twenty-two-foot Cadet Cabin. Is yours a Constellation, a thirty-footer? That beauty will be seaworthy long after we're dead and buried.'

'It is a thirty!' The man extended a callused hand. 'Where are you from, Kate?'

'Eric and I now live in Charleston, but I'm originally from Pensacola.' They all shook hands heartily.

Dotson pointed at his sofa. 'Take a load off. What brought you here from the Gulf of Mexico?'

Kate sat down, while Eric perched on the sofa's arm. 'That is a long story. Right now it's crucial Eric and I reach Elysian Island as soon as possible because we believe our friends are in trouble. We're hoping you'll take us there.'

Dotson's expression turned suspicious. 'Why are you asking *me*?'

Kate shrugged. 'Because we've already asked every boat owner we saw in the causeway marina. Everyone said no.'

The corners of Dotson's mouth turned up. 'You're down to your last choice?'

'At least for tonight we are. It's getting dark. We'll pay you four hundred bucks to drop us off and idle five hundred yards away until we give the signal to pick us up.'

'Four hundred bucks? You must have heard that rich guy doesn't want tourists stopping by or anyone dropping anchor to photograph his guests with a telephoto lens.' Dotson crossed his arms over his overalls. 'What did your pals do to make that guy mad?'

'Honestly, we don't know, but we're both worried.'

The longer Dotson studied his torn cuticles, the more worried Kate became. She upped her ante when the tiny hairs stood on her neck. 'OK, Greg, four-hundred-*eighty* dollars. That's every last dime we brought from Charleston.'

Eric elbowed her side. 'Could we talk for a moment, Kate, outside?'

'Easy there, fella. I'm not interested in taking your last buck. I'll do it for three hundred, but I won't go there at night. If you're back here at five o'clock we'll go at first light.'

Kate jumped to her feet. 'It's a deal.'

'I never could understand securing a protected habitat distinction, but not letting anyone enjoy the flora and fauna of the place,' Dotson added, more to himself than his guests.

Eric rose to his feet. 'Thanks, Greg.'

'Don't thank me until we get your pals off that expensive chunk of real estate.' Dotson walked them to the door. 'Make sure you wear long pants, dark colors, hiking boots, and bring flashlights. If I can get you on shore, you won't find any well-lit, well-marked trails to Frazier's house.'

EIGHT

Elysian Island. Tuesday a.m.

At half past nine on Tuesday, two guards arrived to escort Nate and Izzy down to breakfast. 'You're a little late today,' Nate said when he spotted one guard's black eye. 'Were you boys out on the town last night? That where you got the shiner?'

'Keep it up, Price. I'm just itchin for my trigger finger to slip.'

'Please, both of you,' Izzy begged. 'All I want is to solve the murder and go home.' She grabbed Nate's hand like a naughty child and pulled him toward the dining room, to the great amusement of the guards.

With Michael, Beth, and Nicki already in their seats, they didn't have long to wait for Frazier or for their less than mediocre breakfast. As Nate and Izzy filled their coffee cups, Compton ushered in Frazier, followed by Mrs Norville and her son carrying a cardboard box, a toaster, and half a gallon of orange juice. The pair placed their burdens on the buffet and left.

Nate wondered about the quality of today's coffee, since Frazier sipped his from a travel mug, instead of filling a cup at the silver-plated urn. And, for a change, Jonah Creery was conspicuously absent.

'Good morning, members of the Price team of investigators,' Frazier greeted. 'I trust you slept well.'

'Since you asked,' said Beth, 'I heard strange sounds overhead all through the night.'

Frazier forced a smile in Beth's direction. 'Hard to say who or what made those sounds. Both the maids' quarters and the guards' rooms are on the third floor. Perhaps they all joined hands in a square dance.' He turned his focus to Nate.

'I must apologize for today's breakfast. Mrs Norville refuses to cook a hot meal for guests who display such a complete lack of appreciation. In the crate you'll find a loaf of white bread, jars of peanut butter and various jellies, and individual portions of yogurt. There's also orange juice and plenty of coffee. Mrs Norville will return later to see if you need more. I insisted on strong coffee to help your . . . thought processes.' Frazier studied each guest in succession.

'I'm sure breakfast will be fine. Please thank Mrs Norville on our behalf.' Nate sounded as sincere as possible. 'What do you have planned for us today?'

'Please, Mr Frazier.' Nicki half rose from her chair. 'Before we get started, may I ask how my husband is?'

'Ah, that's the demure young lady your mama raised you to be.' A ghost of a smile brightened Frazier's gray pallor.

Like a wild animal caught in a trap, Nicki didn't move a muscle while she waited.

'He's perfectly fine. Hunter spent the night in an old sleeping bag left behind by the previous owner. He had canned chili for supper and, with any luck, Mrs Norville will give him bread and jam later.'

'Tell Mrs Norville that I would be ever so grateful.' Nicki tucked her long skirt under her as she sat down.

'A fine improvement, Mrs Galen. Now if there are no more questions or complaints about nocturnal noise, I'll give you your instructions. Team one will remain indoors studying a videotape of Bob McDowell, an investigative reporter for one of the Atlanta stations. I use the term *investigative* loosely. As you will see, Bob's specialty is tabloid journalism by sensationalizing every story he covers to boost network ratings. Some of the interviews you'll see aired in the days following my wife's murder, while some of the footage was cut before broadcast. But rest assured, enough innuendo went over the airwaves to muddy the water and besmirch my wife's integrity.'

'May I ask how you obtained this video?' asked Michael, sipping his cold coffee.

Their host frowned. 'How I obtained it isn't relevant to the investigation. Suffice it to say that the right price will buy *anything* in our corrupt, materialistic world. As for the remaining members of team two – Beth and Isabelle – you will be searching for clues on my wild and wonderful island and, with any luck, you'll run into a suspect to interview.'

'That's insane!' Nate slicked a hand through his hair. 'You're sending two women outdoors when a murderer is on the loose?'

'What a sexist thing to say.' Frazier shifted his focus to Izzy and Beth. 'Dear me, Isabelle, I'm surprised your caveman husband doesn't keep you barefoot and chained to the stove all day. As for you, Beth, your boss doesn't think very highly of your abilities. I'm curious why he hired you in the first place. It truly isn't for your fashion sense or charming personality.'

Before either woman could respond, Nate shouted. 'If you want us to play your stupid little game, stop baiting my wife and employees!'

As guards closed in to protect Frazier, their host placed his hands on the table and shouted with equal fervor. 'Rest assured, Mr Price, if you refuse to play my game, every one of you will die.'

Nate stood and rammed in his chair. 'Isn't that what you had in mind from the beginning? You'll never let us go after what we've witnessed.'

Frazier uttered a nasty, contemptuous word. 'What do I care what you *witnessed*? I'm not the one killing people on this island!'

The two glared at each other like angry bulls in a spring pasture.

'I believe you, Mr Frazier,' said Izzy, breaking the stalemate. She walked to where Beth sat and pulled her teammate to her feet. 'You're right – Nate can be a tad sexist. Beth and I are ready to search for suspects.'

'I knew you were the level-headed one, Isabelle.' Frazier's eyes glowed with admiration. 'But you haven't had your breakfast yet. How about toast and yogurt? I know it's not much, but my cook can be downright stubborn at times.'

'Toast will be fine,' Izzy said as she and Beth headed to the breakfront.

The guards kept Michael and Nate in their seats until their wives had eaten a slice of toast, grabbed containers of yogurt, and left the dining room.

Once the double doors closed, Frazier clapped his hands. 'Very well, now team one may get their breakfast. While you eat, I'll set up the VCR to show the reporter's interviews on continuous loop. When you've watched the tape enough times, simply press the machine's stop button.' Frazier rolled over the television, popped in the tape, and pressed play. 'As always, use the button on my chair if you need more coffee or when you're finished and wish to return to your rooms.' Then their host picked up his travel mug and left the dining room.

Finally alone in the ornate room, Nate scrubbed his face with his hands. This was a house of madness, not a place for a happily married couple to retire. His cousin, Nicki, sat at the table, staring into space, as though in a daze. 'Nicki,' he said, breaking through the fog. 'Eat a piece of toast or some yogurt. You should keep your strength up, for Hunter's sake.'

Like a robot, Nicki walked to the toaster and pushed down a slice of bread.

'Same goes for you, boss.' Michael practically yanked him from his chair. 'We'll all eat and watch the video. But we'll keep our eyes open for our chance.'

'A chance to do what?' Nate muttered at the buffet.

Michael shrugged. 'We'll know it when we see it.'

So Nicki with her piece of toast, and Nate and Michael with toast, yogurt and coffee refills sat down at the table to watch TV, where the worst of tabloid journalism unraveled before their eyes.

Bob McDowell was a master at directing an interview where he wanted it to go. In the days following the murder, he canvassed Frazier's expensive suburban neighborhood, looking for a bored housewife or an embittered man eager to talk. Many were willing to cast aspersions on the May–December marriage, even if they'd barely known Ariana and Julian Frazier. In the age of reality television, people were so eager for five minutes of fame that they shamelessly stated Ariana married Julian for his wealth, while others inferred she stepped out on him as often as she could. As the interviews aired, McDowell showed photos of Ariana at several galas, pictured over a span of several years, judging by her hair and clothes. In each photo Ariana was always holding a glass of champagne. And she was always surrounded by adoring fans, instead of on the arm of her husband. Of course, how many of these neighbors spent every minute at a party with their spouse? McDowell did everything he could to portray Ariana as a gold-digging party girl who loved money, expensive jewelry, and a good time.

During one segment which aired during the six o'clock news, McDowell went so far as to describe the murder as 'mysterious,' yet he had nothing but innuendos and suppositions to back up his claims. McDowell even questioned the grieving widower why their marriage lacked a pre-nuptial agreement, implying that in itself made Frazier suspect in her death.

The sleazy journalist had done his homework. He had searched for anything that would muddy the waters of Ariana's murder, instead of reporting the plain and simple truth: Julian and Ariana were victims of a break-in that had turned deadly. And the fact that the Fraziers had no pre-nup or that Ariana liked to drink and socialize had nothing to do with it.

Nate lost his appetite halfway through the first showing, but he let the tape play again to make sure he didn't miss something.

'Bob McDowell is a pig,' Nicki concluded once Nate switched off the machine.

'You'll get no argument from me.' Michael pushed away his plate of bread crusts. 'Journalism sinks to a new low.'

Nate jotted down a few notes. 'Frazier has every reason to hate this guy, but I don't see how watching these interviews helps us figure out who paid the Fallons, if someone indeed did. McDowell's interests lie in high ratings for his news segments. But I doubt even McDowell would set up a high-profile murder to create fodder to exploit.'

Michael rubbed the stubble on his chin. 'I agree. But without internet access, we can't check if McDowell knew either Ariana or Julian prior to that night.'

'Didn't Mr Frazier say if we needed the internet, he would provide it?'

Nicki's question caught Nate by surprise. 'You heard Frazier say that?'

She nodded. 'I'm pretty sure it was the day we checked in.'

'Good work, Nick. As long as no one wants to watch this again, I'll signal that we're done in here. I'll tell whoever shows up we need access to Wi-Fi if Frazier wants us to connect this tape to the killings.'

When Nicki and Michael shook their heads, Nate pressed the button on Frazier's chair.

The charming Mrs Norville and several black-clad guards answered his call. 'Your team's finished *already*?' The cook sounded disappointed, as though she wasn't getting her money's worth after the tasty breakfast. When Nate stated his request, the cook rolled her eyes. 'I'll tell Mr Frazier what you want. Maybe he'll give you a couple hours online tonight or maybe he'll let you talk to McDowell at dinner. But I ain't going out on a limb for you, Mr Price.'

That woman doesn't like me anymore than she likes Nicki, he thought as armed guards led them back to their quarters.

Beth changed into sweat pants, a long T-shirt and a hoodie, making sure her baggy pants hid the only advantage she had. Ridiculously, she checked for a dial tone on the phone by the bed. But no tooth fairy came during the night to reconnect the landline to civilization. At some point yesterday, Frazier had everything removed from her room that could possibly be used as a weapon – the fireplace poker, the cords which tied back the heavy drapes, even the water glasses had been switched with paper cups. There would be no even playing field in Frazier's monstrous game.

'What's taking you so long?' yelled a gruff voice in the hallway.

Beth jumped, but she was even more startled when the guard unlocked her door and walked in.

'Nothing,' she replied, forgoing a sarcastic response. 'I'm ready to go.'

The guard took a quick look around and then hustled her down the back stairs. Curtailing any opportunity to snoop, the nastiest of her captors prodded Beth outdoors. 'Good luck, ladies. Try not to get yourselves killed.' She and Izzy heard raucous laughter after he slammed the door.

'Everything OK?' Izzy asked.

'Just peachy.' Beth pulled a pair of gloves from her pocket. 'Was there anything different about your room?'

Izzy cocked her head to one side. 'Not that I noticed, but I was in a hurry to get this over with.'

'Someone took everything from our room that possibly could be used as a weapon, like the fireplace poker and sash cords.'

'Frazier's worried about letting us have lengths of rope when he's got men with automatic weapons?' Isabelle shook her head. 'He really doesn't know who's killing off the suspects.'

'Which means he's not the one who killed Fallon and Sanborn.' Beth drew the obvious conclusion – one she didn't like.

'Like Frazier said, he could have killed either of them long ago and saved himself all the trouble and expense.' Izzy gazed skyward, where low clouds foretold rain later that day.

'Well, if the killer isn't our peculiar host and it's not one of us, then that leaves the remaining suspects, since Frazier's staff here didn't work for him in Atlanta, and Creery and Frazier seemed to be joined at the hip. So we've got the reporter, the assistant prosecutor, and the former public defender, now Hunter's lawyer. What a bizarre twist of fate that is.'

'You're not kidding. Let's get going. I'm eager to talk to that Jennifer Jacobs.' Isabelle impatiently shifted from one foot to the other. 'I'm afraid if we don't solve this soon, Mrs Norville will be reduced to serving us moldy bread and rainwater.'

An idea popped into Beth's head. 'The cook's lousy menus might not be her fault. Just like Captain Burke hasn't returned to bring us Kate and Eric, I haven't seen any boats delivering food or mail or anything else. And I usually stay up half the night watching out my window.'

'You think Frazier cancelled every boat headed this way?'

'Maybe not Frazier. Maybe it was whoever cut the phone line to the mainland.'

'This is going from bad to worse. Well, team leader, what's our plan for today?' Izzy asked without a hint of sarcasm.

Beth exhaled a weary sigh. 'I was thinking about this last night when I couldn't sleep. When Frazier sent us out two days ago, we checked the barn behind the house and then headed east until we reached the beach. When Nate, Nicki, and Michael left yesterday, they headed around the house to the front terrace and found the path to the dock where the *Slippery Eel* ties up.'

Izzy nodded agreement. 'That's how Nate explained it too. When they realized Eric and Kate weren't coming, they tried to find a different way back, but couldn't. Nate said the undergrowth is so thick you'd need a machete to get through it.'

'We went east; they went west, so today we go south.' Beth pointed. 'That way, judging by the position of the sun. Let's see if we can find a suspect in that direction.'

Izzy gazed back at the house where shadows moved behind the curtains. 'Sounds good. Maybe we'll discover the spot where two lawyers like to hide.'

'Or where they plot who to bump off next.' Beth regretted her words as soon as they left her mouth. Izzy made a living as a part-time real-estate agent and full-time mother. She didn't need anyone scaring her more than she already was.

But Izzy didn't seem remotely shocked by her comment. Maybe the boss brought plenty of work stories home with him. For whatever reason, Izzy was already heading south at a fast walk. Beth had to run to catch up with her.

Although there was no real path in this direction, navigating the terrain proved easier than the path she and Izzy had taken on Sunday. After an hour of walking, the woods thinned to an occasional loblolly pine, interspersed with buckthorns and crepe myrtles, and acres upon acres of tall grass, as though this area had once been farmed by a former resident. As long as they watched for gopher holes, the teammates were able to walk side by side.

'I hope Nate's behavior didn't offend you at breakfast,' Izzy said. 'He's very protective of all his employees, even if you can shoot better than he can.'

Beth grinned. 'I wasn't the least bit offended, but for a different reason. I know Nate. Not as well as you do, but I know he's always strategizing. He didn't want us separated. If we're ever to gain the upper hand with Frazier, we must keep everyone together.' Beth glanced over at the woman she barely knew. 'I was afraid *you* might be mad.'

'Because of Frazier's remark about keeping me barefoot and chained to the stove?' Izzy's laugh sent birds soaring from a nearby tree. 'Truth is I love going barefoot and I love to cook. Why should anyone be offended by the truth?'

'You've got a great attitude.' Beth slapped her teammate on the back.

'I'm not at all like Nate described me, huh?'

'Man, how should I answer that? I think I'll plead the fifth.'

For the next hour, the two women talked and laughed and joked about the quirkiness of married life. They had so much fun getting to know one another, they almost forgot they were captives in a mystery skit gone wrong.

'Stop for a moment.' Beth held up her hand. 'Did you hear that?'

Izzy halted in midstride. 'Waves,' she exclaimed.

Both women ran through the tall grass until they reached the dunes protecting what had to be the prettiest beach on Elysian Island. Judging by wet marks left in the sand, high tide never left less than fifty yards of beach. Uprooted trees, weathered by strong winds and shifting sand, created works of art along the shore.

Beth admired the beach in both directions. 'Too bad more people can't enjoy this little piece of paradise.'

'True, but without Mr Frazier's restrictions, maybe this piece of paradise would soon disappear.' Izzy dug a shell from the sand with her toe. 'OK, now that I'm taking the side of a madman, which way should we head?'

Beth again considered the sun's position. 'If we go to the right, we should come around to the dock where Michael and Nate were yesterday.'

'And the path to the house where they found Sanborn hanging from a tree?' Izzy shivered in the cool breeze.

'Yeah, but the other way will bring us around to where we found Reuben Fallon with a cracked skull.'

Izzy met Beth's gaze. 'Let's go right,' Izzy said without hesitation.

But their journey in that direction was neither long nor arduous. Within five minutes, they rounded an uprooted tree which had washed ashore during the last storm. Its bare and twisted limbs reached for the sky as though in supplication, while powdery sand whorled and eddied at its feet. Bits of Spanish moss stubbornly clung to branches against the strong offshore breeze. Yet it wasn't the macabre dead tree which chilled the blood in their veins. Someone was buried in the sand, similar to how children play with buckets and shovels. Yet, unlike a hapless Dad with sand up to his chest, this victim was face down with his head completely covered, while his legs and torso had been left exposed.

Instantly Beth and Izzy closed the distance, dropped to their knees and began to dig. Frantically they pawed sand away from his head and neck until they could turn the man over.

'Now what should we do?' cried Izzy, brushing sand from his face.

Beth took one look at the man's lifeless, open eyes and knew the answer. Nevertheless, she tried to clear sand from his mouth and then listened at his chest for several minutes.

'There's nothing we can do,' Beth finally answered. 'I believe there's sand in his airway and he suffocated.'

'Which one of the suspects is this?' Tears ran down Izzy's cheeks.

'If I had to guess, I'd say this is the Atlanta reporter, Bob McDowell.' Beth sat back on her heels, focusing on seagulls wheeling in air currents offshore. Every now and then a seagull dove straight into the waves and came up with lunch.

However, Izzy continued to clean every bit of sand from the reporter's face and shirt.

'We're too late, Izzy.' Beth took hold of her arm. 'The guy is dead.'

'I know that.' She yanked her arm back. 'But there's something tucked inside his shirt.' In short order, Izzy removed a manila packet that had been pinned to his undershirt.

Shaking off the last bit of sand, Izzy pulled out a stack of photos. Beth picked up the top picture to study. 'It's our dead guy and I'll bet that's the lady assistant prosecutor we saw at the first dinner.' In the photo, the pair looked to be deep in conversation in someone's office. The professionally dressed woman was smiling rather fondly at the man.

'I'll take that stack of photos, Mrs Price,' said a voice over Izzy's shoulder.

'Jonah Creery, why am I not surprised? You seem to turn up wherever there's a body.' Beth jumped to her feet. 'Where's your merry band of henchmen?'

'They will be here shortly.' Creery's phony smile was short-lived. 'Let's just say I got a head start because I knew where the ADA and her former lover have been hanging out, trying to escape. The photos, please?' He held out his hand. 'You'll be able to study them soon.'

Rising to her feet, Izzy handed him the packet.

Reluctantly, Beth took a last look before giving Creery her photo too. 'You and Frazier will never get away with killing these people. People know where we are and eventually they'll come looking for us.'

'You are such a thick-headed woman, Beth. I don't know how Michael puts up with you.' Creery rolled his eyes. 'Mr Frazier and I haven't killed anyone. You still don't get it? The suspect who paid for the hit doesn't want anyone to talk. Whenever he – or she – gets a chance, they're eliminating the other suspects one by one.'

Beth would have liked to knock the obnoxious man down, but the guards had reached their spot on the beach. 'Now we're down to the last two. Which do *you* think it is?' she asked Creery.

'My money's on the sleazy lawyer. Funny how Hunter Galen hired a former Atlanta public defender to handle his New Orleans legal work. Sleaze does love to stick together.' Creery motioned the guards toward Beth and Izzy. 'Tether the two women together. We don't want either of them getting lost on the way back.'

'What about him?' Izzy pointed at the corpse. 'We can't just leave him here. What if the tide comes up this far?'

'Oh, but we can, Isabelle. You should know by now that we leave the crime scene as we found it. Eventually the police will get here.' With a sneer, he motioned to the guards. 'Make sure their ropes are tight.'

And so team two began the long trek back to the house without Beth seeing the remotest possibility of escape.

When the door opened and his wife entered their suite, Nate ran to greet her. 'What happened?' he asked.

'Oh, nothing out of the ordinary, just another dead body on the beach.' Looking exhausted and frighteningly pale, Izzy peered up with watery eyes. 'Someone suffocated that TV reporter by burying his head in the sand. What a horrible way to die! How could anyone do something so cruel?' Izzy crumbled like a ragdoll against his chest.

Nate swept his wife up in his arms and laid her on the bed.

'I'm so sorry I put you through this . . . that I put all of you through this.'

Izzy shook her head. 'This isn't your fault. You took a rich, successful businessman at his word, and why wouldn't you? Frazier was also a friend of Mrs Baer and we know she's an upright person.' Izzy swept the hair back from his face. 'I don't want you blaming yourself, no matter what the outcome. Psychopaths, sociopaths – whatever you call people like Frazier – can't be predicted. We just need to figure out whether the killer is the ADA or Hunter's lawyer.'

'Are you sure it was Bob McDowell, the journalist who sensationalized the murder and publicly smeared the Fraziers?'

'If that's the guy's name then "yes." When Beth and I found the body, there was a packet of photos pinned to his undershirt. In one picture McDowell had a camera around his neck and he was standing with a woman in heels and a business suit. I'm betting it was the journalist and the assistant district attorney.'

'Where are those pictures now, Izzy?'

'That creepy Jonah Creery showed up and took them from us. Funny how that guy seems to be lurking around every tree on an overgrown nature preserve.'

'Yeah, funny indeed. Either Creery followed you and Beth when you left the mansion, which wouldn't be hard to do, or he simply staked out a place he thought you would eventually find.'

'I can't imagine that Creery followed us. We didn't even take a path this time. We just headed south through the woods and across the fields until we reached the ocean. But I also can't believe Creery staked out a certain spot, hoping we'd find it. This island is much longer, north and south, than it is wide, and altogether bigger than we thought. But I'll tell you one thing – I doubt the killer is Frazier and his assistant. And Creery acting alone makes no sense. What motive would he have? It's got to be the ADA, either alone or in cahoots with the public defender. Judging by the picture, they knew each well, and could have had a falling out.' Izzy settled back against the pillows. 'Now let me rest. I am tired beyond words.'

When she closed her eyes, Nate rubbed her feet like they were at home in Natchez, which seemed like a lifetime ago.

But they weren't at home. They were trapped on an island as remote as the Amazon rainforest.

The next thing he knew, Izzy was shaking his arm. 'Wake up, Nate. We'd better get ready for dinner.' She scooted to the edge of the bed and headed to the bathroom. 'I need a long hot shower. Then tell me what your team learned from your clue.'

When Izzy closed the bathroom door, Nate poured himself a stiff drink from the decanter. *We are gerbils caught inside a maze, waiting for Frazier to toss us scraps of bread.* The visual image did nothing to quell his anxiety.

When guards escorted them to their fourth dinner on the island, Jonah Creery was waiting at the door with Beth and Michael. 'Good evening, Mr and Mrs Price. We're just waiting for Mrs Galen. Ah, here she comes now.'

Nicki fought against the guard's grip on her arm all the way to the dining room.

'I'll see you later, Nicolette,' the guard said sweetly. 'Maybe I'll stop by at bedtime to tuck you in.' Then he puckered up and blew her a kiss.

Nate recognized the same creep he'd tangled with earlier. When he reached out to grab the guard's shirt, his cousin got in his face.

'Don't, Nate!' Nicki demanded. 'He's trying to bait you. He wants an excuse to hurt you badly.'

'But what if—' Nate began.

Creery interrupted his question. 'I'll see that he doesn't.' Creery shot a dagger look at the guard. 'Supper will be delayed tonight, but Mr Frazier will join you later when it's served. In the meantime, you'll find libations to take the rough edges off your day.' Creery unlocked the door and practically pushed the five of them inside.

'Notice anything different about the dining room?' Nate asked when he heard the lock click.

'Yeah, we're alone.' Michael walked to the windows overlooking the garden. 'No guards watching us tonight.'

'What difference does it make?' Nicki whined. 'Maybe they finally realize we can't get out and can't find anything in here we could use. There aren't even any butter knives on the table.' Nicki poured a glass of wine from an open bottle. 'Wine anyone?

Beth, Izzy? However, the brand is a definite step down from Sunday's.'

'I will,' Beth chimed.

'Me, too,' said Izzy. 'But let's stick to one glass each and no more.'

'Good idea,' Nate added. 'I don't want anyone getting tipsy tonight. Too much is at stake.'

For the second time, Nicki got in his face. 'Too much at stake? The outcome will be the same whether we're half-in-the-bag or stone-cold sober. Frazier isn't letting any of us leave this island alive.' She filled her wine glass to the rim.

'We don't know that, cousin.' Nate tried to put an arm around her shoulder.

But she batted him away like a gnat. 'I know I'm taking an empty wine bottle to my room tonight, just in case that guard pays me a bedtime visit.'

Nate's blood pressure shot up. 'I thought that guard was just baiting us?'

'He was, but I still don't want to take any chances.' Nicki filled the other two glasses to the rim too.

'There's got to be something in a dining room we can arm ourselves with.' Nate stomped over to the china cabinet and began to rummage. 'Silverware, an iron trivet – look for anything.'

'We wouldn't stand a chance against automatic weapons.' Izzy pleaded with him. 'Let's just do what we're supposed to – sit down and compare notes.'

Ignoring her, Nate rummaged through drawer after drawer. He found candles but no matches; plenty of spoons but no knives or forks, and enough fancy tablecloths to host a wedding reception.

'Hey, boss, maybe you should listen to your wife.' Michael pulled out the chair next to his. 'Seriously, come over and have a seat.'

As much as he hated feeling so helpless, he hated being this out of control more. Nate closed the drawers and sauntered back to the table. 'Since my wife is stunningly beautiful besides brilliant, I think I'll sit with her.' Nate took the chair next to Izzy's.

'OK, but then you won't get to see the hidden microphone in the candelabra. It just wasn't hidden well enough.' Michael plucked a tiny piece of electronics from the silver filigree. 'Everything we've said in here has been listened to by someone out there.' He gestured toward the door.

Beth plucked the microphone from her husband's fingers, dropped it on the rug and stomped it with her boot heel. 'Guess we know why no guards are in here with us.'

The team barely had a chance to consider Beth's actions when the doors opened. In marched Mr Frazier with his side-kick, Creery, and half a dozen mercenaries. 'Good evening, everyone,' Frazier murmured. 'Forgive me for keeping you waiting.' Their host took his usual place of honor at the table.

Creery, however, walked straight to Beth. 'I just bought that device, Mrs Preston. You owe me two hundred bucks, and I will swipe your credit card before you leave the island.'

Beth blinked like an owl. 'Sure, Jonah, whatever you say.'

Frazier cleared his throat. 'With that settled, why don't we get down to business? I'm quite sure Nate and Michael heard from their spouses about Mr McDowell's untimely death on the beach. Untimely, but not unfortunate, since he was scum.' Frazier glanced around to see if anyone would disagree. No one did. 'Isabelle, for the benefit of Mrs Galen, would you please explain what you and Beth found on your morning walk?'

Izzy took a sip of wine, coughed, and then gave Nicki a brief summary of how and where the reporter died. In an attempt to protect Nicki's fragile state, Izzy omitted many of the graphic details. When she finished, everyone gave Nicki a moment to process.

'So, the reporter's dead,' Nicki murmured. 'You took your revenge on the man who smeared your wife's reputation.' Her shoulders began to shake. 'And that just leaves the lady pros-ecutor and Hunter's lawyer . . . and us. I bet you'll save us for last.'

'Please, Nicki, pull yourself together.' Nate feared Frazier's wrath on his cousin if she lost control again.

But surprisingly, Frazier looked on Nicki with pity. 'It's all right, Mr Price. Perhaps Mrs Galen isn't used to being alone this much and having to process events without her husband's

help. I will excuse her rudeness this time.' Frazier poured himself
a small amount of bourbon and pressed the button on his chair.
'Mr Creery, if you'd be kind enough to ready the videotape of
McDowell for the benefit of team two. Before they too think
the reporter undeserving of his fate, I'd like Isabelle and Beth
to view what team one saw this morning.'

As the door opened, Mrs Norville carried in a huge copper
pot which she set on the marble top breakfront. Her son followed
close behind with a basket covered with a checkered cloth.

'Tonight's dinner will be cubed sirloin of beef with new
potatoes, heirloom carrots, turnips, onions, and frozen peas,
which is just a fancy way of describing beef stew.' Frazier
chuckled at his joke. 'But Mrs Norville also baked fresh bread
and made rhubarb pie for dessert. My cook might have forgiven
you after all.'

Izzy rose to her feet. 'Thank you, Mrs Norville. Beef stew
is one of my favorite meals. I make it often at home.'

'You're welcome,' said the middle-aged woman on her way
out.

Frazier downed his drink in a single gulp. '*Bon appétit*, Price
team. If you don't mind, I won't stay for the final showing of
McDowell's vitriol. I've watched it too many times already.'

'What about the photos of the reporter and the Atlanta
prosecutor?' Nate asked. 'Izzy and Beth were told we would
see them later.'

'Is that what Mr Creery told them?' Frazier turned to frown
at his assistant. 'In that case, you'll see them tomorrow at
breakfast.' He slammed down his empty glass and strode from
the room.

This time the guards remained in the dining room while Nate
and his employees ate dinner and watched the videotape of Bob
McDowell. The beef stew tasted much better than anyone
expected and the fresh bread and rhubarb pie were downright
delicious. However, the videotape did not improve with additional viewings. When Nate switched off the machine, he locked
gazes with his wife.

'I don't feel quite so sorry for the reporter anymore,' Izzy
said, her eyes shiny with unshed tears.

'Me neither.' Beth refilled her glass with wine. 'But now

we're down to two suspects – the lady prosecutor and Hunter's lawyer. What were their names?'

Nate pulled out his small notebook. 'According to the court transcript, the ADA was Jennifer Jacobs.' He flipped back a few pages. 'But I don't remember the name of Fallon's public defender. Nicki, what's the name of Hunter's lawyer?'

'*Who?*' His cousin peered up from her half-eaten bowl of stew. 'Ensley,' Nicki said after Nate repeated the question a second time. 'Kyle or Kevin or something like that.' She returned to her bowl of stew.

'OK,' continued Beth. 'So the killer is either Jennifer Jacobs or this Ensley guy. I'm guessing one or the other withheld evidence.'

'Or they're working together.' Nate pushed away his slice of pie. 'No way could the skinny woman we saw on Sunday kill Detective Sanborn by herself.'

'Two lawyers teaming up to cover up a murder – what a scary thought.' Beth slumped down in her chair.

'That's why we must get to Jacobs and Ensley before they get to one of us.' Michael reached down for his wife's hand. 'You ready, Beth? I don't know about anybody else, but I've had enough of this room for one day.'

Nate pulled Izzy to her feet and then helped up Nicki. 'Let's all get a good night's sleep. Tomorrow it'll be our turn to search the island. And I will insist that Nicki stays indoors with Izzy and Beth.'

Surprisingly, Nicki didn't argue with him. In fact, Nate wasn't sure if she even heard him. As they filed through the doorway, Nate said quietly to Michael, 'You and I will do whatever it takes to find the last two suspects.'

NINE

St Simons Island. Wednesday a.m.

When Kate awoke on Wednesday to a clear, starry sky and a gentle breeze, she took it as a good omen. The first pink streaks of dawn were still thirty minutes away, but Eric had the coffee brewing and the condo's living room in a better condition than how they had found it.

'Wow,' she exclaimed, noticing dust-free furniture and vacuum marks on the carpeting. 'You will make some lucky woman a good husband one day.' Kate arched up on tiptoes to peck his cheek.

'I hope she doesn't marry me solely for my cooking and cleaning abilities.' Eric planted his kiss smack-dab on her mouth. 'Want me to make us something for breakfast?'

She shook her head. 'We shouldn't run the owner out of his last few supplies. Besides, Greg Dotson told us to get there by first light, which means we should leave now. We'll just grab whatever the Price team left behind.'

Thus, their breakfast consisted of one sleeve of crackers, the last two slices of cheese from the party tray and an apple. But Kate knew better than to board a boat without something in her stomach. She'd only been seasick once, but that one time had taught her a valuable lesson.

At this hour, the sleepy island was barely waking up, let alone out and about. Although most inhabitants were yearlong residents, many were retired or worked from home. Enjoying the drive through quiet streets, Kate almost forgot what she and Eric were about to do – show up on an island that for some reason they had been excluded from.

What reason could Julian Frazier have for cancelling the boat? And why hadn't Nate contacted her about what was going on? Elysian Island was visible on a clear day from the top of the St Simons lighthouse. With communication possible between NASA and astronauts on the moon, surely he or Beth could've texted . . . or sent a carrier pigeon by now. Each time she considered her former mentor's assertiveness, Kate knew beyond a shadow of a doubt, Beth and the others were in trouble.

'Penny for your thoughts,' said Eric as they left the village behind.

Kate glanced over at the love-of-her-life. 'Step on it, Manfredi. I'm thinking you and I are all that stands between the Price team and disaster.'

'Then they've got nothing to worry about.' Stomping on the gas pedal, Eric's SUV shot down the two-lane highway.

When they pulled into Dotson's gravel driveway and braked to a stop, Eric leaned over and hugged her. 'It's been good, Weller. I have no regrets.'

Kate stared at him, utterly flummoxed. 'What's gotten into you? You just said the Price team had nothing to worry about.'

'I'm talking about the twenty-two miles of water between here and there.' Eric pointed at the cabin cruiser where Dotson had already started the engine. 'If that boat starts taking on water, no way can I swim back, not even with a life jacket.'

'Will you stop worrying? I'm telling you a Chris Craft is a top-notch vessel, as long as she's been maintained.' Kate grabbed her tote bag and climbed out.

'Like I said, Weller, no regrets,' Eric teased as he followed her down the rickety dock.

'Good morning, Kate, Eric,' Dotson called. 'You're right on time.'

'Morning, Captain. Weather looks good, no?' Kate tipped her baseball cap.

'Weather looks perfect. Climb aboard, mates. I'm just warming Betsy's engine.'

Before Kate stepped from the floating gangway onto the boat, she checked the brass plate on the stern. *Beautiful Betsy* – just like she figured.

Eric remained on the dock to untie the ropes and then stepped aboard at the very last moment. 'Whew, that was close,' he muttered when he dropped down on the seat beside her.

'You did good, landlubber,' Kate said to Eric as she stowed

her bag under the bench. 'Was Betsy your high school or college sweetheart?' she asked the captain.

Greg guided the boat carefully into deep water. 'Yes and yes. I met Betsy in high school. Then we both attended the University of Georgia. We were married thirty-five years before she passed.'

'I'm so sorry for your—'

Keeping one hand on the wheel, Greg held up the other like a traffic cop. 'Don't feel sorry for me, young lady. Betsy and I had what many couples only dream about. Thirty-five years ain't chump change.'

Eric tightened his grip on her hand. 'You're not kidding, Greg. So speaking for both of us – even though Kate went to the University of Florida – go UGA!'

Dotson pumped his fist in the air while everyone laughed. 'Take a bite out of those gators!'

Kate leaned forward to get out of the wind. 'Did you always live on St Simons?'

'No, I grew up across the river in Brunswick. My father was a commercial fisherman until the day he died. Dad wanted me to follow in his footsteps, but there was less and less money to be made and so much competition from commercial fleets. Now that I just fish to put dinner on the table, I enjoy fishing a whole lot more.'

Kate settled back against Eric's shoulder to watch day break over the Eastern Seaboard. Before the sun completely cleared the horizon, Captain Greg slowed the boat's engine to a crawl. 'Elysian Island, mates.' He pointed a crooked finger at the green mass straight ahead.

'We'll circle around the island. Hopefully there'll be a good spot to pull up.'

'What if there's no dock on that side?' Eric shielded his eyes from the sun's glare.

'I'm sure there won't be, landlubber. I'll run the bow up the beach and let you climb out. Then you can push me back into deeper water. Make sure you call when you want me to pick you up.'

Eric saluted his superior officer. 'Sounds like a plan, Captain.'

Yet Greg's well-laid plan didn't come close to fruition. The

Beautiful Betsy was still two hundred yards off the coast when they heard popping sounds coming from Elysian.

Kate jumped to her feet. 'Is that what I think it is?'

At first no one answered. But with the next round of rat-a-tat-tat, they saw a line of shots hit the water next to the starboard bow.

'Yep, that's gunfire all right.' Captain Greg turned the wheel in the opposite direction and accelerated to full throttle.

'Can we go around to the other side?' Kate asked. 'Maybe if you just get us to shallow water, we can wade ashore.'

Greg shook his head. 'No way. Sorry, folks, but those were warning shots to stay away. The owner of that island is serious about his "no trespassing" signs. Next time the guy with the long-range rifle will start blowing holes in my boat. And my wood hull doesn't take kindly to bullet holes.' Captain Greg didn't ease up on the throttle until well out of range.

Kate waited until the engine wouldn't drown out her words. 'I'm so sorry. It wasn't our intention to put you or the *Beautiful Betsy* in harm's way.'

Greg smiled over his shoulder. 'I know that, Kate. Besides, this wasn't the first time Betsy and I have been shot at.' The captain winked with such exaggeration that Kate didn't know if he was teasing or not.

'Got any suggestions on how we might reach our friends on Elysian?' she asked.

He stroked his beard while considering. 'I suppose if you rented scuba gear, I could drop you off out of range of that nutcase's sharpshooter.'

Eric, who'd been quiet for a long while, decided to speak up. 'I've never been scuba diving in my life. Is this something I can learn fairly easy?'

'It's sweet of you to offer.' Kate wrapped an arm around his waist. 'But a person should learn to snorkel first and then learn scuba in a swimming pool. An ocean's unpredictable currents and strong undertows can be tricky even for experienced divers. Besides, I haven't gone in so long my certification is probably out of date. No one will rent me equipment without certification.'

On the way back from Elysian Island, all three were deep in thought. Yet when they reached the saggy dock, only Greg had

come up with an idea. 'If you really think your friends are in
danger, I would go straight to the police. They'll notify the
coastguard if someone reports a crime on the water, but either
of them can get on the island.'

While Eric hopped out to catch and secure the lines, Kate
collected their belongings. 'What have you heard about
the nutcase owner, Mr Frazier?' she asked after Greg killed the
engine.

'Not too much. I know he's very rich, eccentric, and a stickler
for privacy. But to my knowledge he's never really shot anyone,
only warns off potential trespassers.' The captain grabbed his
thermos, climbed out, and offered Kate a hand. 'Apparently,
Frazier went off the deep end after his wife was murdered.'

Kate and Eric stared at each other. 'Did you say *murdered*?'
she asked.

'The Julian Frazier who manufactured auto parts in Atlanta
. . . that multimillionaire?' Eric asked.

'Yeah, I guess so. How many reclusive millionaires can
there be?' Greg double-checked the lines on his beloved
boat. 'The story about his wife made all the papers.'

'That story must not have reached Charleston,' Eric said as
they followed him up the dock.

'I guess Frazier had a reason to go off the deep end. Thank
you, Captain, for risking the *Beautiful Betsy* for a pair of strangers. We're grateful for your attempt.' Kate extended her hand.

Greg shook hands heartily. 'Let me know if you change your
mind about scuba diving, or if you'd just like a pleasant afternoon of fishing. We could drink a few beers and grill whatever
we catch for dinner. After your friends are safe, of course.'

'We might take you up on that.' Eric pulled out his wallet
and handed over the agreed-upon amount. 'Thanks, Captain.'

Greg tucked the money in his pocket. 'Just remember, you
two aren't strangers anymore. Stop back any time.'

'Sounds like a plan,' Kate called, feeling a surge of pity as
the widower walked away.

'Where we heading, boss?'

She climbed in the SUV, lowered the windows, and closed
her eyes. 'Take me back to the airport on St Simons,' she said,
slapping her forehead with her palm. 'If not by land or by sea,

then by air. Let's find someone with a helicopter that's willing
to take us to Elysian Island.'

Unfortunately, she celebrated too soon. The helicopters
landing or taking off from St Simons airport were privately
owned and not available for hire. There were two companies
on the island giving sightseeing tours, but neither wanted to
land someplace else. When they checked other airports, they
found a helicopter pilot at the Jacksonville airport who took
tourists to barrier islands, but he refused to take them to Elysian.

'That's a restricted airspace,' he said. 'I know that every
drone flying over gets shot down. So I won't take a chance on
landing and getting my helicopter impounded by the police.
This bird is my breadwinner.'

'What if you didn't *exactly* land?' Kate asked, unsure where
she was headed.

The pilot laughed good-naturedly. 'Do you and your partner
know how to repel from a hovering aircraft like a Navy Seal?
Because I won't get any closer than that.'

'What's the plan now?' asked Eric, as soon as Kate had
thanked the pilot and hung up.

'The Glynn County Police Department. Time to get law enforcement involved, because after all somebody just shot at us.'

The Glynn County Police Department in Brunswick included
all of the Golden Isles in their jurisdiction. Kate and Eric arrived
a little before eleven, but without an appointment they had to
sit for an hour and a half on a hard bench in the hallway.

Finally, the officer led them to a cubicle to take their statement. 'You told them at the desk that someone shot at you from
Elysian Island?' He flipped to a new page on his tablet. 'What
business do you have out there?'

Kate stole a quick glance at Eric before answering. 'I work
for Price Investigations with offices in Natchez, New Orleans,
and Savannah.' If she thought that information might impress
the young officer, she was mistaken. 'My boss set up a retreat
for his employees and spouses on St Simons at his friend's
condo. It was supposed to be half retreat and half vacation. But
at some point, Mr Price received an invitation from Julian
Frazier to have our retreat there. Mr Frazier own Elysian Island,'
she added.

'I'm aware of that.' The officer tapped his pen against the paper. 'Please go on.'

'Unfortunately, my boyfriend and I . . .' she hooked a thumb at Eric, '. . . were detained in Charleston and missed Mr Frazier's boat on Saturday when it took everybody else to the island. We didn't get to the dock until Monday morning. Then we got a text from Captain Burke – he works for Mr Frazier – that the currents were too strong and that he would try again the next day. We tried calling and texting my boss and the other employees, but our calls didn't go through.'

'Cell phone coverage can be iffy out there.'

'On Tuesday, we went back to the town pier at the end of Mallery Street.'

'I know where the town pier is, Miss Weller, but usually only tall freight haulers pick up navigation pilots at the fishing pier. Boat passengers are picked up at one of the marinas.' The officer sounded like he was losing patience.

'I'm just telling you our instructions. Yesterday we waited for another hour, but Captain Burke never showed up. And again, no message from my boss or anyone else.'

Kate hoped the cop might jump in with a comment, but no such luck. 'This isn't like them,' she continued. 'The other employees are my friends. One of them is my best friend.'

'I understand why you'd be disappointed.' Without an ounce of subtlety, he checked his watch, and Kate realized her window of opportunity was closing.

'So this morning we paid Captain Greg Dotson to take us out to Elysian.'

The officer leaned back in his chair. 'How did that work out, Miss Weller?'

'Not very well. We barely got within a hundred and fifty yards of the beach and someone fired at us. If those shots had hit the hull of Captain Dotson's boat, the *Beautiful Betsy* would've sunk and we would've *drowned*.' Kate emphasized the danger of the situation.

Sergeant Mercer straightened up. 'I've warned Mr Frazier about firing at watercraft to enforce his no trespassing signs. But he assured me his security staff only fires warning shots. They have never sunk a boat yet.'

'What can be done here?' Eric asked, his own patience waning. 'Isn't this assault with a deadly weapon?'

The sergeant pondered for a moment. 'I don't think so. Now let me ask you a question: didn't you see the "No Trespassing" signs posted all around the island?'

'Yes, we saw them, but—'

He didn't let Kate finish. 'No buts, Mr Frazier has a right to keep his *private* island private. If he didn't enforce the request, people would soon be crawling all over the place.'

'But Eric and I received an *invitation* to Elysian Island. Can't you please help us?'

'Help you do what? Seems to me your invitation expired on Saturday when you failed to show up. You were given a second chance on Monday, but after that . . . you're plum out of luck.' Sergeant Mercer tapped the papers on his desk into a neat pile.

'All we want to do is make sure our friends are OK. We're worried about them.' Kate's voice rose in volume.

'Do you have any reason to believe someone's in danger other than no one answering your calls?'

'No, but I don't think those were warning shots. Something bad is happening out there and they don't want anyone finding out.'

The cop shook his head. 'From what I hear, Mr Frazier is really a nice guy who donates millions of dollars to charity. Plenty of people would move mountains for an invitation to one of his parties. You're mistaken if you think either the police department or the sheriff's department is going to storm the beaches just because you showed up two days late and missed the boat.' Sergeant Mercer stood, signaling an end to the interview. 'Take my advice – enjoy yourselves on beautiful St Simons. When your pals get back from the retreat, they can show you photos of whatever you missed.'

'Well, I guess he sure told us,' Eric said as they stepped outside. 'Shall we grab a bite to eat?'

Kate reeled around to face him. 'Why do you sound so amused?'

'I'm not amused, but I do see the possibility that Sergeant Mercer is right.' Eric rested his hands on her shoulders. 'Maybe *nothing* is wrong on the island.'

She sighed. 'That crossed my mind too, but my gut tells me something different.'

Eric lifted her chin with his finger. 'If your gut still disagrees after we eat lunch, we'll figure something out . . . even if it means I have to take up scuba diving.'

And for a long moment, Kate couldn't speak past the lump in her throat.

Elysian Island. Wednesday a.m.

The Price team ran out of patience Wednesday morning at breakfast. The five of them waited in the dining room for forty-five minutes before Mrs Norville showed up with two carafes of coffee, the days of silver urns long gone. Then they waited another fifteen minutes before Frazier and his ever-present assistant showed up.

With the caffeine of his third cup kicking in, Nate wanted to grab the old man by the neck. 'Aren't we still your *guests*, Mr Frazier?'

'Yes, Mr Price, you are.' Frazier slumped into his chair looking haggard. 'Forgive the delay this morning. We had some unexpected activity on the south beach. Your breakfast will be here shortly.'

Nate lifted his hands. 'None of us is worried about food. We're all here and ready to start. We're down to two suspects – the lady ADA and the public defender, and one of them is a murderer. Bring them both here and let us question them. We'll get the answers you want, but don't let them out of your house. It's time to stop playing games with this cat-and-mouse around the island.' Nate all but shouted his final demand.

Frazier startled, but recovered quickly. 'As much as I'd like to honor your request, I can't. When I checked on Miss Jacobs and Mr Ensley this morning, they weren't in their rooms. Someone unlocked their doors and it wasn't me.' He stared at Nate with deeply shadowed, red-rimmed eyes.

'Have you searched the house?' asked Beth.

'I have, and they're not inside anywhere.'

Nate scrambled to his feet. 'Someone is working against you, Frazier.'

'I realize that, Price, and I believe I've figured out who,' Frazier shouted with equal venom.

'Calm down,' Michael said. 'Shouting at each other won't help the situation. It's team one's turn to search the island. Can we get on with it?'

Nate inhaled a deep breath. 'But without Nicki, since she isn't feeling well. I want her to remain indoors today.'

'Of course, Mr Price.' Frazier's tone became saccharine sweet. 'In fact, all of team one will remain indoors. It will be team two, your lovely wife and Mrs Preston, who will bring the pair in for questioning.'

'No,' Nate and Michael shouted simultaneously.

'Beth and Izzy were on the island yesterday,' added Michael. 'It's our turn.'

'This isn't a game of ring-around-the-rosy in kindergarten. I make the rules in my game!' Frazier motioned to Jonah Creery, who slapped the packet of photographs on the table. 'Team one will study the pictures of Bob McDowell and that harlot, Jennifer Jacobs. That woman is no credit to the legal profession.'

Nate forced a reasonable tone to his voice. 'We don't need to study a bunch of pictures to know those two were having an affair. It took my wife only one to figure it out. If Jennifer had been working with McDowell, then those two must've had a falling out. And Kurt Ensley is in trouble. Why can't Michael and I look for her?'

Frazier closed the distance between them in a few steps. 'Because I don't trust you two. You're sneaky. I still think you and Preston killed Sanborn. My guards insist no one else was in that part of the island.'

'But why would we? You're the one with an axe to grind.'

'I'll find out why. In the meantime, you, Preston and Mrs Galen will remain here. Guards, subdue Price and Preston until their wives have had a chance to leave.'

'What about our breakfast?' Beth asked as guards closed in on Michael and Nate. 'I'm frightfully hungry.'

Frazier paused on his way to the door. 'What you are is wily, Mrs Preston, but your cleverness won't work with me. You and Isabelle will get something to eat after you bring in Miss Jacobs

. . . alive! Either she or Ensley knows who paid the Fallons to kill my wife.'

'What about Hunter?' Nicki pushed to her feet.

'*What about him?* You are getting truly tiresome, young lady.'

'And you think *you're not?*' Nicki walked toward Frazier with clenched fists. 'You'd better make sure my husband gets enough to eat and drink or I'll make you very sorry.'

Jonah Creery and several guards laughed, but their host did not. 'As glad as I am you've broken from your stupor, don't threaten me. Or you'll find yourself in worse conditions than Hunter.' Frazier ushered Beth and Izzy from the room, while Creery and the guards followed close at his heels.

Nate, Michael, and Nicki were left alone with a packet of pictures and a carafe of cold coffee.

Nate took hold of Nicki's arm. 'You shouldn't bait someone with a screw loose.'

She nodded, then looked him in the eye. 'I know, but I meant what I said. I will make Frazier pay, even if I get thrown in a Georgia jail for a very long time.'

'You won't be going to jail alone, cousin, because I intend to help you.'

'Count me in,' Michael added. 'But in the meantime, let's learn what we can from these.' He dumped the packet and spread the photos in front of them.

Nate glared at the grainy photos. 'Suppose so, until one of us comes up with a better idea.'

Beth checked for her ace-up-her-sleeve before leaving their room in her heaviest coat. 'This had better be our last tromp through the wilderness,' she muttered when Izzy joined her on the back stoop. 'I'm sick of the mud and insect bites and getting scratched by every thorn in the world.' Beth tugged on her gloves and turned up her collar. 'Not to mention finding two dead bodies.'

'Yeah, not to mention that.' Izzy stomped her feet to get the blood flowing. 'Which way today, team leader, is our best shot at finding Jennifer?'

'I guess we'll head east, the same direction we went on Sunday, since either north or south spans the widest part of the island.' Beth turned her focus skyward. 'At least it doesn't look like rain.'

'Good, another day like yesterday and they'll find me dead on the beach.' Izzy started down the steps toward the back lawn. Beth couldn't believe the change in Nate's wife. The Isabelle Price she'd met in Natchez never would have said something so flip in light of so much death. But experiences like they'd had recently either made a person stronger and more resilient or left them broken and nearly catatonic like Nicki. As an ex-cop, Beth had seen people go both ways and was grateful Izzy had chosen the former and not the latter.

As they had on Sunday, they checked the old stable first. But there were no signs anyone had been inside, except for some mice and a raccoon. Once they left the stable, Beth easily found the path to the east beach through the thickest foliage on the island. Since they couldn't walk side by side, Izzy kept close behind her on the path. Often Beth halted and signaled for silence. Yet no matter how many times they stopped, neither heard any sound other than the wind or an occasional bird.

'What do you think, Beth?' Izzy asked when they resumed walking. 'Did we pick a bad way to come?'

Beth lifted and dropped her shoulders. 'How could that lunatic expect us to find two potential murderers on an island this big?' She hadn't expected an answer and received none. But thirty minutes later, just as they heard the sound of waves breaking on shore, Beth also heard a crunch of twigs in the woods. Pivoting on her heel, she pressed a finger to her lips. 'Listen,' she whispered.

Both women stood motionless for two or three minutes. About the time Beth thought she'd imagined the sound, footsteps came pounding up the path behind them. Beth and Izzy crouched down in the weeds just as a wild creature bolted past them – a wild creature that bore substantial resemblance to Jennifer Jacobs.

'Wait, stop!' Beth broke into a run behind the woman.

And, surprisingly, the woman stopped. Panting, Jennifer dropped to her knees next to a massive tree and gulped for air. 'Help . . . me . . . please,' she begged.

Beth stared at the woman. Her thick hair was matted and

snarled, her face streaked with dirt and sweat. Her once-chic clothes were filthy and torn. Jennifer looked nothing like the young, beautiful professional in the photograph, sharing a glass of wine with her lover.

'We'll help you.' Beth extended her hand. 'I'm Beth Preston and that's Isabelle Price. Let's get you on your feet.'

After a few gulps of air, Jennifer accepted Beth's hand. 'Please help me get off this island. Somebody's after me – somebody who wants to kill me.'

'We know who you are and we'll help, but we need to get you back to the house!' Beth pulled her in the direction of the mansion.

Jennifer yanked her hand free. 'How do you know who I am?'

'We're private investigators sent to find you, but we'll protect you from whoever wants to kill you.'

'No way. Frazier wants you to bring me back.' As soon as the words left her mouth, Jennifer bolted down the path toward the beach.

Beth realized the stupidity of telling the truth too late. She sprinted after her, but Jennifer was in good shape and had a head start. Beth didn't catch up until they reached the soft sand past the dunes. Then she lunged forward and tackled the former assistant prosecutor. 'Stop!' Beth yelled. 'I swear we're not going to hurt you.'

Jennifer struggled to regain her footing, but Beth managed to pin down both wrists until Izzy caught up and threw her body across Jennifer's midsection.

'I know Bob McDowell is dead,' Jennifer sputtered, 'which means I am next. If you really want to help, don't take me back to the house. Frazier blames me for his wife's death, but I had nothing to do with it.'

Beth pulled her into a sitting position, while Izzy made sure she wouldn't get away. 'OK, tell us your side of the story.'

'I did everything possible to bring the Fallon brothers to justice, but I can't prosecute without solid evidence. After Mack died of an overdose in county lockup, I had no choice but to ask the judge to drop the charges against the younger brother. We found none of Reuben's prints in the bedroom or bathroom. The only proof we had Reuben was there that night was his prints on the wrench. And Chuck Sanborn made sure I had nothing to work with when the wrench was thrown out as evidence.' She tried to shake the sand from her face and hair.

'Detective Sanborn paid dearly for his poor job performance,' Izzy said wryly.

'I know he's dead, along with Reuben Fallon, who's been free all these years. Now with Bob dead, I will be next. I can't go back to the house. Frazier has practically starved us. He barely gives us enough water to drink. You gotta help me,' she pleaded, her dark eyes wild with fear. 'I'm married and have a seven-year-old daughter. Are either of you mothers?'

Izzy shifted some of her weight off the woman. 'I'm a mother of a little boy, but giving birth doesn't give you a free pass with Ariana Frazier's murder.'

Jennifer focused on Izzy. 'I swear I had nothing to do with the break-in or murder of Mrs Frazier.'

'We saw those photos of you and Bob McDowell.' Izzy sounded like a PI instead of a part-time real-estate agent. 'And we know that sleazy journalist was involved in this up to his eyebrows.'

'Yeah, I had an affair with him,' Jennifer admitted. 'I was young and exceptionally naive when I moved to Atlanta after passing the bar exam. But if McDowell had a bigger agenda than smearing the Fraziers to boost ratings, I had no part in it.'

Beth locked gazes with Izzy, who seemed to be buying the story, hook, line, and sinker. 'Let's say we believe you.' Beth pulled the prosecutor to her feet. 'Your best chance of survival is with us. There's no way off this island – no boats, no jet skis, and no wave-runners.'

'I know that. Bob talked me into trying to leave in a rowboat we found behind the dunes. I despise that man but I wanted off this island. We barely got a hundred feet away when the boat sank and we had to swim back. Someone had drilled holes in the bottom. Frazier's guards were waiting for us on shore.'

Jennifer brushed the sand from her clothes. 'Do you still have your cell phones? We need to contact the coastguard.'

'No, they took them from us. The phones didn't work anyway.'

'What about a satellite phone? Nobody even knows I'm here,' Jennifer wailed.

'Who carries a sat-phone on vacation?' Beth's question dripped with sarcasm. 'No. And we can't send emails either. They took our laptops. According to Frazier, his landline was cut. So unless you're unafraid of sharks and can swim back to St Simons, your best chance of survival is with us. Strength in numbers.'

Jennifer wiped her runny nose on her sleeve and took one last look at the ocean. 'You'll protect me if I go back? All I want is to see my husband and daughter.'

Izzy was first to speak. 'Yes, you've got my word.'

'You've got mine too,' Beth added.

And if she had planned to elaborate on her lofty promise, her opportunity was cut short by a sudden, sharp prick to her neck. The last thing Beth remembered was the sensation of falling and her world turning black.

TEN

B eth opened her eyes to blue sky with a few wispy clouds overhead. When she tried to raise her head, she tasted blood and felt a stabbing pain behind the eyes. Lifting up on her elbows, she retched in the sand and tried to regain her bearings. Then the memory of searching the island and finding Jennifer flooded back. Despite the pain in her head, Beth forced herself to look left and right.

Isabelle Price was on her belly in the wet sand with her head cocked oddly to one side. And she wasn't moving.

'Izzy!' Beth pushed to her knees, then to her feet, and staggered over to her friend. She rolled Izzy on her back and pressed her ear to Izzy's chest. Hearing the faint *thrum* of her heart, Beth pulled the limp woman into her arms. 'What on earth happened?' she asked, tucking a lock of damp hair behind Izzy's ear. When she got no response, Beth checked Izzy's mouth and nose for sand and shook her gently, all to no avail. Finally, Beth slapped Izzy on the back several times. But nothing roused her teammate to consciousness.

'Help!' she screamed at the top of her lungs. Over and over Beth shouted for help. Not only did no one answer her, Beth didn't hear a sound in any direction. But she did spot footprints – lots of them – around the area where Izzy had lain in the sand.

Beth checked her friend's pulse once more and then followed the footprints to a tangled pile of driftwood near the dunes. Amidst the bleached-white branches and drying seaweed lay the corpse of the assistant prosecutor of Atlanta. There was no question that it was Jennifer Jacobs and no question she was dead. Her brown eyes stared sightlessly at the sky, still waiting for help that wouldn't arrive in time.

Very carefully, Beth turned the body far enough to spot two

gunshot wounds – one on the left which had probably pierced her lung and a second to the right of her spine, which most likely struck her heart. Small-caliber bullet, no exit wounds. Beth studied the footprints and trail of blood in the sand. Someone had shot Jennifer in the back as she ran – someone who was a fairly good shot. Jennifer had staggered forward and died atop the pile of twisted tree limbs.

Like the trained former cop she was, Beth checked the area around the body, careful not to corrupt the crime scene. Lying in the sand twenty feet from the driftwood was a handgun, probably cast off by the murderer in haste. *A small handgun, the kind that fits nicely into an ankle holster.* With a bad taste in her mouth, Beth pulled up her right pant leg to reveal an empty holster. Her Ruger .380 semi-automatic was gone.

'Nooo!' She let out a howl that could've been heard on the mainland. Heedless of the need to preserve the crime scene, Beth ran to the gun and plucked it from the sand, obliterating several footprints along the way.

It was a Ruger .380.

It was her gun, no doubt about it.

Beth checked the clip and the chamber. Empty of all seven bullets, except for the three in Jennifer's back. Suddenly Beth felt weak in the knees and sick to her stomach. For the second time that day, she retched in the sand, further compromising the crime scene.

Someone followed us to the beach and shot Jennifer with my gun?

No one knew about my second weapon except for Izzy and Michael, and those two would die before telling a soul.

The thought of Isabelle brought Beth to her feet. But before she could return to her friend, several black-clad guards stepped from the brush and surrounded her, their automatic weapons aimed at her chest.

'What have we here?' Jonah Creery sauntered through the tall grass like he'd been strolling in a park. 'Beth Preston, with a smoking gun in her hand. I'm not sure if Julian will throw you in the dungeon with Hunter Galen, or give you the other special place we set aside.' Creery chortled like a lunatic.

Beth pointed her weapon at him. 'I didn't shoot anyone. You

had better tell your goons to lower their weapons or I'll put an extra hole in your head.'

This time his laugh was less convincing. 'Shoot away, Beth. You can't do much damage with an empty Ruger.' Creery nodded to the guards.

'How would you know that,' Beth sneered, 'if I was the one who shot Jennifer Jacobs?'

In a flash two snapped handcuffs on her wrists, while another tethered her ankles together with a short cord. She'd be able to shuffle along but not run.

Creery got right in her face. 'Because my guards and I heard you arguing with Miss Jacobs in the forest. By the time we got to the beach, we found Mrs Price out cold and the ADA gone. You must have emptied your gun into Miss Jacob's back when she tried to run. You're not a very good shot, are you?' His smile could've turned water into ice. 'Pretty heartless for a former Natchez Police detective.'

'Actually, I'm a crack shot.' Beth struggled against her restraints. 'And what do you mean by *your* guards? I thought Mr Frazier hired the mercenaries for security.'

'Mine, Julian's, just a matter of semantics. He and I are on the same side.' Creery glanced at his watch. 'Take Mrs Preston back to the house. It's almost the cocktail hour and I don't want to miss any of Mrs Norville's canapés.' He turned on a heel and started walking.

'Wait a minute.' Beth kicked and fought with all her strength. 'We can't leave Isabelle. She's back there on the beach and needs medical help. Please!' she begged.

Creery paused to consider. 'Julian is awfully fond of her. Of course, he always was partial to blondes.' He spoke more to himself than anyone. 'Very well, I'll send the team back for her. But right now I need them to make sure you don't get away.'

Three six-foot-plus men with automatic weapons and one five-foot-five-inch unarmed woman . . . yet Creery was afraid?

With her wrists already bruised, Beth had no choice but to shuffle back to the mansion, praying the entire time for Izzy's survival.

*   *   *

Nate paced from window to window until he wore a path in the thick carpet. After several hours alone in his suite, he finally heard the click of a lock and his bedraggled wife staggered into the room.

'Izzy! Where have you been? I've been worried sick.' He tried to take her into his arms, but she shrugged away and slumped down on the ottoman.

'To the other side of this hideous island and back.' Izzy unzipped and tugged off her boots. 'Remind me when we get home – if we ever get home – to throw these straight into the trash. Why on earth did I buy such uncomfortable boots?' She threw the boot across the room.

Izzy's face and clothes were dirty and a long scratch ran down her cheek from her brow to her chin. Yet she was rambling about bad footwear? Nate crouched in front of the ottoman and reached for her foot to rub. 'Take it easy and tell me what happened.'

She tossed the second boot where the first had landed. 'After checking out that abandoned barn, Beth and I took the same path that we did on Sunday. We kept stopping to listen, but we didn't hear anything but birds.' Izzy focused on the fireplace instead of him. 'Then we heard someone coming. It was that lady prosecutor. She begged us . . . to help her get off the island. We said . . . no way. Then Beth told her we were PIs . . . she took off running.' Izzy's sentences became increasingly fragmented.

Nate picked up the other foot to rub. 'Take a deep breath and slow down. Did you follow this woman, Jennifer Jacobs?'

Exhaling a shaky breath, Izzy nodded. 'Beth sort of tackled her on the beach. Jennifer was a mess. She was still wearing the same clothes as the day she arrived. Frazier hasn't given them much to eat either. I hope he's giving Hunter enough to eat.' Tears began to stream down Izzy's face.

Nate jumped up to get a glass of water. No doubt she was totally dehydrated. 'Here, drink this nice and slow.' He thrust the glass into her hand. 'What happened after Beth tackled Jennifer?' he asked after she finished.

Izzy reached for a tissue to blow her nose. 'Beth convinced her to come back to the house. That it would be safer if we all stuck together. Jennifer knew Bob McDowell was dead. That reporter used to be her boyfriend when she was young and stupid, but not anymore. Now she's married with a young daughter.' More tears ran down her dirty cheeks.

'Go on,' Nate prodded after several seconds of silence. 'Tell me the rest.'

'Jennifer agreed to come back to the house if we would protect her. So Beth helped her up and we started walking. Then Beth stopped . . . and slapped her neck . . . and fell over . . . just like that.' The fragmented sentences returned as Izzy's tears turned to sobs.

Something tightened in Nate's chest. 'Did Beth get shot?'

She shook her head. 'No, I don't think so. Not with a bullet anyway.'

'Did you see blood? Tell me everything you saw, Izzy.'

'I didn't see any blood, but Beth just lay there on the beach. Then Jennifer took off running and I felt a pinch.' Izzy reached up to the back of her neck.

'Bend your head down.' When Nate pulled her hair forward, he found a small red mark similar to the kind made by a vaccination with a hypodermic needle. 'If you don't think anyone sneaked up behind you, you and Beth could've been shot with a tranquilizing pellet.'

Izzy shrugged listlessly. 'Maybe.'

'What happened to Jennifer?'

She offered another shrug. 'I don't know. All I remember is waking up in the sand, but now the sand was wet.'

He muttered an oath. 'The tide was coming in. Was Beth still lying in the sand too?'

'No, she was gone. I was all wet and all by myself. So I started walking down the beach and calling Beth's name.' Izzy locked eyes with him. 'That's when I saw Jennifer on a pile of branches. Dead, I'm sure of it. She was staring at the sky with her eyes open, blood all over the place. That sand was still dry.' She exhaled as though she'd been holding her breath.

'Jennifer, but no Beth?'

'I already told you – no Beth. There's something else too. Jennifer swore she had nothing to do with Mrs Frazier's murder and I believed her. If that sleazy McDowell was part of a conspiracy, he duped Jennifer into this mess.'

'But then again, you usually take the word of another woman, especially if she happens to be a mother.'

Izzy's chin snapped up while her eyes flashed. 'Maybe that's because there are fewer heartless murderers among women than among men.'

'That's true.' Nate lifted his hands in surrender. 'Go on. I didn't mean to interrupt you.'

'There's no more to tell. I backtracked to the same path we took this morning and didn't see another soul until I reached the house. A group of guards was coming out the door. They said they were on their way to get me. I asked about Beth, and one said I would find out soon enough. Then he escorted me to our room.' Izzy rose shakily to her feet. 'That's all I know, and right now I'm cold and need a long hot shower.' On her way to the bathroom she halted midway. 'I'm scared, Nate. Beth brought two guns on the retreat and only turned one in to the butler. She told me not to tell you. She said it would be her ace up the sleeve. I hope that little hidden gun didn't get her killed.' With that Izzy closed the bathroom door, and Nate soon heard water running.

Beth had brought her Ruger .380? He should have remembered Beth's ankle holster. *Never leave home without a security blanket*, she always said.

Nate spent the next thirty minutes staring into the fire and mulling over everything Izzy had told him. The death of the assistant prosecutor didn't surprise him, but Beth's disappearance did. Frazier had promised nothing would happen to any Price employee as long as they played the game by his rules. *By his rules.* Did the fact that Beth kept a hidden weapon break the rules sufficiently to warrant her death? The queasy feeling in his gut compacted into a solid mass.

'Why aren't you ready for dinner?' Izzy asked, startling Nate from his woolgathering.

Izzy was dressed in the same cocktail dress and high heels she'd worn on Saturday night, their first dinner with Frazier. Gone were the dirt, sand and leaves in her tangled hair. Izzy had fixed her hair in a fancy bun and covered the long scratch on her face with plenty of makeup.

'I *am* ready. What the heck, Isabelle? You got all dressed up to eat supper with a madman and his assistant?'

'You bet I did.' She pulled a curl in front of each ear. 'Frazier seems to like me more than Nicki and Beth. I plan to use that to our advantage.'

'And what exactly does that mean?' Nate ran a hand through his hair.

She stopped primping and looked at him. 'The players in Frazier's game are dropping like flies around us. I don't want one of your employees to be next. I also want Hunter to get adequate food and water. And Beth too, if she's still alive,' Izzy added with a hitch in her voice. 'You and Michael can't overpower that many guards. And you can't fight automatic weapons with butter knives. I plan to charm Frazier into having mercy on us. Now go change out of those baggy sweatpants while I look for my lipstick.'

'I'll put on jeans, but that's it.' Nate stomped into their bedroom, piqued with his wife for no reason. He felt powerless when Izzy cried and sobbed, yet somehow this new assertiveness scared him more. For the first time in their marriage, Nate feared for his wife's sanity.

Or maybe she was the only sane member left in the group.

Five minutes later, Izzy hooked her arm through his elbow and they were escorted down the hallway like royals dining with the Queen.

Even the butler looked taken aback. 'Mr and Mrs Nathan Price,' he announced as he opened the door.

'Ah, Nate and Isabelle,' crooned Frazier, rising from his chair. 'Since you look so lovely, Isabelle, I'll forgive your tardiness. Come, sit next to me.' He pulled out a chair.

Nate noticed only Nicki and Michael were at the table. No Beth and still no Hunter. And Michael looked like he could kill Frazier with his bare hands.

Primly, Isabelle smoothed down her dress and fluffed out her napkin. 'Are we late? I'm so sorry. It took me a long time to walk back from this afternoon's venture.'

This afternoon's venture? Izzy sounded like a tour guide at a living history museum. Nate gritted his teeth.

'Yes, according to my assistant, you and Mrs Preston had quite an afternoon. Compton, bring Mr and Mrs Price some wine. I remember Isabelle enjoyed the chardonnay that we

served on Saturday.' Frazier barked orders at the butler like a
drill sergeant. 'And replace this basket of bread with some fresh
dinner rolls.'

When Compton nodded, Nate's mouth fell open.

Maybe my wife isn't so crazy after all.

'That's very kind of you, sir,' Nate murmured, keeping his
tone as neutral as possible. 'May I ask where Mrs Preston
is tonight? My wife didn't recall what happened to her.'

Frazier blinked with confusion. 'But I thought Isabelle was
a witness to the murder of Ms Jacobs. I was counting on her
to give a statement to the authorities when they finally reach
the island.' He paused as Compton filled three glasses with
wine, skipped Nicki and Michael, and left the room. 'According
to Mr Creery, Beth demanded that ADA Jacobs return to the
house with them to face questioning over the death of my wife.
There was a struggle between Beth and the ADA. When the ADA
broke free and took off running, Beth shouted for Jacobs to halt
and pulled her weapon. Then Mrs Price passed out on the beach.
When Mr Creery found Beth, she was standing over Jacob's
dead body with an empty gun in her hand.'

'You're a liar, Creery,' Michael shouted.

'Kindly control yourself, Mr Preston. I won't tolerate such
outbursts at my table.'

'I'm telling you, Mr Frazier, Beth would never do that.' A
flush rose up Michael's neck.

'I must take the word of Jonah Creery, a man who has worked
for me for years, over the word of Beth Preston, a *disgraced*
Natchez Police detective.'

'And you're a crazy old man, who will spend the rest of his
sick life in jail.' Michael lunged from his chair and almost
reached Frazier before finally being subdued by the guards.

'That outburst will cost you dinner.' Frazier clucked his
tongue. 'If I didn't need you tomorrow, I'd throw you in the
same hole as Hunter. Take Preston to his room and keep a guard
posted all night.'

'But how could she?' Nate asked, fighting to maintain his
own composure as Michael was dragged from the room. 'Beth
surrendered her firearm in the foyer when we all did.'

'Yes, but Beth had a second gun hidden in an ankle holster.

I saw the holster myself when the guards brought her back in handcuffs.'

Beth was still alive. Nate felt the tight muscles in his neck relax.

'Get it through your head, Mr Price, one of your detectives will face charges. Whether Beth was licensed to carry in this state or not, she wasn't Georgia law enforcement, and thus had no right to take justice into her own hands.' Frazier sounded more disappointed that Beth broke his rules than that an Atlanta assistant prosecutor was dead. 'We'll keep Beth locked up with Mr Galen until the police arrive.'

'You'd better be giving Hunter enough to eat.' Nicki shook her finger at their host.

'Nicki,' Izzy admonished. 'Of course, Mr Frazier will give Hunter and Beth plenty to eat and drink. He has been nothing but a gracious host since we arrived.' Izzy picked up her glass of wine and sipped.

'Thank you, Isabelle.' Frazier drank, too, without taking his eyes off Izzy.

Before Nicki grabbed Izzy by the throat, Nate whispered in his cousin's ear. 'Relax and roll with this. Izzy has a plan up her sleeve.' Nodding, Nicki focused on her lap as though answers could be found in linen napkins.

'As a matter of fact, Mrs Galen, I instructed the cook to deliver Hunter and Beth's dinners first this evening. Now I wonder what's keeping our meal.' Frazier pressed the button on his chair.

'Other than Mr Creery's *eyewitness account*, how can you be sure it was Beth's gun that killed ADA Jacobs?' Nate didn't try to hide his skepticism.

'I wouldn't be so quick to insult my assistant if I were you. As I mentioned, Jonah has been loyal to me for years.' Frazier motioned to Creery standing sentinel at the door. 'If you would be so kind, Jonah?'

After Creery left the room, wax dripped from the candles; the mantel-clock's ticking became unbearable, and Nate's shirt stuck to his back until Creery's return.

'Is this what you wanted, Mr Frazier?' Holding a plastic bag high in the air, Creery marched triumphantly to his boss, Frazier. Inside the bag, everyone could see the outline of a handgun.

'Yes, thank you, Jonah.' Frazier inspected the contents and then passed the bag to Nate. 'Do you recognize this weapon, Mr Price? This gun was found twenty feet from ADA Jacobs's body. I'm confident the police will match the serial number to a weapon registered to Beth Preston, your employee. According to one of my guards, the gun holds .38-caliber bullets, which would match the three wounds found on Ms Jacobs's body.'

'This is a frame-up,' Nate roared, as guards closed in on both sides. 'If Beth had emptied the clip at ADA Jacobs, you would have found seven bullet holes in her body, not just three. Beth never misses.'

'Everyone misses occasionally,' said Frazier, nonplussed. 'All I know is that Mrs Preston had been instructed to surrender her weapons upon arrival to protect the safety of all my guests, even my so-called suspects. The fact that she didn't, and because she took her gun with her this morning, tells me Beth had an ulterior motive.'

'What reason would Beth have to kill a former assistant prosecutor, a woman she'd never met before this week?'

'My head of security described Beth's behavior as survival mode – kill or be killed. She viewed Ms Jacobs as a threat to her safety and the safety of her friends, since either she or Kurt Ensley is a murderer. At any rate, I am not Beth's judge and jury. We'll let the authorities sort this out. She will be safely confined until then.'

Nate slammed down his wine glass hard enough to crack the stem. 'How can you be certain the police are on their way? Is your phone line suddenly working now?'

'Anything you break you shall pay for, Mr Price,' Frazier cautioned. He let several tense moments pass before continuing, 'No, it's not working. But I get my regular delivery of groceries on Thursday. I don't know why Captain Burke hasn't been back with the other couple by now, but I'm sure tomorrow's tugboat will arrive on schedule. That fearless captain makes deliveries even with ten-foot swells. He will take word back to St Simons that we need the coastguard or the Glynn County Police Department, or whoever has jurisdiction.'

'Since there's no way off this island, I don't see why Beth can't be—'

'Enough, Mr Price!' Frazier shouted. 'You're getting almost as tiresome as Mrs Galen with her butter knives. I assure you your employee is fine, and we have more important matters to discuss.'

'What matters are those?' Nate asked, clenching down on his back molars.

At that moment, however, the dining-room door opened and Mrs Norville entered with her son. As they set down a steaming kettle and basket of crackers, Norville seemed surprised to see Frazier.

'What is this?' Frazier demanded.

'A pot of chili, sir. I thought you'd be dining with the staff, not with these people.'

Frazier glared at his cook. '*These people* are my guests, Mrs Norville. Immediately bring whatever you prepared for the guards and staff.'

Norville put her hands on her hips. 'Who's gonna eat all this chili?'

'You and your son can eat it. Now go! What were we saying, Mr Price?' Frazier's grip on reality seemed to slip another notch.

'You said we had another matter to discuss.'

'Oh, yes. The untimely death of Ms Jacobs complicates solving my wife's murder. As part of a plea deal, Mack Fallon agreed to name the person who paid him in exchange for no death penalty. Then the evening before he was to testify, Mack mysteriously overdosed on drugs. Only two suspects had access to Mack's cell that night – the assistant district attorney and his public defender, namely Jennifer Jacobs and Kurt Ensley. Now one of them is dead and I still don't know who paid for the hit.'

Izzy chose that moment to rejoin the conversation. 'I met ADA Jacobs this afternoon,' she said. 'Although Jennifer admitted to having an affair with that disreputable journalist, she insisted she had nothing to do with the break-in at your home. Strange as it sounds, I believe Jennifer was telling the truth.' Astonishingly, Izzy placed her hand on Frazier's arm.

Nate had to look away or he might be tempted to drag Izzy from the room by her hair.

Frazier refilled their wine glasses from the carafe. 'Jennifer

Jacobs advanced her career by sleeping with people in power. Behavior like hers isn't something you would be familiar with. Trust me when I say nothing from that woman's mouth can be trusted.'

'Why do you think either Jacobs or Ensley gave Fallon the drugs?' Nate asked, trying to distract Frazier from Izzy. 'One of the guards could've supplied the fatal overdose or they could have been hidden on Fallon when he was arrested.'

'It's possible, I suppose,' Frazier admitted. 'But the jail searches prisoners thoroughly at intake and why would a guard pass out free drugs to the prisoners? Doesn't make sense.'

'Unless this unknown third party paid one of the guards.'

Frazier scowled at Nate's logic. 'For now, let's stick to what we know: early this morning Jennifer Jacobs and Kurt Ensley were set free on the island. Now Jacobs is dead and none of the guards can find Ensley.'

'If Ensley was on the island, he could have shot the ADA to keep her quiet,' Nate suggested.

Their host sighed. 'All of the suspects were searched when they arrived, so we know Ensley didn't have a weapon. How could he have gotten Beth's gun, which I'm sure the police will determine was the murder weapon?'

'I don't know! Maybe Ensley had been following Beth and Izzy and took Beth's gun after he knocked them out.'

It was a stalemate. Fortunately, Compton and Norville broke the uncomfortable quiet by delivering roast beef, mashed potatoes, mushroom gravy, creamed corn and warm dinner rolls. Not exactly gourmet, but better than chili with saltines. Nate had lost most of his appetite when Izzy flirted with Frazier under the misguided notion it would keep them alive, so while the Price team picked at their food, Frazier ate heartily and drank two more glasses of wine. It was the most uncomfortable meal they had ever endured.

When Frazier finally finished, he summoned the guards and walked them to the door.

'Good night, Mr Frazier,' Izzy murmured. 'Thank you for supper.'

'Good night, Isabelle. Thank you for your company.' Frazier ignored Nicki as she walked out, but he grabbed onto Nate's sleeve. 'Remember, Mr Price. You better hope my men locate Ensley tonight or you and Michael find him tomorrow. That public defender is *our* last hope of discovering the truth. If I don't find out who was behind the break-in, things won't go well for you and your investigators.'

As the guards took Nate by the arm, Frazier strode away in the other direction. He didn't give them as much as a backward glance.

ELEVEN

St Simons Island. Thursday a.m.

On Thursday morning, Kate decided to jog around John's neighborhood while Eric was still asleep. Running was good for the body and good for the mind. Hopefully she'd be able to figure out their current dilemma, as well as their long-range plans.

Eric wanted to leave his well-paid career as head chef in his family's restaurant to become a private investigator like her, a job where hours were long and paydays few and far between. And Eric looked to her for a plan of action, as though crime-solving was as simple as following the steps in a lasagna recipe. She hated to disappoint him, since her affection for the gourmet cook had gone far beyond their former landlord–tenant relationship. So when Kate had circled the block without a single epiphany, she went around a second time at a slower pace.

'Good morning, sunshine,' Eric crowed the moment she walked through the door. 'Coffee is hot and I've got soft boiled eggs with whole-wheat toast for breakfast.'

Since Eric was already showered and dressed he must have gotten up the moment she left the house. 'How did you get breakfast done so fast?'

'I faked being asleep, so you would have some time alone. You're not used to people hovering around you twenty-four/ seven.'

Kate took a bite of toast. 'Wow, a man who can cook and read minds? My gal-pal Beth would call you a keeper.'

Eric handed her a cup of coffee. 'Beth is a very smart woman. What's our plan to rescue her and your co-workers today?'

'We don't know they actually need rescuing. Everybody could be having such a good time, they forgot all about the newest hire and her boyfriend.' Kate finished the toast in three bites.

'You know that's not true. Sit down and eat.'

Kate slid into a chair and pulled her plate of eggs closer. 'Here's what I came up with. The people in the marina all seemed to know each other. So why wouldn't they also know this Captain Burke who works for Mr Frazier? He might not lease a slip, but I'm sure someone has run into him at the diesel pumps or in some bar. We just need to find the spot where boaters congregate.'

'That's why *you're* a keeper – beautiful and smart.' Eric kissed the top of her head and dug into his eggs.

As soon as they finished eating, Kate loaded the dishwasher and jumped in the shower. Thirty minutes later, she was dressed in combat-ready clothes, prepared to run, jump, or – if necessary – leap tall buildings to find her friends.

Of the first dozen people they asked at the bar in the Morningstar marina, most had met Mike Burke once or twice, but didn't know where he lived or where he docked Frazier's yacht on this side of Elysian Island. However, the thirteenth boater knew Captain Burke quite well and provided specific directions on how to find his home near Gascoigne's Bluff. According to the old-timer, Captain Mike and his wife bought a yellow bungalow near Epworth-by-the-Sea after the kids grew up and moved out. In fact Kate and Eric could barely pry themselves away from the chatty neighbor who apparently had never heard of privacy laws.

They had no trouble finding the two-story home with dormers and a wraparound porch. As soon as Eric parked across the street, Kate spotted a deeply tanned man cutting the lawn in Bermuda shorts, someone who looked far too distinguished to be a gardener despite his ball cap.

'Captain Mike Burke?' she called, halfway up the driveway.

'Yep, that's me.' He killed the mower's engine. 'Can I help you?'

'I hope so. May we have a word with you?' Kate waited until they were face-to-face to elaborate. 'I'm Kate Weller and this is Eric Manfredi. We've been trying to reach you, but you're not answering your calls or texts.'

'When I'm not working, I throw my business cell phone in the drawer and carry only my personal cell.' Burke pushed his sunglasses atop his head and stared at them. 'Did you say Weller and Manfredi? I was told you had changed your mind about attending the corporate retreat.'

'Who told you that?' Eric stepped up to Kate's side.

'Mr Creery relayed the information from the boss. Mr Frazier said he doesn't need me until Saturday and that I had time off with pay until then.' Burke looked from Eric to Kate and back again.

Kate crossed her arms over her chest, unable to hide her irritation. 'We didn't change our minds and have been cooling our heels in the village since you stood us up on Tuesday.'

Burke swept off his Atlanta Braves cap. 'I am so sorry, Miss Weller, Mr Manfredi. Mr Creery called me early Tuesday morning to say you two had changed your minds.'

'Please stop saying that,' Kate muttered. 'We didn't change anything.'

'This Creery guy *called* you?' Eric asked. 'Using what?'

Burke blinked several times. 'I'm assuming he used the phone in Mr Frazier's office. An underwater cable connects Elysian Island to the mainland because cell coverage can be unreliable.'

'Yes, we found that out.' Kate felt beads of sweat form on her lip.

'Come with me into the house. We'll call the island right now and find out how I got the wrong information.'

Kate and Eric followed him into a neat-as-a-pin kitchen where a redhead was taking cookies from the oven.

'Hello,' the redhead greeted. 'I'm Celine Burke. You're just in time for chocolate chip cookies.'

'That's very kind of you, ma'am, but no thank you,' Kate said.

'Maybe a little bit later,' Eric added.

'We need to get to the bottom of a communication breakdown first,' Burke explained as he reached for the phone.

As a thought popped into Kate's head, she grabbed hold of his arm. 'Wait a moment, Captain. Did you actually speak to Mr Frazier?'

'Why don't we sit down?' Burke pointed at the kitchen table. 'No, I spoke to Jonah Creery, his assistant. But Jonah said the directive came from Mr Frazier.'

'And you're the one who took my boss, Nate Price, and his employees to Elysian on Saturday?'

'Yes, I am. It was Mr Price, his wife, and two other couples. Sorry, I don't remember their names, but they seemed like a nice group of people.'

'How well do you know this Jonah Creery?' Eric asked.

Burke shrugged. 'I don't know him well at all, but Mr Frazier sure does. Creery was the chief financial officer of the company Julian founded years ago. In fact, to my knowledge, Creery stayed on as CFO even after Julian retired. He's a bit younger.'

'To be clear, which company are you talking about?' Kate pulled out her trusty notebook as Mrs Burke set down a pot of coffee and three cups.

'The Resilient Automotive Systems Corporation in Atlanta. Mr Frazier started out in his garage years ago, then kept expanding as his business grew. Now it's an international billion-dollar enterprise and the elder Mr Frazier still owns fifty-five percent of the stock. Julian's nephew, Alexander, is the current CEO. Would either of you like coffee?'

Kate answered for them. 'Yes, please, cream and sugar for me and black for Eric.'

'Such a shame,' interjected Celine Burke, slipping into the fourth chair at the table. 'Not long after Mr Frazier bought Elysian Island and retired, his wife died, leaving him to rattle around in that huge house alone. And in such an awful way, no less.'

The captain patted her hand. 'Now, Celine, these folks want to know why I received erroneous information about them, not hear about some old tragedy.'

Kate exchanged a glance with Eric. 'Actually, Captain, *anything* you can tell us about the Fraziers might help. We suspect someone has been purposefully keeping us away.'

'It certainly isn't me.' Burke pressed a hand to his chest.

'We believe you,' Eric said. 'Can you tell us how Mrs Frazier was killed?'

Celine stared into her cup for a moment. 'She was beaten to death during a home invasion and, although the police caught the thugs, Mr Frazier insisted other people had been involved.

The poor man went a little nuts after she died. That's why he seldom comes to St Simons or the mainland.'

Mike waved his hand through the air. 'That's not fair, Celine. Julian isn't nuts. He's just eccentric and he's always been very good to us.'

'All right,' Kate said. 'Before this discussion goes completely off-track, I need the names of everyone you ferried to the island during the last month.'

Burke lifted an eyebrow. 'Don't you think I should call the island first? There could be a completely logical explanation. I would hate to compromise Mr Frazier's privacy without good reason. If I call Jonah Creery on his satellite phone, then Julian won't have to learn about the confusion.'

Now somebody is worried about privacy? Kate thought. 'No, give me Creery's number. I want to talk to him myself.'

Again, Burke looked reluctant. 'I don't think I should.'

Kate's blood pressure was rising rapidly. 'Look, Captain, we believe something has happened out on Elysian. We'll need time to do some research before deciding how to proceed. But if you call out there, and my suspicions are correct, I'll see that you're charged with obstruction of justice or possibly even as an accomplice.' It was a lofty threat, one that Kate wasn't sure would stand up, but it worked.

Celine gasped while every bit of color drained from Captain Mike's face. 'I have no wish to obstruct anything. I'll cooperate with you.'

'OK, start by getting that list of passengers for the last four weeks. We also plan to contact Frazier's nephew and see if he wants to involve the police.'

Burke sprang to his feet. 'My logbook is on the yacht, the *Slippery Eel*, which is moored at a protected dock not far away. I'll go get it and come right back.' Burke raced out the door.

'And don't make any calls,' Kate hollered after him.

Celine looked from one to the other. 'While Mike is gone, would either of you like more coffee or some cookies?'

Thoroughly impressed by the woman's hospitality, Kate didn't hesitate. 'Yes, ma'am, we would. That's very kind of you.'

While Celine's back was turned, Eric rolled his eyes at her, then proceeded to devour five cookies.

True to his word, Captain Burke returned ten minutes later with the logbook. He copied down a list of names along with dates on a sheet of paper. 'I took these guests to Elysian Island last week, a few days before I picked up Mr Price's group. I took the first group over a three-day period. I put the date next to the passenger's name.' Then Burke added the names of Michael and Beth Preston, Hunter and Nicki Galen, and Nate and Isabelle to the sheet. 'Here you go, Miss Weller. Celine and I will be home all day if you still need me. And I promise not to call Elysian Island.'

Kate tucked the list in her purse. 'Thanks, we'll be in touch. And Mrs Burke, those were the best chocolate chip cookies I've ever had.'

Celine blushed to a pretty shade of pink. 'Don't be silly. It's just the recipe from the bag of morsels.'

Kate grinned at Eric as they left the house.

'Smirk all you want now,' he teased. 'You won't be smiling when I tell Granny what you said.'

Eric drove back to the condo as fast as the speed limit allowed. For the next few hours they learned everything they could about Frazier's company and his wife's murder. From newspaper archives, they discovered that a pair of brothers, Mack and Reuben Fallon, had been arrested and charged with the break-in, robbery and death of Ariana Frazier. But Mack Fallon died before standing trial and Reuben was subsequently released on an unnamed technicality.

Reuben Fallon was the first name on Captain Burke's passenger list.

Thirty minutes later, Eric matched a second name on the list to the Frazier murder case. 'The Atlanta cop who caught the burglary/break-in case was Detective Charles Sanborn,' Eric said, looking up from his laptop. 'Captain Burke took him to the island the day after Reuben Fallon, along with Kurt Ensley, whoever he is.'

Kate studied the list. 'Then Jennifer Jacobs and Bob McDowell were delivered to Elysian on the third day. I'm guessing all five are somehow connected to the murder of Ariana Frazier.'

'I'll take McDowell; you take Jennifer Jacobs,' Eric suggested.

His next revelation came on the heels of his first. 'I thought the name Bob McDowell sounded familiar. He's a television news reporter from Atlanta. Sometimes the Charleston stations carry his segments if they're newsworthy enough. McDowell must have covered the story on the evening news.' Eric leaned back in his chair. 'But why would Frazier bother with a journalist? They just report whatever they see or hear.'

Kate shook his head. 'Journalists aren't always one hundred percent truthful with their stories. See if you can find any of McDowell's coverage of the murder, while I try to get ahold of Julian's nephew, Alexander Frazier.'

Before long, Eric had listened to enough of Bob McDowell's recent segments to know he was the tabloid news type, although he found nothing about the murder. And Kate had found out enough about the Resilient Automotive Systems Corporation to make an intelligent stock purchase for her portfolio – if she had one – but still didn't know where Alexander Frazier, the current CEO, lived or how to reach him. Every call to his office yielded the same result: 'I'd be happy to take a message, miss,' said his secretary, 'or make an appointment for you. But unless you describe your so-called emergency, I can't let you speak to him directly. Mr Frazier is a very busy man.'

Indeed. 'My name is Kate Weller and I work for Nate Price Investigations. Our team was invited to Elysian Island for a week-long corporate retreat. My partner and I have been unable to join our team, but we feel something is very wrong on the island. Instruct Mr Frazier to call me *before* trying to reach his uncle or his assistant, Jonah Creery. This is of upmost importance.'

Kate had to repeat her message three times, including her phone number, before the secretary correctly repeated it back. Then the secretary barraged her with a series of questions:

What is very wrong on the island?

Why shouldn't Mr Frazier call his uncle first?

Why have you been unable to reach the island?

'None of that is important,' she blurted, rapidly losing patience. 'I will explain everything to Alexander Frazier. Please have him call me ASAP.'

Kate hung up, feeling confident her message would be relayed intact immediately and she would be talking to Frazier's nephew within the hour.

Elysian Island. Thursday a.m.

Nate and Izzy had argued for an hour before going to bed the previous evening. Then both had tossed and turned for another hour before falling asleep. Nate felt his wife had gone overboard flirting with Frazier in hopes of preserving their lives and securing humane treatment of Hunter and Beth. Isabelle, however, thought him to be a typical jealous husband and that Mr Frazier simply wanted to solve his wife's murder before dying of cancer. The fact that there were already four dead bodies somewhere on the island didn't promote much caution with Izzy.

Nate apologized on their way to breakfast, yet Izzy's acceptance seemed half-hearted at best. When Compton ushered them into the dining room, only one person was at the table.

'Where have you two been?' Michael asked. 'I'm already on my third cup of coffee.'

'Overslept.' Nate saw no need to elaborate. 'Where's Nicki?'

'In her room, refusing to come down. She sent a note to Frazier instructing him to give her share of breakfast to Hunter.'

'That poor girl,' murmured Izzy, pouring a cup of coffee. 'She's so worried about him. I'll send a note to Mr Frazier asking if I could spend the day with Nicki while you two search for Kurt Ensley.' Izzy took her regular chair.

'Hang on.' Irritation spiked up Nate's spine. 'Let's think about this before you rush off, writing notes.'

Izzy's expression spoke volumes as she sipped from her mug.

Michael turned his back to the door. 'I'm going to make a request,' he whispered to Nate. 'Give me all your cash when Compton steps into the hallway. Mr Compton, may I trouble you for another pot of coffee?' Michael asked in his most cordial voice. 'I'm afraid I didn't leave enough for Nate and Isabelle.'

The moment the door closed behind the butler, Nate pulled out his wallet and handed over several twenties. 'Don't know what good these will do you. The guards won't be easily bribed considering Frazier's per diem.'

'I know, but just play along.' Michael shoved the bills into his pocket. Then he walked over to the coffee service and – to Nate's astonishment – drank the contents of the milk pitcher.

'I guess we'll have our coffee black,' muttered Izzy.

Michael was still at the breakfront when Mrs Norville and her son delivered the carafe and their paltry morning meal. 'Ahhh, that toast smells wonderful, Mrs Norville. Thank you.'

The woman's lip curled. 'Smells like it always does.' Norville placed the toast and butter on the table while her son plunked a basket of assorted cereals next to the coffee carafe.

'Oh, good.' Michael pulled out one with bran flakes and raisins. 'This one's my favorite.'

'Mine, too,' her son agreed.

'May I trouble you for milk for my cereal, Mrs Norville?'

The cook turned and glared at Michael. 'It's right there in the blue pitcher.' She pointed with a stubby finger.

'Yes, ma'am, but the pitcher is empty.' Michael offered every bit of charm he could muster.

'Too bad,' Norville snapped. 'I gotta fix those creepy guards their breakfast and the boss wants a soufflé today. Like I have time to fuss on a day like this?' she added, halfway to the door.

'Perhaps your son can refill the pitcher?'

'Yeah, I can do it,' the boy answered before Norville could refuse.

When Norville gazed at her son, her expression changed to true compassion. 'You won't spill it in the hallway, will you?'

'No, Ma. I promise.'

'Fine, Paul. You can refill the pitcher.' Norville strode from the room with her son at her heels.

'Thanks, Paul,' Michael called.

'Mind telling me what that was all about?' Nate asked.

'Just wait and see.'

So Nate waited until the young man returned with a pitcher of milk. Paul walked so slowly, none would have spilled if they'd been on a ship in high seas.

Michael checked to make sure Compton was still in the hallway, then met the boy at the breakfront. 'Thanks, Paul.' He poured milk on his bowl of dry cereal. 'Say, Paul, may I borrow your gaming device for one day? It's so boring when we're stuck in here or locked in our rooms.' Michael whined like a teenager.

The boy shook his head. 'No way. My ma wouldn't like that. This baby cost her plenty.' Paul patted his back pocket.

'I promise your mom won't find out. I'll give it back tomorrow, plus I'll give you eighty dollars.'

'Eighty dollars?' Paul's eyes grew round as saucers. 'For real?'

'Yes, for real, but you can't tell anyone. Not Mr Frazier or Mr Creery or any of the guards.'

Paul nodded vigorously, pulled the device from his pocket and slapped it down next to the pitcher.

'Remember, this is our secret.' Michael handed him the wad of bills and tucked away the device just in time.

When Paul knocked on the door, Compton re-entered the dining room. 'Eat up, Price employees. Mr Frazier is on his way to give the men final instructions and escort Mrs Price back to her room.'

'But I'll be going back to Nicki's room, not ours,' Izzy said softly.

'Good, because I don't trust crazy old people any better than crazy young people.' Nate brushed her lips with a kiss.

The three of them barely had enough time to finish breakfast before Frazier marched in with Creery and two guards.

'Good morning, Mr Preston, Mr and Mrs Price. I hope you enjoyed the meal.' Frazier walked to the head of the table but did not sit.

'Yes, sir, everything was fine.' Izzy's exaggerated drawl matched the one from last night.

'Good to hear. I put a stack of magazines in your room, Isabelle, along with cheese and crackers in case you get hungry. Now if you're ready, I'll escort you.'

Izzy dabbed her mouth and stood. 'That is so kind of you, sir. But could you please move those magazines and snacks to Mrs Galen's room? While the men search for Mr Ensley, I'd like to spend time calming down Nicki so she doesn't disrupt dinner tonight.' Izzy punctuated her request with a warm smile.

'Of course, if that's what you prefer.' The muscle in Frazier's jaw tightened. 'Nate, Michael, I gave you my instructions last

night. Since the guards couldn't find Ensley in the dark, don't
bother returning until you find that lawyer. And he'd better
still be breathing. Come along, Isabelle.' Frazier extended his
hand.

Nate swallowed the bad taste in his mouth. 'Another moment,
please?'

'What is it, Price?'

'We would like to talk to Beth before we leave. She wasn't
around when Izzy woke up on the beach, but Beth might have
seen something or spoken to Jennifer Jacobs before she was
shot.'

Frazier sauntered over to Nate. 'You mean before Beth shot
her?'

'With all due respect, Beth had no reason to kill that prosecutor. She grew up in Mississippi and lived there her entire
life until she and Michael moved to Savannah last year.'

'We've already explained that – survival of the fittest.'

'I know, but Jacobs might have told Beth something about
Ensley. This is a hard island to find people.'

Frazier pondered Nate's request, then he turned to Creery at
the door. 'Go get Mrs Preston.'

'You can't be serious, Julian.' Creery's fingers curled into
fists. 'These two are wasting time. Just send them out and see
what they come back with.'

'How much time would this waste – ten, fifteen minutes?'
Nate argued. 'Beth might know something helpful.'

Creery needed only a few long strides to reach Nate. 'You're
not much of an investigator, are you? You have failed in every
attempt to question the suspects. Now you want some woman
from Natchez to make your life easier?'

Nate and Creery glared at each other like junkyard dogs
separated by a chain-link fence.

'One more thing, Mr Frazier.' Nate didn't take his eyes off
Creery. 'Please keep your assistant and the guards indoors until
Michael and I return. Funny how those guards keep turning up
wherever there's a dead body.'

Creery yanked Nate from the chair with a handful of shirt.
'Who do you think you are, Price? You don't give orders around
here.'

'Go get Beth Preston,' Frazier thundered. 'And stop wasting my time, Jonah.'

'Fine, but if you fail, it'll cost Hunter and Beth their lives. Right now, where they're being held has plenty of air. But I might just cut off the ventilation as an added incentive. And considering what a windbag Beth is, Hunter might suffocate if you don't find Ensley fast.' Creery laughed as he walked out the door.

'Jonah,' Frazier called, his voice raspy. 'Don't *you* forget who's giving the orders. This is still my game.'

'For some reason, my assistant doesn't seem to like Mr Price,' Frazier said to Michael. 'But I'll see that Beth has plenty of air. You just find Ensley.'

Ten minutes later, the guards dragged a kicking and struggling Beth into the room. 'Are you OK?' Michael rushed toward his wife, but two other guards kept them apart.

'Nothing I can't handle, baby,' she answered, cocky as ever.

'Ask your questions, Price, and be quick.'

'Beth, tell us everything you remember from the beach. When Izzy woke up, the tide was coming in, you were gone, and the ADA was dead.'

'The three of us were coming back to the mansion when I felt a prick in my neck like from a tranquilizer dart. Then I blacked out. When I came to, I tried to wake Izzy up, but these creeps must've given her a stronger dose than mine.' Beth managed to elbow her captor's gut before they tightened their hold.

Creery opened up his palms. 'After Beth shot the prosecutor, we felt we needed to subdue both of you. I apologize if Mrs Price's dose was too strong.' He bowed rather nobly to Izzy.

'I didn't shoot anyone.' Beth struggled against her restraints. 'I found Jennifer lying in a pile of driftwood, dead.'

'She appeared to have been shot with your gun, the gun you were still holding when we captured you.' Calmly, Creery turned to Izzy. 'I sent the guards back for you with a stretcher, but you were gone, so they brought back the ADA. Again, I apologize for any discomfort you suffered.'

'This is a pile of you-know-what, Mr Frazier,' Beth spat. 'I didn't kill that woman. Jennifer was willing to tell you what she knew.'

'Did she say where Kurt Ensley might be hiding?'

Frazier's question took Beth by surprise. 'No, I don't think she knew.'

'Then this is a waste of time,' Frazier concluded. 'The police will check the weapon for fingerprints and run ballistics when they get here.' Frazier spoke to the guards. 'Take Mrs Preston back and make sure they get breakfast.'

'Wait!' Beth pleaded. 'Please let me kiss Michael before you throw me down that rabbit hole.' But she was quickly dragged away.

'Isabelle, are you ready to go?' Frazier asked. After she nodded, Frazier said to Nate and Michael: 'I suggest you not disappoint me again.'

Nate understood what they were up against, but not what Michael had up his sleeve. However, he waited until they were outdoors and far from the house to ask, 'What on earth do you want with that kid's gaming device?'

Michael patted his pocket. 'I recognized the device is just like one my niece owns. Although you can't make phone calls, you can still send texts. It must have a cheap, limited data plan. As soon as we're far from Frazier's spies, I'll send Kate and Eric a text. If at any point today we get within range of St Simons, the message might go through. It's worth eighty bucks to try.'

Once they were deep in the woods, Michael pulled out the device and searched for the correct screen. 'Trouble is I can't remember Kate's number. I always use speed dial.'

'I know it.' Nate took the device, entered the cell number, and tapped in a message.

Price team fine. But 4 other guests dead. Bring help. Trust NOBODY here except us.

Nate recited the message for Michael and then hit the 'send' button. 'That ought to do it, if we're lucky. Let's head toward the boat dock where we were dropped off. That's got to be the closest spot on Elysian to St Simons or the mainland.'

'Let's hope the gaming device works.' Michael tucked it back in his pocket.

'We'll walk slowly so we can listen and watch for signs of Ensley.'

When they reached the dock, Michael typed and sent the message again, yet they'd found no signs of the lawyer. Along the way back to the house, they checked the old barn and found only small footprints in the dust, which had to be Izzy's and Beth's.

'You know what Frazier said.' Michael wiped sweat from his neck and face.

Nate peered up at the curtained windows of the second floor. 'Don't bother coming back without the lawyer.' He gazed up at the sun's position. 'How long have we been out here – an hour and a half? And we've only searched the island at the narrow, rocky part. Let's head to the beach at the widest point and see if we can find Ensley. If I were him, I'd be trying to flag down a fishing boat or shrimp trawler. And you can't walk through sand without leaving footprints.'

'Which way?' Michael turned away from the house.

'Izzy said she and Beth headed south yesterday. So we'll head due north and hopefully come across a path.'

But after hours of hiking through fields of spartina, stepping in plenty of water-filled holes, crossing paths with two snakes, and getting bitten by insects, the only trails they found had been made by crabs. And there was no sandy beach on the northern end, only acres of swampy marsh which eventually became open water.

Nate and Michael had no choice but to turn around and head back the way they had come. After hours of slogging across tidal marsh and through the tall weeds on higher ground, Nate finally spotted the closest thing to a path they'd seen all day. 'This is ridiculous.' Nate lowered himself to a fallen log. 'Either that guy grew wings and flew off the island, or Creery already killed him and disposed of the body.'

'Maybe Ensley flagged down a passing boat.' Michael swatted an insect against his neck.

'Have you seen even one boat come near this island? I haven't, and neither has Izzy. Right now we only got a couple more hours of daylight. Then we won't be able to see two feet in front of us. I say we head down this path and see if it leads to the house.' Nate pointed in the direction he wanted to go.

'You heard what Creery said.' Michael scuffed his boot heel

in the hard-packed sand. 'We're not going back without Ensley. It's not your wife who'll be running out of oxygen.'

'You didn't let me finish,' Nate snapped. 'This path should cut through the island at the widest part. If we keep yelling Ensley's name in every direction he should hear us, as long as he's still alive.'

'What if that lawyer thinks we're as big a threat as Frazier and Creery?' Worry and fatigue deepened every line on Michael's face.

'Unless you got a better idea, it's the chance we must take.' Nate didn't say another word, giving Michael time to decide.

'You're right. This is our best shot.' Michael tied the bandana around his forehead. 'You lead the way and watch everything left of the trail. I'll follow behind at twenty paces and keep watch on the right.'

Every minute or two the men yelled Ensley's name at the top of their lungs. At least searching became easier as the path entered the maritime forest. Unfortunately, those trees cut off the last of the setting sun just as Michael spotted human footprints in the dirt.

As Michael knelt down to examine the prints, Nate searched for a dry place to spend the night. 'It will be dark soon. Maybe we should stop here and continue at first light.' He pointed at a sprawling live oak tree.

Michael jumped to his feet. 'No, let's keep calling Ensley's name until we can't see a foot in front of us. Then we'll stop.'

Suddenly, a commotion overhead curtailed their argument as a man dropped from the tree in front of them. 'Who in the world are you two?' he asked. 'And why are you looking for me?'

TWELVE

St Simons Island. Thursday p.m.

K ate soon realized that 'urgent situation' and 'please call ASAP' meant something different to a corporate CEO from Atlanta than to a private investigator from the Panhandle of Florida. Although she'd watched her phone throughout dinner at a local pizza shop and kept it on her lap for the rest of the evening, Alexander Frazier didn't return her call until almost eleven o'clock. She and Eric had fallen asleep on the couch when the ringtone jarred her awake.

'Kate Weller.' She poked Eric in the side and hit the speaker button.

'This is Alexander Frazier. I'm sorry for the delay, Miss Weller, but my secretary didn't relay your message until *after* the company's board meeting. You believe something is wrong out on Elysian? Is it my uncle's health?'

'We don't know exactly what's wrong out there, but either your uncle or one of his employees has purposefully kept us from joining the company retreat. My partner and I have been unable to reach co-workers, and when we hired a boat to take us to Elysian, someone shot at us.'

Frazier paused. 'If that's all that's wrong, Captain Mike Burke ferries the guests from the mainland to the island. You should get ahold of him.'

'No, sir, that's *not* all that's wrong. We talked to Captain Burke yesterday. He said Mr Creery specifically told him we had changed our plans and weren't coming to the retreat. He told Captain Burke to take the rest of the week off with pay. None of that was true.'

'Mr Creery?' Frazier asked. 'Mr Jonah Creery?'

'I guess so. How many assistants named Creery does your uncle have?'

'You're right, Miss Weller. Something is wrong on the island. I'm calling my uncle right now.'

'Wait, please!' Kate begged. 'Tell me what's going on first. You don't want to make matters worse.'

Frazier took a moment to consider. 'Jonah Creery is the chief financial officer of Resilient Automotive Systems. He's been absent all week without taking vacation or telling anyone where he's going. Since Creery wasn't taking my calls, I had my auditor run a quick check on our balance sheets.'

'*And?*' Kate prodded when Frazier fell silent.

'What I'm about to tell you is extremely sensitive information. It could cause a panicked sell-off of the company's stock.'

'Look, I'm not going to say anything, but lives may be at stake on the island, including those of my friends.' Kate wanted to reach through the phone and shake the guy. 'Tell me what your auditor found out.'

'Jonah Creery has been skimming from the company for at least fifteen years. At first, he took only small amounts. Then, after my uncle retired, Creery became bolder with the money he stole.' Frazier huffed with contempt. 'What's particularly disgusting is that my uncle trusted Jonah. They had been friends for years. If Creery told him the books were being regularly audited as bylaws require, Uncle Julian took him at his word. After my accountant reported the theft, I called an emergency board meeting for this evening. I have my uncle's proxy to vote his shares whenever he's not in Atlanta.'

'What happened at the meeting?' Kate asked.

'What do you think? We voted to replace Creery with an interim CFO pending a full investigation. Look, I don't mean to sound harsh with you, Miss Weller. I'm just totally disgusted. My uncle trusted Creery with his life.'

'Let's hope it hasn't come down to a life-and-death struggle out there.'

'I still don't understand the connection between Creery's theft and you not reaching your company's retreat? Creery couldn't possibly know what my accountant discovered, or that he'd been removed as the CFO. Everyone at the meeting was sworn to secrecy under corporate privacy laws.'

Kate then told the nephew everything she knew as succinctly

as possible, including the passenger list from the previous week.'

Frazier swore under his breath. 'Those are the people Uncle Julian blamed for his wife's death. This might have nothing to do with skimming profits. Creery could be helping my uncle get justice for Aunt Ariana.'

'Then why wouldn't Creery take vacation time?'

'I don't know. But if I can't get ahold of my uncle, I'm taking the company helicopter to Elysian Island with my own security force. I gotta stop those two before they end up in jail.'

'No, Mr Frazier, you're not. If you want your secrets to stay that way, you'll fly your helicopter to the St Simons Airport. Then Captain Burke will take you, me, and my partner to Elysian like normal.'

'How will I explain myself?'

Kate voiced the first idea that came to mind. 'When you couldn't reach your uncle, you decided to come for the weekend to make sure Julian wasn't sick or something.'

'Let me check with the pilot. Don't hang up.' Frazier was gone for several minutes. 'Fine, I'll leave Atlanta first thing in the morning. I can be on St Simons by ten o'clock. Where should I meet you?'

Kate couldn't remember Captain Burke's address off the top of her head, so she picked the next best location. 'Meet my partner and me by the Seaside Kitchen off the Causeway. The *Slippery Eel* is docked in that marina.'

'I know the place. Just remember to keep quiet about the independent audit and voting Creery out as CFO. I want to hear Jonah's explanation as to why he's been missing all week.'

'You've got a deal.' Kate hung up, feeling more optimistic than she had in a while.

Elysian Island. Thursday p.m.

Neither Nate nor Michael was prepared for someone to drop out of the trees like Tarzan. Yet the moment they recovered their senses, they sprang into action. Michael tackled the smaller man, while Nate slipped his arm around Ensley's neck.

'We're private investigators hired by Mr Frazier to find you . . . if you're Kurt Ensley,' Nate added.

'I . . . am,' he croaked. 'Please get off me. I can't breathe.'

Nate released the headlock. 'Where have you been?'

'Hiding in big trees with plenty of Spanish moss.'

Michael sat back on his haunches. 'You've been in a tree *all this time*?'

'Not in the same tree. I've been moving around the island. Do you have anything to eat? All I've had is a few apples and some raw oysters. And I had to drink from puddles of standing rainwater. I'll probably die of intestinal parasites, if Frazier doesn't kill me first.'

'Here.' Michael pulled three dinner rolls, several packs of crackers and a bottle of water from his pocket. 'Eat slowly. It's everything I could store up.'

Nate watched Ensley eat, unsure if they could trust him. 'It'll soon be completely dark, so unless you've got a flashlight, we can't go anywhere until morning.'

'Frazier took everything away from us.' Ensley shoved the second roll in his mouth while still chewing the first.

'Then we've got plenty of time to talk.' Nate leaned his back against a tree. 'You were Mack Fallon's court appointment attorney eight years ago?'

Ensley nodded affirmatively while chewing.

'Then why on earth would you come here?'

The lawyer took a long swallow of water. 'I received an invitation to spend a weekend of duck hunting and card playing with Hunter Galen, my best corporate client.'

Nate frowned. 'So you didn't know Julian Frazier owned the island?'

'Oh, I knew. I did my research before boarding the flight from New Orleans to Jacksonville. But why would Frazier hold me responsible? I was court-appointed after the fact.'

Nate exchanged a look with Michael. 'You thought it was a pure coincidence you got invited to the one-time home of Ariana Frazier?'

Ensley finished the water and crumpled the bottle noisily. 'Why wouldn't I? I've known and trusted Hunter Galen a long time. I've considered him a friend besides my client.'

'Just for the record, Hunter didn't know about the invitation,' Michael said wryly.

Ensley leaned into a thin patch of moonlight. 'I knew Frazier might have found out, but I wanted this nightmare behind me once and for all.'

Nate leaned into the moonlight, too, so there would be no misunderstanding. 'If you want us to help you, Ensley, I suggest you stop playing games. How are you involved?'

'As his lawyer, I should have asked for the security tape of the cellblock on the night Fallon overdosed. But I never did. I had so many other cases.' He dropped his face into his hands. 'Everybody thought Mack brought the drugs in with him. The guards didn't watch the tape because they're the ones who should've searched him better. I didn't request the tape until long after the case was dismissed.'

'Look, if it wasn't you who gave Mack the drugs, it was ADA Jennifer Jacobs.'

Ensley lifted his chin and looked Nate in the eye. 'It wasn't either of us. That reporter handed the guard a bunch of money to look the other way so he could accompany the ADA to the cellblock. McDowell wanted an early scoop on Fallon's big confession scheduled for the next day.'

Nate blew out an exasperated breath. 'You're saying McDowell gave Fallon a hot dose of heroin so there would be no confession to the cops or the press. Why would he do this?'

Ensley started eating the crackers slower than the rolls. 'Because someone paid him much more than a boost in his ratings was worth. And, for the record, Jennifer didn't know what McDowell had done until she read it in the papers.'

Michael grabbed ahold of the lawyer and shook him like a ragdoll. 'Why didn't you take that tape to the judge? McDowell has gotten away with murder all these years.'

'I was afraid the only thing it would accomplish was to get me and the ADA fired and potentially disbarred. After all, Mack Fallon only got what he deserved. And I was young, stupid and . . . a coward.'

'Why the big change of heart eight years later?' Nate didn't hide his contempt.

'I know it's hard to believe, but nothing has gone right since I covered up that conspiracy.'

Nate snorted. 'You left the public defender's office years ago and seem to be doing well as Hunter's big-time lawyer.'

'Is that how it looks?' Tears ran down Ensley's haggard face. 'Hunter Galen is my *only* client. The law firm told me to find more clients or look for another job. Then, last month, my fiancée broke off our engagement because she met someone else.'

'You think you've got it tough?' Michael sneered. 'Four people are dead because of your cowardice. The Atlanta detective might have done a poor job, and the ADA shouldn't have helped McDowell, but they didn't deserve to die.'

'I know,' Ensley wailed. 'I should've done the right thing years ago. But if I can take down the last person responsible for Mrs Frazier's death, maybe I can look myself in the face without feeling shame.'

Nate and Michael exchanged a confused look. 'Who would that be? Please don't tell me Frazier took out a hit on his wife.'

'No, not Frazier, but his assistant, Jonah Creery. The two probably had some trouble brewing for years, then a tiny blonde sealed the deal between Creery and Frazier.'

Nate remembered the picture of platinum-haired Ariana sipping champagne in very high heels. 'Ariana?'

'Maybe Frazier kept his wife on a short leash financially. I don't know, but Creery fell in love with her. He paid the Fallons to kill Julian so he could marry Ariana. But Mack must have accidentally hit Ariana too hard when he knocked her out.'

Michael smacked Ensley so hard he fell over backward. 'You're making all this up. You hadn't even been appointed Mack's legal counsel yet.'

Ensley returned to a sitting position and brushed off his hands. 'I don't know all the whys and hows of their relationship, but I know Creery paid for the break-in and gave the Fallons the security code. And I've got proof right here.' Ensley patted his jacket. 'I copied the security tape onto a flash drive and brought it with me. I want Frazier to know the truth and then I'll take whatever I got coming.'

Nate glanced around in the dark. Their path had disappeared, while overhead only a few stars twinkled between the treetops. 'We'll have to sleep here and find our way back in the morning.'

'And if Creery has harmed one hair on my wife's head, you'll end up alongside the other four in the morgue.' Michael thumped Ensley once more for good measure. 'Try to get some rest, Nate. I'll make sure this creep doesn't crawl off into the trees.'

Following Michael's dire warning, Ensley curled into a tight ball by their feet, while Nate listened to crickets and tree frogs for hours. He couldn't sleep either. He had to make sure Ensley lived long enough to show Frazier the truth.

St Simons Island. Friday a.m.

With so many things that could go wrong with her newly concocted plan, Kate couldn't eat a bite of breakfast Friday morning. Yet sooner or later her luck had to change. Using the company helicopter, Alexander Frazier would arrive at McKinnon Airport on St Simons Island at ten o'clock. So she and Eric needed to bring Captain Burke up to·speed. For her plan to work, the captain must play his role perfectly.

'Captain Burke?' she called as Eric knocked on his front door. 'It's Kate Weller and Eric Manfredi.'

After a flurry of activity, the front door opened. 'Come in, Miss Weller, Mr Manfredi.' Captain Burke, tousled-haired and unshaven, stepped to the side to let them pass. 'I thought you would call last night to tell us what's going on.'

'I had planned to, but it was late when I got off the phone with Alexander Frazier.' She and Eric followed the captain to the kitchen where Mrs Burke was making coffee.

Clad in a pink bathrobe and fuzzy slippers, Celine looked as though she had just climbed out of bed. 'This will be ready in five minutes,' she said.

'Sorry, ma'am,' Kate murmured. 'We shouldn't have dropped in so early but I'm afraid we need an early start.'

Eric walked around the room as though checking for clues. 'You didn't contact anyone on the island, did you?'

'Absolutely not.' Burke ran a hand through his tangled hair.
'I followed your instructions exactly.'

'Good. Let's sit, and I'll bring you up to speed.' Kate relayed
the gist of her conversation with the nephew, but withheld the
details about Creery's thievery. Even if Burke had no stomach
for insider trading, Kate wanted to keep her promise to
Alexander.

'You're saying the younger Frazier believed you that something is wrong?' Burke slurped some coffee the moment his
wife set down a cup.

'Yes, Creery hasn't been at the office all week. So, if for no
other reason, the nephew wants to ask him why, besides checking
on his uncle.'

'He's on his way to Elysian now?'

'No, his helicopter will create too much fuss. He will meet
us at the Maritime Center at ten o'clock. You'll take him over
on Frazier's yacht, taking Eric and me secretly there as well.'
Kate sipped her coffee, hoping for more cookies. 'OK, you
need to tell me everything you can about the Frazier house –
the location of doors and ground-level windows, the layout of
rooms, and which staff members may be on the island.'

Burke did better than explain. He drew a map to the
mansion, then sketched a layout of the first floor. He also
marked the location of a cellar door that was usually left open
in case the cook's son locked himself out. 'Frazier normally
has three maids to serve, but Creery had me pick them up
late Wednesday night. So the only staff present should be
the cook, Mrs Norville, her son, Paul, and the butler, Alfred
Compton.'

Kate jotted their names and roles on the side of the map.

Eric scratched his chin. 'Didn't you find it strange for Creery
to dismiss the maids when Frazier had a bunch of houseguests?'

'Mr Manfredi, I'm paid rather well not to question *anything*
that eccentric man does. Besides, Creery said the guests doing
for themselves was part of the game Frazier planned for the
week.' Burke finished his coffee in one long swallow. 'If you'll
excuse me, I need to shave and change clothes. If I show up
in shorts and a T-shirt, someone will get suspicious.'

While Burke became presentable, Celine fed them cinnamon

toast and refilled their mugs twice. She also explained the best sights to see on St Simons for when they return.

If we return, she thought. But when Burke appeared in his starched captain's uniform, Kate banished her pessimistic thoughts. Nate, Izzy, and her co-workers were counting on them. And if Eric had aspirations of one day joining the Price team, this would be his big chance to prove himself.

'If you're ready, let's head over to the marina and get the *Slippery Eel* ready.' Captain Burke positioned his cap on his head.

'Eric and I will drive there too, since we'll need a car available when we come back. We're meeting Alexander Frazier outside the Seaside Kitchen restaurant. Do you happen to own a weapon, Captain?'

Burke's blond eyebrows knit together. 'Do you mean a gun?'

'Handgun, rifle, cannon, bowie knife or bow and arrow,' Kate said. 'Eric needs something to defend himself with on the island.'

'I have an old spear gun for fishing. Will that do?'

'It's better than nothing,' said Eric. 'Find it and put it on the boat.'

'Thanks for breakfast, Celine,' Kate called on their way out.

Burke disappeared into the garden shed and reappeared with a gruesome-looking weapon which he waved in the air.

Kate gave him the thumbs-up. 'Whatever happened to a worm, bobber, and bamboo pole?' she muttered under her breath.

Her question went unanswered on their short drive. Eric might have beaten Captain Burke to the marina, but not the nephew's helicopter and subsequent taxi. Three impeccably dressed men stood waiting under the covered canopy of the marina's retail area.

'Check out the suits,' Eric said as they approached from the parking lot. 'Frazier and his staff look ready for another board meeting, not a friendly visit to his uncle's island.'

'Hold up a second.' Kate pulled her vibrating phone from her pocket. 'I can't believe this. It's a text from a number I don't recognize.' Staring at the screen, Kate read the cryptic words through twice.

'What does it say?' Eric tried to read over her shoulder.

'*Price team fine. But four other guests dead. Bring help. Trust nobody here but us.*' She and Eric locked eyes. 'Holy cow,' Kate said, for lack of something better.

'How do you want to handle this?' Eric asked.

Kate glanced over at Frazier who kept shifting his weight from foot to foot. 'I guess we have the proof that law enforcement needs to storm the island. I'll forward that text message to your phone. As soon as you get it, head to the sheriff's office and show someone in charge. Four people dead ought to rally them to action.'

'Come with me, Kate. Let Frazier's nephew go to the island alone.'

'No, it might take time for law enforcement to implement a plan; time that the Price team doesn't have. I'll go over with Alexander and gauge the situation at the mansion.'

Eric shook his head like an angry bull. 'I won't allow it! It's too dangerous.'

'Look, I love you too, partner.' She stretched up to kiss him. 'How 'bout if I promise not to do anything until you storm the ramparts with the cavalry?'

Eric glared at Frazier who was walking in their direction. 'I don't like this, but OK. Just remember your promise – stay out of sight until I arrive with backup.' He kissed her again, then strode back to his car.

Kate smiled and waved at the impatient-looking man. 'Mr Frazier? Sorry we kept you waiting. My partner got an urgent message he needed to take care of. I'm Kate Weller.' She stretched out her hand, noticing that Frazier wore a Rolex to accompany his expensive suit, but at least he had on Sperry's instead of hard-soled shoes.

'Nice to meet you, Miss Weller.' Frazier shook hands, shot his cuffs, and finished introductions. 'This is Baker and Nguyen from my personal security staff.'

'Are you gentlemen armed?' Kate asked, noticing that both Baker and Nguyen also wore boat shoes.

Both stared as though she'd grown a second head. Baker answered in a soft drawl. 'We wouldn't be much use to Mr Frazier if we weren't.'

'Of course, I'm just making sure everyone understands the danger we might run into.' Kate looked toward the water as a blush rose up her neck. Fortuitously, she spotted Captain Burke waving a hundred yards down the dock and waved back. 'Captain Burke has the *Slippery Eel* ready for our trip to Elysian. Shall we get going?'

Accustomed to taking charge, Alexander Frazier rattled off orders. 'Baker, walk back and cancel the idling taxi. Nguyen, please see what Captain Burke needs to get under way. And Miss Weller, would you please walk with me?'

'Of course.' As soon as his men headed in opposite directions, Kate took Frazier's right side. 'I hope I didn't offend your staff with my question.'

The nephew smiled. 'Not at all. The question might have surprised them, but a trained security team knows better than to take anything for granted. And I agree with your assessment of the island. Things could turn ugly in a hurry.'

'Is there anything else I should know?' Kate asked.

'Only that my uncle is dying. He has non-operable, non-treatable cancer. This could be why Creery is up to something. Maybe Creery is afraid of being left out of the will, or that he'll be replaced in the company once my uncle is gone. Maybe he fears his shenanigans will be uncovered. At any rate, I wouldn't underestimate either Creery or my uncle.'

As they neared the slip for the *Slippery Eel*, Burke stepped onto the dock. 'Watch your step, Miss Weller,' he cautioned. 'We are at low tide. You'll have to use the ladder down to the yacht.'

'We'll manage, Captain,' said Kate. 'Have you met Mr Frazier's nephew, Alexander?'

'Yes, many times,' Burke replied. 'Nice to see you again, sir.'

'Thank you, Captain. Whenever you're ready, Captain, Mr Nguyen will release your lines. Miss Weller, let me climb down first so I can offer my hand.'

Having grown up near the Gulf of Mexico, Kate probably had more familiarity with boats than someone from Atlanta. Nevertheless, she took his hand midway down the ladder.

As soon as Nguyen was aboard and Burke disappeared into

the pilothouse, Frazier turned to face her. 'What have you told Captain Burke, Miss Weller?'

'Nothing about Jonah Creery. Only that you wished to check on your uncle. And I'd like you to call me Kate.'

'I am grateful for your discretion, and please call me Alex.' His smile revealed perfectly straight teeth.

With the *Slippery Eel* under way, Kate and Frazier took seats in the stern, while Baker and Nguyen went up to the bow, presumably to keep an eye on Captain Burke.

'Do you have some sort of a plan, Kate?'

'I want you and your security force to disembark as soon as we dock. I will remain on board, hidden.'

Frazier nodded. 'My uncle's butler, Compton, usually welcomes new guests. Most likely he won't today, since I'm arriving unannounced.'

'If no one shows up to meet the *Slippery Eel*, can you still find the house?' Kate asked.

'I've been here a few times for corporate parties, but usually I imbibe on the way over and don't pay much attention. But I remember a path through the woods that leads to the mansion. How will you find it?'

Kate unfolded her crude map. 'Captain Burke drew me this map of the island and, on the other side, a layout of the house.' She handed him the map for his inspection.

'This is how I remember it too.' Alexander handed back the drawing. 'Once I reach the house, I plan to look for Uncle Julian . . .' Alex let his statement hang in the air, waiting for her response.

'I plan to enter his mansion unseen,' Kate said. 'After that, I'm hoping for a brilliant insight.'

'I wish you luck. Now, tell me where your partner went in such a big hurry.'

As the yacht bounced over the waves, Kate studied the handsome, thirty-five-ish corporate mogul. 'I suppose I have no choice but to trust you.'

'You should – you're the one who called me.'

'Only because your family's mess has jeopardized my friends' lives, not to mention ruined a perfectly affordable company retreat.'

Alex's grin was slow in coming. 'Let's sort out the details later. Regardless of what my uncle has done, I mean *nobody* any harm. So tell me where Mr Manfredi went.'

Kate dug her phone from her pocket, tapped the screen a few times, and handed him the phone.

Alexander's grin vanished. 'Exactly who is dead on Elysian?'

'I'm not sure, but so far they're not my co-workers. It could be the people your uncle holds responsible for his wife's death.'

'Has Uncle Julian lost his mind?'

'That remains to be seen. As for right now, we're almost at the island. I'll slip down below and hide, while you remain in view like nothing is amiss.'

'While traveling with two bodyguards?' Alex sounded like his cool composure was rapidly slipping away.

'If anybody asks about Baker and Nguyen, say someone phoned in a threat to your office. So you're playing it safe for a few days.'

'That sounds good.' Alexander stood and smoothed the wrinkles from his suit. 'Will you be all right?'

'I'm a trained professional. The only things I fear are very large spiders,' Kate lied as she ducked down into the stern.

Although well appointed, with teak furniture and expensive bedding, the sleeping quarters had only a few tightly sealed portholes. Kate couldn't hear the conversation between Alexander and his bodyguards, or with Captain Burke, and she couldn't see much beyond a small, circular scope. But from what she could gather, no one came down to meet the *Slippery Eel*.

Kate waited a few extra minutes after she could no longer see anyone or hear anything. Then she crept quietly from her hiding spot and stepped onto the aft deck.

'What do you want me to do, Miss Weller?' whispered Captain Burke.

Ridiculously, she'd forgotten about the captain in her haste to exit. 'I thought you got off with Alexander Frazier,' she whispered back.

'He told me to remain on the yacht. If he doesn't come back or send word within the hour, I am to head to the mainland and contact the coastguard.'

'Good idea,' Kate said after a short consideration. 'No sign of the butler?'

'No sign of anyone at all. This is unlike Mr Frazier's usual hospitality.'

'I doubt anything is *usual* at the house. Besides, hopefully no one knows we're here yet.' Kate climbed up the gangway and surveyed her surroundings. As Burke had described, a thick growth of trees reached the rocks at water's edge, but she saw the path that led to the house. 'Remember, if someone asks, you brought no one to Elysian but Mr Frazier's nephew and his bodyguards.'

'I understand. Good luck, Miss Weller.' Burke opened one of the deck's storage compartments. 'And don't forget this.' He handed her the ghastly spear gun. 'I hope you don't have to use it.'

'You and me both.' Kate slung the weapon over her shoulder and ran up the dock. As she'd seen on countless television shows, she bent from the waist to keep a low profile as she headed for the woods. When no one shot at her, she slowed her pace to a fast walk on the path.

Low branches scratched her face, while tree roots hidden by leaves caused her to stumble twice, but Kate soon reached a rambling stone house surrounded by a landscaped lawn. French doors, wrought-iron balconies, and a flagstone courtyard shaded by a vine-covered pergola gave the mansion a romantic feel, not in keeping with *four guests dead* and *trust no one*.

From behind a tree, Kate watched for movement at the windows or on the grounds. After seeing and hearing nothing, she bolted across the lawn and hid between the arborvitae and the house, then circled the house until she found the steps down to the cellar. Thick grape vines almost obscured the entrance but, as Captain Burke had promised, the door was unlocked and the knob turned easily. Kate entered the gloomy, dank basement with enough cobwebs for a scary movie set. Using her phone's flashlight, she stepped carefully around crates of empty wine bottles, stacks of newspapers and unmarked cardboard boxes piled from floor to ceiling. Hopefully, the cook's son never snuck a cigarette down here, because the whole place could quickly go up like a roman candle. A thin shaft of light guided her to a set of stairs, presumably leading to the kitchen.

Taking each step as quietly as possible, Kate heard a woman humming as she neared the top. Unfortunately the top step gave off a loud squeak, giving away her location. The off-key humming abruptly ceased. But when the door opened, Kate was ready.

'What the devil?' the grey-haired woman asked. 'Who are you?'

Kate leveled her gun with the woman's belly. 'My name isn't important, Mrs Norville. But if you want to see your son again, you'll keep quiet and press no silent alarms.'

'What silent alarm?' Noticing the weapon, Norville took several steps back. 'How do you know my name?'

'I'll ask the questions,' Kate hissed under her breath. 'Where is your son?'

'Paul's in his room, grounded, because he lost his gaming device somewhere on the island.' Soup dripped from her spoon onto the floor tiles, while something sputtered on the stove.

'Stir your pot. Then tell me where's Alexander Frazier?'

While she stirred, her face registered confusion. 'You're mistaken, young lady. Julian Frazier owns this island. His nephew lives in Atlanta where he runs the company.'

'I know that,' Kate snapped. 'But he's on his way.'

'I haven't heard the company helicopter.'

Sighing with exasperation, Kate followed the cook across the kitchen. 'If you're playing games, lady, you'll be sorry. Where are Nate Price and the other members of his team?'

Norville pondered while stirring the pot. 'When I delivered breakfast this morning, Mrs Price and Mrs Galen were in the dining room with Mr Frazier and Jonah Creery. Mr Price and Mr Preston never came back to the house last night. I suppose they'll be back today, hungrier than bears.'

'What about Hunter Galen and Beth Preston?'

'I don't know where those two are.'

Kate stuck her weapon in the holster and pointed at the table. 'Time for you to sit down and explain what's going on. And if you try anything, I'll shoot you and then shoot your son. I know four people have already died on this island, so what's two more?'

Norville dropped heavily into the chair and started to

whimper. 'I'll tell you what I know, but please don't hurt us. Paul and I had nothing to do with those people's deaths.'

'I'll believe that once I hear it from somebody else.'

Kate didn't like threatening a middle-aged cook and her son, who may indeed have nothing to do with the murders. But, on the other hand, the words *trust nobody here* kept running through her mind like a radio jingle.

THIRTEEN

Elysian Island. Friday a.m.

Despite his best intentions, Nate had slept for a few hours. Michael shook him awake just as the sun's first rays pierced the thick canopy of trees.

'Wake up, Ensley.' He nudged the man's side with the toe of his boot. 'Time to straighten out the nightmare you created.' Nate dragged the lawyer to his feet none too gently.

Michael checked Paul's gaming device and gave Nate the thumbs-up. 'At some point last night, our message was delivered,' he said while Ensley was distracted in the bushes.

Nate took a sip of water and handed the bottle to Michael, who finished the last swallow.

'Any left for me?' Ensley asked.

'Sorry, it was our last bottle. We'll see that you get plenty to drink before you start talking.' Michael pushed him in the direction of the path, once again visible in daylight.

Nate took the lead, followed by Ensley, and then Michael, who eagerly shoved the attorney each time he dropped back. But the uneven terrain and swampy patches made the going slow. Judging by the position of the sun, Nate figured it was almost noon when they reached the landscaped gardens around the mansion.

Panting and sweating, Ensley stepped from the woods, but Nate grabbed his arm. 'Hold up there. We don't want the guards to see us before Mr Frazier.'

'Why not?' Ensley gasped, trying to pull free. 'I need water and I don't care who sees me first.'

'I suspect that those guards work for Jonah Creery and not Mr Frazier. We don't want you ending up dead before you have a chance to tell your story.'

Pale and weak, Ensley stopped struggling. 'What do you suggest?'

Nate watched the back of the house. 'The guards will expect us to return the same way we left. So we'll stay out of sight, circle around to the front, and make a break for the door. Let's just hope the butler reaches the foyer before the guards.'

Michael had to drag Ensley, not because he wouldn't cooperate, but because he was weak from hunger, thirst, and lack of sleep.

Nate counted to three, then the three men bolted from the woods and up the brick steps. While Michael held the last suspect upright, Nate pounded his fist on the solid wood panel.

'What on earth?' Alfred Compton demanded indignantly as he opened the door. 'Why didn't you men enter at the—' When Compton recognized Ensley, he stopped short. 'I never thought we'd see him again.' The butler pointed at Ensley.

'No time to explain, Compton. Where is Mr Frazier?' Nate and Michael shoved past the butler, dragging Ensley with them.

'He's in the dining room with the ladies. When Mr Frazier found out Mrs Preston hadn't received her intended meals, he insisted she be brought to him immediately.'

Nate pressed on several spots on the paneling, trying to find the secret cupboard in the wall.

'Your weapons are no longer there, Mr Price,' intoned the butler. 'Mr Creery moved them to an unknown location.'

'Then we're all going to the dining room, and you will go first and deal with any interference.' Nate shoved Compton toward the main hall.

He sniffed with indignation. 'No need to push. I didn't move your precious guns.'

'Maybe not, but I still don't know whose side you're on.'

As Michael half carried the lawyer, Nate prodded the butler through several hallways. Yet, the party of four encountered no one along the way. At the dining room, Compton lifted his hand to knock.

'No, don't,' Nate warned. 'Use your key to open the door.'

Just as Compton turned the key, Nate and Michael threw their combined weight against the door, throwing the guard on the other side off-balance. The foursome surged into the room before anyone could react.

'Mr Frazier, we followed your instructions!' Nate shouted, pulling Kurt Ensley up beside him.

Beth's, Nicki's, and Izzy's eyes grew very round, while Frazier's mouth dropped open.

However, no one looked more surprised than Jonah Creery. 'Yes, but you're late, Mr Price.' The assistant's expression turned to one of pure hatred. 'You had until sundown yesterday to return with the lawyer. Guards, take Mr Ensley and Mrs Preston back to the holding cell to await the police.'

'Nothing doing, Jonah.' Frazier rose shakily to his feet. 'I want to hear what Fallon's public defender has to say.'

The guards looked from one to the other, confused.

'What do you think he'll say, Julian?' Spittle flew from Creery's mouth as he spoke. 'He would say anything to buy himself time. Ensley was the one who gave Fallon the heroin to keep him from talking. Then he killed the other three *suspects* for the same reason.'

Released from Nate's grip, Ensley staggered toward the water glasses on the table. He drank the contents of two and then wiped his mouth. 'I didn't kill anyone, not on this island and not eight years ago.' The words tumbled out, raspy and garbled, as Ensley slumped into a chair. It sounded painful to talk. 'But I did cover up for the person who did . . . *you*, Creery.'

Izzy carried the pitcher of water to where Ensley sat. 'Drink more. You're dehydrated.' She filled both glasses.

'You were a lazy nobody when you graduated from law school, and you're still backwater scum now.' Creery moved closer and shook his fist at Ensley. 'I won't stand by while you tell lies to a dying man, a man who happens to be my best friend.'

To the shock of everyone, including the guards, Creery pulled out a gun and shot Ensley squarely between the eyes.

The former public defender – the final suspect in Frazier's game – fell forward, dead before his head hit the table.

Nate and Michael rushed toward Creery, but the guards quickly blocked their path.

'I suggest you sit down with your wives, gentlemen, before the guards forget you're the *good guys*.' Creery's sly grin reappeared.

With automatic weapons aimed at them, Nate and Michael had no choice but to do as he said.

'What have you done, Jonah? How will you explain this when law enforcement arrives?' Frazier braced both palms on the table for support, as every bit of color drained from his face.

Creery tucked his gun inside his sport coat. 'I'll worry about the police later. That thug systematically killed everyone who had been connected to your wife's murder.' He pointed to where Ensley was face down in a pool of blood, which grew larger by the moment. 'Only Ensley and Jennifer Jacobs had access to Mack Fallon's cell in county lockup. Someone paid Ensley to slip Fallon the drugs to keep from talking.'

'And, thanks to you, we'll never know who that someone was!' Frazier had tried to shout, but he sounded like what he was – a very sick old man.

'What difference does it make? The game is over, my friend.' Creery closed the distance between them and slipped his arm around Frazier's shoulder. 'Everyone connected to that horrible night is dead and nothing will bring your sweet wife back. Let's concentrate on making each day you have left a tribute to Ariana's memory. I'll face whatever consequences I have coming down the road.'

Surprisingly, Frazier released his grip on the table and clung to his old pal, allowing Creery to help him toward the door.

Nate pushed to his feet. 'Ensley said he covered up for you, Mr Creery.'

Creery looked back over his shoulder. 'Yes, I heard him, Mr Price. But, considering your wife and Mrs Preston were outdoors when every suspect died except for Detective Sanborn, wouldn't you prefer that the police believe Ensley was the killer?'

'We prefer that the truth comes out.' Izzy rose to stand beside him.

'Ah, Isabelle.' Frazier continued his slow progress toward the door. 'The truth died with Kurt Ensley.'

'Actually, sir,' Michael interjected, 'that's not completely true.'

'Stop, Mr Preston,' Creery said. 'Hasn't this man suffered enough? This ridiculous mystery game is finished. I'll send for the yacht and have Mr Galen released immediately. Each member of the Price team will be generously compensated for their time and trouble.'

'We didn't come here for money or prizes,' Nate said. 'Ensley brought proof of the conspiracy with him. If you allow me, Mr Frazier, I will find it on his body.'

Nicki, who had been staring at the corpse, stood up abruptly. 'I need to use the restroom. I'm going to be sick.'

Although Isabelle rushed to her side, Nicki didn't get eight feet away when she created a second mess for Mrs Norville to clean up.

'Good grief, Price,' Creery exclaimed. 'Haven't these ladies been through enough? Let them wait in their rooms until the *Slippery Eel* arrives.'

'Great idea,' Nate agreed. 'The guards can escort the ladies to their rooms while the men view the flash drive Fallon brought to the island.'

'Wait just a minute. I'm a PI, not a *lady*!' Beth let her indignation be heard.

'I agree with you on that point, Beth,' Creery sneered. 'Take her back to the holding cell and the two ladies to their rooms.'

'Please, Beth, don't put up a fuss.' Nate leaned Ensley's body upright in the chair, trying not to see his ruined head which lolled pitifully to one side. Swallowing down a gag reflex, Nate patted the bloody jacket until he located the memory stick in an inside pocket. 'I found it, Mr Frazier. We'll need a computer that has the PowerPoint program.' He placed the flash drive in Frazier's hand.

As the three guards left the dining room with Nicki, Izzy and Beth, Frazier caught the arm of the last guard. 'Go to my office and get my laptop. If the door's locked, Mrs Norville has the key. Take my computer to the library. We'll watch the flash drive in there.'

When the guard glanced at Creery for a split second, the action wasn't lost on Frazier. 'Why are you looking at him?' Frazier demanded. 'I'm the one paying your outrageous per diem. You will do as I say while in my employ.'

Creery wore a smug smile as he helped Frazier down the hall to the library.

Michael noticed Creery's expression too as they followed him down the hall. 'I hope you know what you're doing, boss,' he said softly.

'I hope so too,' Nate replied. 'But at least we'll soon know who our enemies are.'

Creery deposited Frazier in the overstuffed recliner and brought him a glass of water. Nate and Michael took the two chairs on Frazier's left to wait. After a long interval of silence, three guards entered the library, including one with a laptop.

'Plug it in there.' Frazier pointed at a wall outlet. 'Then aim the projector at the white wall. Jonah, bring up the PowerPoint program and then pop in this flash drive.'

Like the dutiful assistant he'd been for years, Creery did as instructed without displaying an ounce of emotion. After a few moments of blank tape, Kurt Ensley appeared on screen. 'What you are about to view,' Kurt said, 'is the security tape of the cellblock from the night Mack Fallon died. Unfortunately, I wasn't smart enough to request this from police evidence until long after the judge dismissed the case against Reuben Fallon. I will go to my grave regretting I didn't do my job when I had the chance.'

'And to your grave you shall soon go.' Creery's singsong-like words filled up a few moments of additional blank tape.

Then everyone's focus locked on the wall where Jennifer Jacobs walked into view with Bob McDowell close at her heels.

'So it was ADA Jacobs, not Ensley!' Frazier gasped. 'And that lowlife Bob McDowell. I knew those two had something going on.'

'Let's just keep watching, sir,' Nate instructed.

When the ADA stopped in front of Fallon's cell, McDowell was not in view, but the security tape showed the back of her head along with fairly clear dialogue between the two. 'Good evening, Mr Fallon,' Jacobs said. 'I trust the Fulton County jail has been treating you well.'

'Can't complain so far.' Mack Fallon, a taller, heavier version of his younger brother, Reuben, walked up to the bars. 'Seeing a pretty woman right before bedtime never hurts.' Mack ogled Jennifer rather rudely.

'The state of Georgia will be grateful tomorrow for your

guilty plea to first-degree manslaughter in exchange for testimony against the party who paid for the break-in.' Jacobs's drawl was slow and melodic.

'And I'd be grateful for another open button on that pretty silk blouse of yours.' Fallon pressed his face against the bars. Thankfully, Jacobs's back was to the security camera as she undid a button. 'For a *third* open button, you'll have to do me a little favor.' The ADA purred like a cat.

'Name it, pretty lady.' Fallon was practically drooling.

'I have a very good friend who's a reporter. He begged me to bring him along today. My friend wants the inside scoop on your big story. Would you mind talking to this reporter for a few minutes?' When Jennifer lifted her arms to chest-level, everyone in the room knew what she was doing by Fallon's expression.

'Do we really want to watch this tramp?' Creery whined.

Frazier's reply was short and to the point. 'Yes.'

'Is this reporter on television? So I'll get my five minutes of fame on TV?' Fallon asked.

'Absolutely,' Jennifer drawled.

'Then send in your friend. I don't care if I spill the beans before tomorrow's big court appearance.' Fallon pursed his lips as though blowing her a kiss.

As the assistant prosecutor walked down the cellblock, Bob McDowell stepped into view. The newsman looked younger and in better condition than when Nate had seen him the night Frazier marched his suspects into the dining room.

'Hey there, Mack. I'm a reporter with Atlanta's News Channel Eleven. I would love to hear the gist of what you plan to say in court tomorrow. But first, the man who hired you also asked me to bring you a little present. He said it's for a job well done.'

Fallon grabbed ahold of the bars. 'Are you saying Mr Creery wasn't mad?'

'Nah, at first he was, since the wife ended up dead instead of the husband. Then he said, "What the heck? I was getting a little tired of Ariana anyway."'

McDowell used a foul word to describe Mrs Frazier before he passed Fallon a small, foil-wrapped packet.

'That swine, McDowell,' Creery muttered. 'I never said that!'

'You were seeing *my* Ariana?' Frazier's hands gripped the arms of the chair so hard his fingers turned white. 'How could you, Jonah?'

'*Your* Ariana?' Creery spat. 'You didn't own her. Ariana was a grown woman whom you treated like a child . . . and not a very bright child either. You decided everything in your marriage – from what she bought, to what she ate, to what friends she was allowed to see.'

'I was trying to protect her.' Frazier's voice faltered. 'Ariana used poor judgement when she was young.'

Creery stood so he could loom over Frazier. 'Which you never let her forget. It wasn't hard to steal Ariana away. All I had to do was listen to her opinions and treat her with respect.'

Frazier covered his face with his hands. 'All these years . . . I thought you were my friend. You earned plenty of money working at my company.'

'*Your* wife, *your* company? I helped to build Resilient Automotive Systems into what it is today. It wasn't just you.'

When Nate heard Frazier sobbing, he decided their argument had gone on long enough. 'That's enough, Mr Creery. Sit down.'

Creery reared around as though he'd been poked with a stick. 'No, you sit down, Price.' Creery pulled out his gun.

'Guards,' commanded a sad, weary Julian Frazier. 'Lock up Mr Creery where we've been keeping Mr Galen. Let Hunter rejoin his wife and friends.'

Despite the direct order, none of the guards moved. In fact, some of them sneered at the elderly man while aiming their weapons at Nate and Michael.

'What's the matter with you? I'm still in charge here!' Frazier pushed down on the arms of the chair.

'Sit down, old man. You haven't been in control of this island for a long time.' Creery pushed Frazier back down. 'I did everything in my power to prevent this stupid game of yours. But you refused to listen, even after I warned you that you might not like the ending. And for the record, out of respect for our friendship, I tried to protect you. You could have gone to your grave believing Ariana had been the perfect wife. But now you'll die knowing *the truth* you so desperately sought.' Creery addressed one of the guards. 'For now, lock him in his room and make sure he takes his medicine on the bedside table. I don't want to see his pathetic face again.'

'Wait!' Creery said as they dragged Frazier across the carpet. 'Don't leave by that door. I don't trust the butler.' Then Creery pressed a carved rosette on the wall and a panel slid back, revealing a hidden staircase. 'Take him up this way, while you men gag and cuff Price and Preston. We'll keep them locked in here until I figure out how to fix this.'

While Nate and Michael squirmed beneath three sets of restraints, a sudden pounding on the door commanded everyone's attention.

'What's the matter with you, Compton?' Creery shouted. 'I told you that Mr Frazier and I were not to be disturbed.'

'Begging your pardon, sir,' the butler said through the door. 'But Mr Frazier's nephew has arrived and wishes to see his uncle.'

Nate thought the former assistant might faint dead away.

'Alexander is on the island?' Creery asked.

Someone pounded even harder than before. 'Yes, I am here,' said an irate voice. 'Compton, unlock this door immediately or you're fired.'

The lock clicked, the door swung open, and in strode a much younger and more dapper version of their host. He was followed by two bodyguards, judging by the fact their right hands were hidden inside their suit coats. 'What on earth is going on in here?' Alexander Frazier looked from face to face in the library.

'We didn't hear your helicopter, sir,' Creery murmured. 'What a nice surprise.'

'The pilot dropped us off at the St Simons airport because someone needed the helicopter this evening. When I finally got ahold of Captain Burke, he brought me over on the *Slippery Eel*.' Alexander wandered the perimeter of the room, as though assessing the situation. 'Someone had given Burke the impression he had the rest of the week off with pay.' His gaze came to rest on Creery.

'I don't know how that happened, but it does explain why Burke never delivered the last two guests,' Creery mused. 'I wonder why Thursday's supply boat never showed up either.'

'I'd like to know who these men are and why they're bound and gagged.' The nephew pointed at Nate and Michael. 'And why are those security guards carrying automatic weapons?'

Creery offered a placating smile to his boss. 'You'll have to ask your uncle that question. By the time I got here, Julian had hired a team of mercenaries and bribed everyone he thought responsible for Ariana's death to come to Elysian Island. Once they arrived, he took them prisoner. Then Julian invited a team of private investigators to solve some crazy murder mystery. I'm afraid your uncle has lost his mind, probably due to the chemo and radiation treatments.'

'None of that makes a bit of sense.' Alexander slumped into the chair formerly occupied by his uncle. 'But first, why didn't you tell anyone you were coming here? Your secretary has been calling you. I've been calling and sending texts – everything but smoke signals – yet no one at the office has been able to reach you.'

Creery sat down too, as though weary from spinning his web of lies. 'I arrived last Saturday because Julian said he needed help with the mystery game he planned for his guests. He said it would be similar to those dinner theaters he and Ariana enjoyed so much. I thought it would be business as usual – people stomping all over the island, searching for a bunch of clues, and drinking far too much alcohol. I told Julian I didn't like the idea of armed guards, but your uncle insisted. Julian said people often tried to crash his parties and he would take no chances this time.'

Nate tried to snag the nephew's attention, but he seemed to be buying Creery's story hook, line and sinker.

'Go on,' Alexander prodded. 'This ridiculous party scheme doesn't explain why you didn't tell anyone at the office where you were.'

'I'd planned to return to Atlanta on Monday,' Creery continued. 'But by then things were spinning out of control. I felt Julian was losing touch with reality, so I stayed to control the damage.' Creery leaned toward Frazier. 'One of his guests – Julian called them "suspects" – was found dead on the beach.'

'*What?*' Alexander jumped to his feet. 'Did he drown while swimming?'

'No, and this gets much worse.' Creery rubbed his face with his hands. 'I wanted to call the sheriff's department and the coastguard, but Julian had severed the landline. While I was running crowd control on the island, his mercenaries confiscated the guests' cell phones and laptops.'

Finally, the nephew's expression turned skeptical. 'But you have a satellite phone, Jonah, for just such emergencies.'

'Your uncle knew where I kept it. When I got back to the house, it too had been confiscated. I couldn't call the authorities or my office or you. Julian insisted he would free the team of detectives once they solved Ariana's murder.'

Alexander began pacing the room. 'My uncle *knows* who killed Aunt Ariana – Mack Fallon. And that creep died of a drug overdose in jail.'

'I'm telling you your uncle's not himself. Julian believes everyone connected to the case was somehow part of a grand conspiracy – the assistant prosecutor, the Atlanta detective in charge of the case, Fallon's public defender, even that slimy newspaperman who smeared Aunt Ariana's reputation on TV. One by one they turned up dead somewhere on the island.'

The nephew stopped pacing in front of Nate and Michael. 'No way could my uncle have done this alone. Did these two help him pull off the murders?'

Nate squirmed in his chair so much that the chair fell over. One of the guards yanked the chair upright.

'Yes, those are two of the investigators Julian hired. The rest are locked in their rooms, awaiting law enforcement.'

'Why would a group of PIs help Uncle Julian if he was as crazy as you say?'

'I don't know the details, but I heard Julian threaten them once or twice. He said if they didn't help bring the "suspects" to justice, he would kill them one at a time. Julian said Hunter Galen would be the first to go and nobody has seen him for days. I think Galen was a stockbroker from New Orleans.'

Nate fought down the bile creeping up his throat, hoping that this too was just another of Creery's lies.

'And that one there.' Creery shook his finger at him. 'I watched him shoot Kurt Ensley, the public defender, in cold blood. Ensley's body is still in the dining room. Nate Price and his employee, Beth Preston, hadn't turned in all their weapons at the front door. Preston shot Jennifer Jones in the back on the far side of the island.'

Alexander slicked a hand through his hair. 'This is a matter for the police to sort out.'

'I agree, sir. But since we can't get ahold of them, I suggest we have the armed guards take the Price team back to St Simons on the *Slippery Eel*. The guards will contact the proper authorities and turn over the prisoners. You and I can wait for the forensic experts out here with Julian.'

'Whatever you think best, Jonah.' Alexander dismissed the matter with a flourish of his hand. 'But right now, I'd like to see my uncle.'

'I understand, sir, but Mr Frazier is sleeping. Why don't you and I discuss corporate damage control until he wakes up?'

'What kind of damage control are you talking about?'

The corner of Creery's mouth twitched. 'Five people have been murdered on Elysian by one or more guests. Although you're the CEO of Resilient Automotive Systems, your uncle is still a majority shareholder. If news of this gets out, our stock could take a major nosedive. That certainly won't do anyone any good.'

Alexander rubbed his jawline. 'I see your point, but I don't see how we can sweep five dead bodies under the rug.'

'I suggest you position your security men outside Julian's door. The housekeeper can show them the way. As soon your uncle wakes up, we'll visit him together and you can gauge his mental condition for yourself. In the meantime, I'll fill you in on the week's events so you understand before the police arrive. Then we can plot our corporate spin to this disaster.'

'Fine, but I don't need both bodyguards standing vigil at Uncle Julian's door.' Although Nate tried his best to catch the nephew's eye, Alexander paid him no mind as he crossed the room. 'Mr Nguyen, you'll remain with me. Mr Baker, have the housekeeper direct you to my uncle's suite. Text me the moment he wakes up.'

Creery addressed his henchmen. 'You four move Price and Preston down to the boat and make sure they're well secured. Two guards should stay on the boat while the other two come back for the wives. Both Nicki and Isabelle are together in the Price suite. Then my entire security team will deliver the private investigators to the authorities on St Simons. I want to make sure nothing goes wrong.'

As the guards dragged Michael and him from the room, Nate got a bad feeling about the Price team's future . . . and that of the nasty men-in-black as well.

FOURTEEN

Elysian Island. Friday a.m.

When Eliza Norville had finished her convoluted tale of million-dollar bribes, kidnapping, and sneaking maids off the island in the middle of the night, Kate only had one question: *how on earth did Nate Price and his employees get dragged into the madness?* According to Norville, her employer thought a bunch of private investigators would make the murder mystery 'game' more interesting, but she had no idea how Frazier had selected Nate out of hundreds of agencies in the Southeast.

Some game. Over the last six days, all five so-called suspects had ended up dead, and Norville had no idea what had happened to Hunter Galen. After she'd caught Hunter breaking into the office, Creery had dragged him off. As Frazier's assistant, he took care of everything Frazier didn't want to do. But Kate knew Creery was responsible for so much more, thanks to her phone conversation with Alexander.

Just as the cook returned to the stove, they both heard feet shuffling down the hallway. 'Eliza, where are you?' asked a male voice.

Kate pressed a finger to her lips and then slashed it across her throat. Just as the kitchen door banged open, she slipped into the broom closet.

'Why haven't you delivered more coffee to the library?' the man asked. 'The boss has been talking and looking at videos with Price and Preston and their breakfast carafe is empty.'

From between the louvers, Kate saw a tall, sixty-ish man wearing a fancier suit than any her father had ever owned.

'I've been chopping vegetables for soup,' Norville stammered. 'I thought everyone would be outdoors by now.'

'Well, they're not. Is that pot fresh?' The man pointed at the coffeemaker.

'No, it's leftover from early this morning.'

He pulled a silver tray from the shelf. 'For now I'll take everyone bottles of water. You deliver fresh coffee as soon as it's done, then get busy fixing more than soup for lunch. Mr Frazier's nephew arrived on the *Slippery Eel*. If we serve weak broth and last summer's produce, we'll embarrass the boss.'

'Alexander is here, *now*?' Norville shifted her weight from foot to foot.

'That's what I said,' he snapped. 'So dig through the freezer for something decent for the one o'clock meal.' He let the door slam behind him.

'Who was that guy and what's his problem?' Kate asked, slipping from her hiding spot.

'That's Alfred Compton, Mr Frazier's butler.' Norville wiped her palms down her long apron. 'He's usually nice, but Mr Alexander's showing up unannounced made him flustered. Alfred doesn't like surprises.'

Kate put her ear to the kitchen door. 'I'm not fond of them either. That's why I'm going with you to deliver that coffee. Get that pot started.' Kate sat down at the table, tucked her weapon in the holster, but didn't take her eyes off Norville. However, just as the pot finished brewing, the butler stomped back into the room, his face ashen.

'Eliza, come quick,' Compton wailed. 'It's Julian!'

Norville turned to face him. 'What's happened? Did Mr Frazier fall?'

'No, but he might be dead. When I took water to the library, Mr Creery said Mr Frazier was sleeping. But when I checked, Julian didn't seem to be breathing.' The butler finally spotted Kate at the table and froze, his jaw falling slack. 'Who are you?' he demanded.

'Kate Weller. I was invited to the island, remember? But someone has done everything in their power to keep me away from my friends.'

Compton stared at Kate and then shook his head. 'You'll have to be patient, Miss Weller. We're in the middle of an emergency. Please, Eliza, come to Mr Frazier's room. You've had some medical training. Hopefully, Julian has lapsed into a

Isabelle's suite until the guards come back to get them and there's a guard watching their door. Creery doesn't trust anyone.'

'What about Beth and Hunter?'

'Beth was taken to wherever they have been keeping Hunter. That's what I overheard, but I have no idea where, only that they are not inside the house.'

Kate placed a hand on his shoulder. 'Think, Compton! You must have some idea where prisoners could be locked up.'

Suddenly, the door opened and one of Alexander's bodyguards walked in with his weapon drawn.

'*Baker?*' Kate asked.

'*Weller?*' he asked almost simultaneously. 'What's going on in here?'

Kate glanced up and down the hallway before closing the door. 'Mr Frazier was murdered and it wasn't any of us. My guess is he was poisoned with an overdose of sleeping pills.'

Baker pushed the butler and the cook aside on his way to the bed. Then he checked for signs of life. 'Creery,' he muttered. And, by the expression on his face, Baker wasn't asking a question.

'That was my guess too. Where's Alexander?' she asked.

'In the library, but Nguyen is with him.'

'Good, because we have more pressing problems. We need to free two PIs from one of the suites before Creery's guards return for them. Do you have more than one weapon?'

Baker revealed a pair of shoulder holsters under his jacket, along with a third gun tucked into the waistband on his pants. 'Why?' he asked.

'Both Isabelle and Nicki can handle firearms. We need to take out the guard at the door, liberate my friends, and get to the dock to rescue Nate and Michael. According to the butler, Creery might have wired the *Slippery Eel* with explosives.' Kate hooked a thumb at Compton who nodded affirmatively.

Baker re-buttoned his coat with great dignity. 'I'm sorry, Miss Weller, but I'm paid to protect Mr Frazier. I will help free your friends and provide them with weapons, but then I'm returning to the library. You're on your own to save the two already on the yacht.'

Kate knew pleading would be useless. 'Fine, but let's hurry. Creery's henchmen may already be on their way back.'

'What do you want us to do?' asked the cook. 'We'll help if we can.'

Kate had almost forgotten about them. Then an idea popped into her head. 'If your son is like most teenagers, he has roamed over every inch of this island. See if Paul knows where Creery might be holding the prisoners.'

Norville nodded and hurried from the room.

'Why don't I deliver this coffee to Mrs Price's suite?' the butler suggested. 'She's in number seven down the hall off the foyer. I might be more useful to you there than in here.' Compton cast another glance at his sheet-covered employer.

'Good idea,' Kate agreed, hatching a spur-of-the-moment plan. 'When you get to Izzy's door, insist that you're let in immediately. Don't let the guard take the carafe. We'll try to get a drop on him.'

While Compton argued masterfully, Kate and Baker knocked the guard out cold without anyone firing a shot. Baker entered the luxurious suite first . . . and narrowly missed getting whacked with a curtain rod.

'A curtain rod, really?' Kate easily disarmed Nicki. 'That's the best weapon you could come up with?'

'Kate!' Isabelle flew at her like a bullet. 'It's so good to see you!'

'Glad you finally made the party, Weller,' Nicki sneered. Then she joined Izzy in a three-way hug. 'And I challenge you to find a better weapon in this lame suite.'

While the Price team members celebrated their reunion, Baker dragged the unconscious guard into the room, bound his wrists with his own cuffs, and hogtied him with sash cords. When the guy came to, he wouldn't be going anywhere soon.

'And who might *you* be?' Nicki stood over Baker's shoulder, with curtain rod back in hand.

'This is Mr Baker, Alexander Frazier's bodyguard. He's a good guy. Full story later. Right now you and Izzy need to get down to the dock. They're holding Nate and Michael on the *Slippery Eel* which might be wired with explosives. Baker will provide weapons. Just make sure none of you are on that yacht if it leaves the dock.'

Baker handed over his extra firepower to Izzy and Nicki. 'You're going with them, right, Weller?'

'No, since no one knows where Creery is holding Beth and Hunter, I'm coming to the library with you.'

The mention of Hunter's name got Nicki's attention. 'No way, Kate,' she said. 'You go with Izzy. I'll get the location out of Creery, one way or the other.' She checked the magazine of the Glock pistol and tucked it into her jeans.

'No, Nicki. If you show up, the guards will know you two escaped. It has to be me.'

Baker, who had been following the discussion curiously, arched an eyebrow. 'How do *you* plan to pull that off?'

'I'm an invited guest, remember? I hitched a ride on the *Slippery Eel* when Captain Burke brought Alexander Frazier here.'

Baker shook his head. 'You think Creery will believe it took a week to track down the yacht and captain? Who in their right mind shows up on the last day of a retreat?'

'Maybe not, but at least I'll be inside the library.' Kate opened her jacket to reveal her weapon. 'One way or the other, Creery will tell me where Beth and Hunter are.'

After a bit more convincing, Nicki agreed to the plan. She and Izzy left the mansion through the cellar entrance while the cook ran interference.

After allowing enough time for them to reach the woods, Kate turned to the butler. 'Compton, I want you to deliver that pot of coffee to the library in exactly ten minutes.' She glanced at her watch.

'This pot, Miss Weller?' The butler's lip twitched. 'The coffee is quite cold by now.'

'It doesn't matter. That coffee might just provide another necessary diversion.'

Baker also checked his watch. 'Mind telling me your plan?'

'My plan? I'm just a hardworking PI from Pensacola who's looking for her co-workers.' Kate accentuated her drawl. 'Luckily I ran into you while wandering around the house, because you know the way to the library. Give me a moment to text Eric back on St Simons. He's my partner.'

'This might just work,' Baker said. 'I'll text Alex to say his uncle is still sleeping.'

Baker gagged the guard in Izzy's suite and led the way with Kate behind him. Kate had the time it took to get to the library to come up with ideas. *After all, who in their right mind showed up on the last day of a retreat?*

Outside the library stood one of Creery's unsmiling goons. 'How is the old man?' the guard asked. 'And who the heck is she?'

Baker glared with haughtiness to rival Compton's. '*Mr* Frazier is still sleeping. And this is Miss Weller, an invited guest. She arrived with Alexander Frazier.' His contempt could not be plainer.

'Hi, I'm Katie,' she gushed. 'Pleased ta meet ya.'

The guard ignored Kate's outstretched hand. 'Where has she been since the boat docked?'

'Eating in the kitchen with Mrs Norville,' she bubbled. 'I never should've got on that boat hungry. That cook's plate of cheesy grits settled my stomach just fine.' Kate made a circular motion over her midsection.

'I can confirm that Miss Weller was on the boat with my boss. Now unlock this door immediately!' Baker thundered.

The guard complied. Then he followed them into a room where Creery and Alexander sat at a table with spreadsheets covering the surface. Both executives rose when Kate approached.

'Who on earth are you?' Creery demanded.

'Hello again, Miss Weller,' Alexander greeted. 'I trust the cook gave you something to eat in the kitchen?'

'Hi, Alex,' she drawled. 'Yes, Mrs Norville took good care of me and then directed me here. But this place is so confusin', I got lost. Good thing I ran into your man, Baker.' Kate elbowed the bodyguard in the ribs. 'Say, you must be Julian Frazier.' She approached an astonished Jonah Creery with her hand out. 'How ya doing? I'm one of Nate Price's investigators.'

'I am not Julian Frazier. I'm Jonah Creery, his assistant. *You're* Kate Weller?' Like his henchman outside the door, Creery ignored Kate's outstretched hand.

'Yep, I finally made it, but it wasn't easy. My boyfriend, Eric Manfredi, got so mad about the endless delays, he refused to come along.' Slowly retracting her hand, Kate rambled on. 'Oh, well. Boyfriends are a dime a dozen these days.' She circled the table while assessing the room. Nguyen and Baker were near the door, flanking Creery's guard. 'Hope you don't mind me asking, but are you married, Alex?'

'I'm afraid so.' The nephew seemed to be biting his cheek.

'Why are the good ones always taken?' Kate muttered, stopping on Creery's left. 'Could you take me to see Mr Julian now? I'd like to explain in person why I'm so late to his mystery party.' Although Kate tried her best to look and sound earnest, Creery's astonishment faded into barely concealed rage.

'It was pointless to come now, young lady. The game is over, the mystery solved. You should have remained on St Simons with your dime-a-dozen *boyfriend*.' Creery practically snorted flames from his nostrils.

'Gosh, I'm sorry to hear that. But I brought a little hostess gift for him. Of course, Mr Frazier is a *host* not a hostess.' Kate hiked her tote bag up her shoulder and giggled for good measure. 'Alex, do you think I could see your uncle just for a minute or two?'

Asking the nephew instead of Creery sent the assistant over the top. 'You may certainly not! Mr Julian isn't feeling well. He asked that his rest not be disturbed. What's more, Miss Weller, you have interrupted an important business meeting. Considering the events of the last few days, the future of a major corporation may be at stake.'

'What kind of events, Alex?' Kate's tone turned anxious.

'Unfortunately, there were a few deaths on the island, but Jonah assured me that your co-workers are fine.'

'Oh, my goodness, that's awful. What happened? Was it a shark attack? Maybe food poisoning?' Kate pressed both hands to her belly. 'Please take me to Nate and Izzy Price,' she pleaded, taking hold of Creery's arm. 'I won't be able to relax until I know everyone is OK.'

Creery brushed away her hand like a bug. 'I told you, Miss Weller. The mystery is over. Your friends are no longer inside the mansion. They have been escorted to the yacht in preparation to return to St Simons. In fact, I must notify Captain Burke not to leave without *you*.'

'You want me to leave now?' she squealed. 'I don't get to spend even one night in this cool house?' Kate addressed her question to the nephew.

'I'm sure one night can be arranged,' Alexander said. 'Why don't you take your gift to my uncle while Creery and I discuss business? Baker can show you the way to his suite.'

Creery was obviously beginning to question the believability of Kate's story. 'I thought you were so worried about your friends. And why would you want to spend the night in a house where five people recently died?'

Kate didn't have time to respond to the assistant, since Compton, who'd apparently been eavesdropping, chose that moment to stomp into the library with his pot of coffee. 'Please don't send Miss Weller to see your uncle, Mr Frazier, because Julian is dead. I'm sorry to say.' Without missing a beat, Compton threw the contents of the carafe into Creery's face. And then he threw the carafe. Unfortunately, the coffee was no longer hot.

For one split second, the butler's brash action stupefied everyone in the room. Fortuitously, Kate and the bodyguards recovered first. Kate whipped out her weapon and aimed it at Creery's dripping face, while Baker and Nguyen easily over-powered the mercenary.

'Down on the ground, Jonah.' Kate pressed the barrel of her gun to his neck. 'Your game here is over.'

'Careful, Kate,' Alexander warned. 'Creery has a gun under his jacket.'

Kate reached under his suit coat until she felt the touch of cold steel. 'Not anymore he isn't.' She slid the weapon toward Baker while Nguyen snapped handcuffs on Creery's guard.

'I don't know what this woman told you on the ride over, Alexander,' Creery sputtered. 'But if Julian has passed, it's by her hand not mine.'

Kate bent down to Creery's ear as Baker handcuffed him as well. 'Save your breath, you stinkin' murderer. Alex will soon know you were sneaking around with Aunt Ariana *and* stealing from the corporation. Or maybe you two hadn't reached that point in the business meeting yet.'

Creery lifted his face from the floor. 'I should've had you taken care of back on St Simons.'

'Would've, could've, should've . . . it's too late for regrets.'

'With any luck it's too late for the rest of the Price team,' Creery hissed from the side of his mouth.

'I don't think so.' Kate motioned for Baker who hauled Creery to his feet. 'Nicki and Izzy are armed and on their way to the dock. Captain Burke is also aware of your machinations on Elysian.'

Betraying his crude manners, Creery spat on the Oriental rug. 'Nicki has turned into a lunatic, while Isabelle is a vapid little housewife. You think those two can overpower well-trained mercenaries?'

'Yep, I do,' Kate boasted, although she felt far less confident than she sounded. 'You have no idea how creative women can be. In the meantime, you're going to tell me where Hunter and Beth are, or Mr Nguyen and Mr Baker will turn you into a punching bag.'

Nguyen and Baker each took a well-placed gut punch that made Creery double over and struggle to breathe. 'I don't care if . . . you kill me,' he gasped. 'I loved Ariana and . . . now she's dead, thanks to those worthless miscreants. I only stole money from the company because she wanted me to.'

Alexander uttered an expletive. 'That's a pack of lies. My aunt has been dead for eight years, yet you continued to defraud the company. Your only hope of avoiding the death penalty is to release the two prisoners.'

Without warning Eliza Norville burst into the room with a roll of papers. 'I found an old map of the island in Mr Frazier's study. This morning Beth referred to the place where she's locked up as a "rabbit hole." According to this map, a previous owner built a fallout shelter many years ago.' Eliza unrolled the papers on the desk. 'My son is on his way there now with a pickaxe and bolt cutters.'

'Paul will never get there in time,' Creery wheezed.

'You'd better hope that's not the case.' Kate delivered her best shot to his solar plexus.

Eric hadn't liked the idea of Kate arriving on Elysian without him. But he could never have rallied the Glynn County Police Department and the Glynn County Sheriff's Department into action without the physical proof of the text. Even with it, mustering the coastguard into action took Kate's urgent message that Creery had planted a bomb aboard Frazier's yacht to get rid of the witnesses and his overpaid guards. Then, coordinating a strategy between the three departments took more time than anyone could have imagined. Finally, Eric boarded a coastguard vessel for the thirty-minute ride to the island's dock on the western side. The police and sheriff's department would land on the Atlantic side and approach the mansion from the eastern beach.

Eric breathed a sigh of relief when he spotted the *Slippery Eel* still tied up at the dock. And getting the armed guards to release Nate and Michael proved easier than expected. Not even trained mercenaries wanted to remain on a ship carrying explosives.

'This is the US coastguard,' the voice of the commander thundered across the water once their vessel reached a safe distance from Elysian. 'We are coming ashore. This island is completely surrounded by law enforcement watercrafts. Release the hostages, lay down your weapons, and disembark the vessel. Keep your hands in plain sight or you will be shot. The *Slippery Eel* has been armed with explosives. If you attempt to escape to open water, we will fire upon you and detonate the device. This will be your only warning.'

One warning was all it took.

Soon Nate and Michael staggered up the gangway of the *Slippery Eel* with their hands raised. Both looked thin and exhausted, yet were smiling nevertheless. After Captain Burke exited the boat, the coast guardsmen swarmed aboard to take four killers into custody.

Eric met his friends halfway down the dock. 'Hey, Nate, Mike! How was the party? Is the gourmet food and expensive wine all gone?'

Despite his physical appearance, Nate managed to laugh. 'Yeah, we saved you some bad soup and stale white bread if you're hungry.'

Michael threw his arms around Eric. 'Sure happy to see you, old buddy, but don't think for a minute you guys rescued us.' Michael hooked his thumb back at the boat where two handcuffed thugs were being marched up the gangway. Judging by their expressions, they might start spitting bullets from their mouths.

'What do you mean?' Eric asked.

'Take a good look at the group exiting the vessel.'

Nicki and Izzy were climbing the gangway surrounded by coastguardsmen. '*Your wife and Nicki Galen?*' Eric asked Nate. 'How on earth did they get aboard and then overpower those guards?'

'First, they took out two on the path who'd been coming for them. Then, with a little help from Captain Burke, they boarded the boat, put on those maids' uniforms, and offered the two guards a cocktail. By the time the guards realized who they were, it was too late. They were staring down the barrels of a pair of Glocks.' Nate wrapped one arm around Nicki and one around his wife as they were herded toward the woods.

Eric approached the commander. 'The five of us are heading to the house. That's where my partner and Mr Frazier are.'

The officer nodded. 'As soon as I contact an explosives team and secure the prisoners abroad the vessel, my men and I will join you. We will also need from you—'

Eric waved acknowledgement, but they had no time to make statements or fill out paperwork for the police. Kate was somewhere in that house of horrors with a man who'd already killed plenty of people.

All that could wait until after Kate was safe.

Kate had never run so hard in her life. After leaving Nguyen behind to watch Creery, she and Baker took off to the location marked on the map. Why anyone would need a fallout shelter way out in the middle of nowhere made no sense to her. But anyone escaping foreign invaders by sea or fallout from a nuclear attack would need a supply of air. And hopefully that supply would support two adults a while longer.

She and Baker found Paul Norville on the other side of the island, almost to the dunes. The paranoid former resident had dug deep into the side of a hill, creating an underground bunker with a stand of bamboo and palmetto palms obscuring the entrance. Although Paul had chopped away the vegetation, he still hadn't broken the heavy padlock on the door, although scratches in the steel indicated numerous attempts.

'Well done, young man.' Baker spoke softly to the teenager. 'Now may I have a crack at it?'

'It's too thick to use bolt cutters,' Paul explained to Kate. 'We need to break the lock.'

'We'll give Mr Baker a turn whacking at it.' Kate patted Paul's sweaty back. 'You did a good job finding this place. We couldn't have done it without you and your mother.'

Smiling, the boy rocked back on his heels.

Since Baker had arms the size of tree trunks, he only needed a few cracks to spring the lock. Then he pulled open the heavy metal door.

Ducking her head into a cave that smelled like sweat, dirt and mildew, Kate let her eyes adjust to the dark. 'Beth?' she called. 'Hunter? Are you guys in here?'

'*Kate Weller?*' A voice emanated from the corner. 'Is that you?'

'Yes!' Kate rushed forward, bumped her head on the low ceiling, and practically tripped over her friend and mentor.

'Glad you finally made it to the retreat,' Beth squawked, 'but where's your flashlight? I taught you to never leave home without a flashlight, your cell phone, your weapon and water.' The woman who'd taught Kate everything she knew about PI work hugged her tightly.

'I brought three out of the four. Can I have partial credit?' Kate held out the bottle of water.

'Let's give that to Hunter,' Beth said. 'He's in bad shape from hunger and dehydration. I've tried to keep him awake, but he keeps passing out.'

Baker moved past them in the dark, located the unconscious man, and carried him from an almost certain tomb.

Once back in the sunshine and fresh air, Beth dropped to her knees next to Hunter. 'I sure am happy to see you two.'

'This is Baker.' Kate chose the simplest explanation possible as Baker checked for signs of life on their unconscious friend. 'I rode across on the *Slippery Eel* with him.'

'What should I do, Miss Weller?' Paul shuffled his feet in the dirt.

'Run as fast as you can to the beach! Wave your arms at any boat you see. Hopefully my friend, Eric, is on his way with the police.'

'Am I your friend too?' he asked.

'You bet you are – one of my best.'

After the boy sprinted off, Kate crouched down beside the bodyguard.

'He's got a weak pulse,' he said. 'But at least he's alive. Let's see if he'll drink some water.'

While Beth and Kate held Hunter upright, Baker dripped water into his mouth. On the second attempt, Hunter opened his eyes, parted his lips and swallowed. With his first major gulp, he coughed and sputtered.

'Easy, Hunter,' Kate advised. 'Your throat is parched.'

After a few more sips, Hunter focused on Kate. 'Beth said you always come late to everything, Weller,' he whispered hoarsely. 'But better late than never. Where are Nicki and the others?' Dark circles ringed his eyes and his skin was the color of skim milk, but with each swallow his breathing improved.

'Your wife is fine. You're the one everyone has been worried about.' Kate didn't know if Nicki was fine or not, since she'd given her and Izzy handguns to fight men with assault weapons. But she saw no reason to stress out a suffering man.

'Take me to Nicki.' Hunter tried to stand.

But Baker's firm hand held him down. 'You're not going anywhere. Medical attention is on the way.'

'Who the heck are you to give me orders?'

Kate smiled, knowing that Hunter Galen was coming back to life. 'This is Baker – don't know his first name. But he and Nguyen are Alexander Frazier's bodyguards. They arrived today on the *Slippery Eel* and helped me save the day. So be nice to him.'

Hunter took another gulp of water and held out his hand. 'Forgive my bad manners. Hunter Galen, how do you do?'

'*Marcus* Baker, and I'm fine.' Baker winked at her and shook hands. 'Kate's partner should be here soon with the cavalry. Let's have medical personnel look you over before you walk back to the house.'

'Kate's partner . . . *Eric*?' Hunter frowned at her. 'The stuff you drag that poor man into! Eric doesn't even work for Nate, yet you probably put him through the worst week of his life.'

'Maybe I'm worth it,' Kate teased. 'And *you* don't work for Nate either but look at the pickle Nicki put you in.'

'You gotta point, Weller,' Hunter growled. 'Marcus, if you help me up, I'll be indebted to you for life. I've just spent days in a cave with very little to eat or drink. If I have to crawl on my hands and knees, I'm getting away from this place.'

Suddenly they heard shouts coming from the dunes. 'Kate, I found them!' Paul Norville bounded into view. 'There's a whole bunch of boats beached in the sand. I told the cop at the boat we needed help and he spoke into his radio.' Panting, Paul sat down next to her. 'How'd I do?'

'Magnificent.' Kate slipped an arm around his shoulder. 'And you ran all the way back.'

'Yep. Hey, here comes my ma. Did you bring water?'

Eliza Norville trudged through the cordgrass. 'Of course, I did.' She handed a six-pack of water to Kate. 'This sure didn't look so far on the map.'

Hunter's eyes flashed with hatred at the cook. 'Easy, Galen,' Kate murmured. 'Without this woman's help, we never would've found you.'

'Sorry about the bad food, Mr Galen, but the delivery boat never arrived.' Norville pulled her son to his feet and hugged him protectively, in case Hunter decided to exact his revenge.

However, the arrival of deputy sheriffs and EMTs curtailed discussions about menus or thoughts of revenge. Besides, Kate knew Hunter Galen was a gentleman. As medical personnel swarmed in, Baker pulled Kate away from the group.

'Since the situation with Hunter is under control, I'm going to slip away and get back to Mr Frazier. If the police want to talk to me, I'll give my statement at the house.'

'Absolutely, Marcus. I owe you one.'

'No, Kate, I'd say we're just about even.' Baker grinned, then vanished into the forest.

Kate told what she knew to one deputy, while another deputy talked to Mrs Norville. After a twenty-minute infusion of fluids and electrolytes, EMTs wanted to transport Hunter via stretcher to the sheriff's boat. Needless to say, the stockbroker from New

Orleans refused to go along with that idea. So the entire entourage trekked back to the Frazier mansion. Hunter walked every
step, although at times he leaned heavily on one burly EMT.

When they reached the back door, Kate grabbed Paul's arm.
'We'll let the deputies go in first, and then Beth and me. You
keep your mom safe out here until we know what's going on.'

The teenager nodded. 'OK, but just holler if you need me,
Kate.'

When the deputies headed in one direction, Kate drew her
weapon and headed in the other with Beth. They checked room
after room until they found a crowd of friendly faces in the
front parlor. Then everyone started talking at once and things
happened fast.

'It's about time you showed up, Weller,' said Nate. 'Don't
think I'm paying you for goofing off on St Simons.' Nate crossed
the room and wrapped his arms around her. 'Thank you,' he
whispered in her ear.

'Did you turn your phone off? I've been calling you and
texting you.' Eric joined them in a three-way hug.

'Where you been, Beth?' Michael swept his wife off her feet.
'I'd better not hear you've been hanging with that Galen guy.'
Beth buried her face in Michael's shirt and, for once, had nothing
clever to say.

When Kate extracted herself from Eric and Nate, Nicki was
waiting for her. 'If Beth is back, where's Hunter?' she asked.
'Is he OK?'

'The EMTs are bringing Hunter to the house. He will be here
soon.'

'Is this soon enough for you?' Hunter asked, braced against
the doorjamb.

Nicki approached slowly, as though afraid he might be a
mirage. But once Hunter wrapped her in his arms, Nicki began
talking and kissing a mile a minute.

Izzy wanted to talk to Eric and her next. She took each of them
by the hand. 'We owe you our lives. How can we ever thank you?'

'Just see that Kate gets paid,' Eric said, laughing.

'Oh, we'll do much better than that. Name your favorite place
to go on vacation . . . or maybe a cruise to somewhere exotic.
Nate and I will make the arrangements.'

Kate thought for a minute. 'I think we've had enough fun in the sun and boats on the water for a while. I'd like a week in Charleston with Eric's family – gourmet Italian food and the *normal* kind of crazy people.'

'I can take care of those details.' Eric wrapped an arm around her waist.

After another ten minutes of sharing details in the parlor, the Price team of investigators headed to the kitchen in search of food. But Kate had a different idea. 'Let's go find Alexander Frazier, along with Baker and Nguyen,' she whispered in Eric's ear.

'They're upstairs with the police and Julian Frazier. The elder Mr Frazier passed away this morning,' Eric added.

'That much I know. Let's make sure no one misses the teacup as evidence. I believe Julian was poisoned.'

With her new friend, Paul, leading the way, they went straight to Mr Frazier's suite on the second floor. True to form, Baker and Nguyen were just inside the door when she knocked.

'Hi, Kate. How is Hunter?' Marcus asked when he motioned them into a room filled with forensic techs, medical personnel and sheriff's deputies. One tech was slipping the teacup into an evidence bag at that moment.

'Hunter is fine, thanks to your help. Marcus, this is Eric, my partner and boyfriend.'

The men barely had a chance to shake hands when Alexander Frazier summoned them from across the room. 'Miss Weller,' he called. 'May I speak with you a moment?'

Kate had just begun the introductions when Alexander interrupted her. '*This* is the boyfriend who refused to tag along at the last minute? He doesn't look dime-a-dozen at all.'

Kate felt her cheeks grow warm. 'Yeah, about that . . .'

'Nice to meet you. Because of your loyalty and persistence, a murderer was stopped before he killed even more people.' Alexander pumped Eric's hand like a handle. 'You should have heard the tale Kate wove to Jonah Creery. I could hardly keep a straight face.'

'I can't wait to hear the story.' Eric crooked an eyebrow. 'But I am sorry about your uncle.'

'Thank you, Eric.' Alexander's face sobered. 'But Creery

might have actually done Uncle Julian a favor. The type of cancer he had can be very painful at the end. Besides, even in light of Creery and Aunt Ariana's affair, I know those two had been very happy for a while, so hopefully Uncle Julian will rest in peace.'

'We'd better let you get back to it.' Kate nodded toward the deputies still waiting to question Frazier. 'We'll talk more on the boat ride back. Besides, I've some explaining to do.'

FIFTEEN

It was very late on Friday when the Price team and spouses returned to the marina on St Simons Island. Coastguard officers questioned each of them during the trip back and then several guardsmen drove those who wouldn't fit into Eric's SUV to John's condo. Nate and his employees had been ordered to remain on the island for another twenty-four hours for more questioning by the Glynn County Police and the Sheriff's Department, so no one wanted to chitchat when they walked through the door. Three couples retreated to their bedrooms to call their respective families, who doubtless had been worried about them. They would all sleep soundly for the first time in a long while. Kate and Eric volunteered to sleep in the living room since their ordeal had been less traumatic.

Kate curled up in a corner of the sofa. 'Why do you think Julian Frazier invited us and then kept us away all week?'

As soon as the last bedroom door closed, Eric stretched out in the recliner. 'Maybe he decided four couples was just one too many.'

'I think when all the details come out, we'll learn that Creery had been pulling the strings from the beginning. But that doesn't explain why Creery kept us away. The Price team were very lucky,' she added.

'You're not kidding, although Hunter probably hasn't felt very lucky for the last five days.' Eric ran a hand through his thick hair.

They were both quiet for a few minutes while events on the island ran through their heads like a bad dream. As she and Eric had listened to their friends answer questions, they more or less pieced together what happened on the island. Any missing details could be filled in down the road. No one would be forgetting the past week anytime soon.

'I suppose the Atlanta detective, the former assistant prosecutor and Hunter's lawyer weren't very lucky.' Kate tucked the afghan around her legs. 'Even though each had a hand in this by commission or omission, they didn't deserve to die. Only Reuben Fallon and that reporter got their just comeuppance.'

'Julian Frazier waited so long for justice to be served in his wife's death.' Eric locked gazes with her. 'Me? I wouldn't have waited so long if someone beat you to death.'

A shiver ran up Kate's spine from the mental image. 'I never took you for a man capable of vengeance, Manfredi, and certainly not a plot for revenge.'

Eric sauntered into the kitchen, then returned with two glasses of wine. 'I could picture Hunter or Nate strangling someone if they found their wife dead; maybe even a mild-mannered man like Michael Preston. No one really knows what they're capable of until faced with the situation.'

Kate shivered for a second time. 'As PIs weren't committed to upholding the law, let's hope you and I are never put to the test.'

'About that, Miss Weller.' Eric took another sip of wine and set down the glass. 'Investigative work no longer seems as exciting and action-packed as it did in Pensacola.'

Kate stared out the window where one streetlight cast a yellow pool of light. 'Having second thoughts about putting Bella Trattoria fully in your sister's hands?'

'There are worse careers than being part-owner and head chef in one of Charleston's *finest* restaurants.' He laughed at his boastful but true description. 'Usually the worst thing that happens to me is someone sends back their dinner.'

'Or a bad review in *Gourmet Magazine*,' she suggested.

'Bite your tongue, woman.' Eric clutched at his throat. 'All kidding aside, I couldn't work beside you like Michael does with Beth. I'm not afraid of walking into danger or even dying, but I couldn't stand by and watch you risk your life.'

'We're not first responders; we're seldom put in harm's way.' Kate finished her glass of wine.

'I know that, but working alongside me would drive you crazy. I would hobble you with overprotectiveness.' Eric offered a lopsided grin – the same smile that had won her heart. 'I'm better off in the kitchen dreaming up new pasta sauces, and picturing you doing nothing more dangerous than photographing cheating spouses or county workers sleeping on the job.'

Kate fluffed up the pillows behind her head. 'When I come home after a long stakeout at the Winn Dixie, will you have my glass of Chianti and plate of pasta Bolognese waiting?'

'You bet I will. Maybe I'll even throw in a foot rub.' Eric closed his eyes for a few moments. 'Were you pulling Izzy's leg about the perfect week's vacation?'

The air in the room seemed to change, similar to how the air feels when a thunderstorm approaches. 'You mean about spending it with your family in Charleston? No, I wasn't joking. Sorry about the crack about your *crazy* family. At least none of them is in jail like mine.'

'My father would be if not for you.'

Kate chose her next words carefully, knowing they were important. 'I look forward to a week at Bella Trattoria. I like the food; I really like your family, and I'm a tad fond of you. Despite Beth's noble training attempts, maybe I'm not cut out to be a private investigator either.'

Eric rubbed his eyes. 'You handled yourself well on Elysian Island. Nate was very proud of you. Right now we're both tired, so this isn't a good time to figure out the rest of our lives. Let's get some sleep.' Eric rubbed his eyes, set his keys and phone on the coffee table and leaned back.

Kate stretched out on the sofa and pulled the afghan to her throat. Yet sleep refused to come, because each time she opened her eyes to check, Eric was watching her. And they couldn't be any safer than in that condo.

In the morning Eric went out for bagels and donuts, while everyone else slept in. Kate found his note when she was making the first pot of coffee.

'Good morning, Nicki.' Kate greeted the third person up. 'Are you ready for coffee?'

Instead of answering yea or nay, Nicki kissed both of Kate's cheeks. 'I don't think I properly thanked you yet. If you hadn't shown up when you did, Hunter would be dead. My daughter and I will be forever grateful to you.'

Handing her a mug, Kate blushed to her hairline. 'You're welcome. How's Hunter feeling?'

'He's still sleeping, but I think he's back to normal. Last night he lectured his mother about giving Evangeline cupcakes right before bed.' Nicki rolled her eyes. 'Our daughter operates at full throttle without eating sugary sweets.'

Michael and Beth emerged from their room as Eric walked in with two bags and a box. 'What do we have here, Manfredi?' Beth took the two bags from him.

'Healthy multigrain bagels with low fat cream cheese in one bag,' Eric said. 'Buttery French croissants and Danish fruit pastries in the other.'

Beth looked in a bag and handed it to Michael. 'Here you go, Mr Decathlon.' Then she gave the other bag to Nicki. 'I knew you two love anything from Europe. As for me, if there aren't greasy donuts in that box, I'm going to cry.'

Eric handed her the box. 'No tears for you today. Eat your fill. I bought two dozen.'

Nate and Izzy showed up during the second pot of coffee. Nate headed straight for the donuts, while Izzy nibbled a blueberry Danish. Kate had just started their third pot of coffee when a tousled-haired Hunter appeared in the doorway.

'Good morning,' he drawled. 'I hope I haven't missed any mini-dramas.'

Izzy sipped from her mug. 'Only Nate and Beth fighting over the last chocolate-filled donut.'

'Who won?' Hunter asked, pouring a cup of coffee.

'I did.' Nate licked his fingertips. 'I reminded Beth about what Michael said on the island . . . something about crazy people shouldn't carry guns.'

And so went their reunion breakfast – eating, drinking coffee, and poking fun at each other. It felt like any other Price employee gathering in many ways. Yet none of them would ever be the same again.

Soon they cleaned John's condo, left him a thank-you note with five hundred dollars' worth of gift cards, and drove to the Glynn County Police Department in Brunswick. After each of them gave their statement to law enforcement, they finally were released to go home – the Prices to Natchez, the

Galens to New Orleans, and the Prestons up the coast to Savannah.

And Kate and Eric took the long, scenic way back to Charleston to his family's restaurant. Kate had been given two weeks off with pay and promised a fat bonus in her next paycheck. But she didn't care much about the money. She'd finally found what she'd been looking for – someone to love who also loved her and an honest-to-goodness family. Who in the world needed more than that?

Charleston, South Carolina

Who would have thought a two-week vacation at a restaurant would be enjoyable? When Kate and Eric returned from their 'retreat' on St Simons Island, the Manfredis welcomed them home with open arms. With Eric back to work full time and Kate helping out for the next two weeks, his father and sister reduced their hours and Bernadette's husband went back to his real job. Everyone was happy.

Then one of the Manfredis spotted an opportunity. Maybe it was Alfonzo because he feared losing his son to the exciting life of a PI. Or maybe Irena was afraid her son would marry Kate and move to her hometown. But most likely, his sister realized they both could get the life they wanted.

Eric loved to cook, but like Bernadette, he didn't want to work ten hours a day, six days a week. Eric usually spent his mornings working out, running along the battery, or meeting friends for breakfast. With Kate in town, they could see Charleston's historic sites or head to the beach in the morning, then arrive at Bella with enough time to check the wine inventory and prep for dinner. Eric didn't mind staying late to catch up on paperwork.

Bernadette, however, got all the exercise she needed at the restaurant. So she would come in early, cook for Bella's busy lunch crowd, and leave before Danielle got home from school. Aunt Estelle baked the breads and desserts every morning; Nonni continued to make the pasta noodles, and Alfonzo prepared each sauce from scratch. As the evening head chef, Eric grilled the meats and seafood, sautéed the mushrooms and vegetables, and prepared the lasagnas, stuffed manicottis and raviolis to order. Kate began her career as a salad girl and worked her way up to pasta once she learned the difference between tender, firm and al dente. Although at times the kitchen seemed like chaos, everyone pitched in and helped. With three chefs, there were plenty of disagreements, but no one stayed mad long. And no one was happier than Kate. The Manfredis were a family who loved each other, and she would soon be one of them.

After the last dinner reservation had been served, the Manfredis usually sat down and ate together. Sometimes Bernadette and her family joined them, sometimes not. During Kate's two-week vacation, she and Eric often dined alone in the courtyard. On one warm night under the stars, eating food prepared by their own hands, Kate thought life couldn't get any better. Then Eric popped the question she'd been anticipating . . . and had been terrified of for so long. But Kate wasn't terrified anymore and, without a moment's hesitation, she said yes. That night, after a second glass of wine, she and Eric decided on a dinner party to announce their news.

Now Kate wasn't sure that was a good idea. Telling her friends and co-workers about their engagement was one thing, but announcing she was leaving PI work was quite another. Who throws a resignation party? Most likely, only Michael and Beth would show up since Savannah was only ninety minutes away. They couldn't expect the Galens or the Prices to hop on a plane so soon after their harrowing getaway, especially since Hunter and Izzy had careers and both couples had small children. But once again, Kate was wrong. Izzy and Nicki called to say they were coming as long as kids were welcome. Of course, they were. Little Nathan and Evangeline would provide diversion while Beth pulled her hair out.

On the morning of the dinner party, Kate sipped her first cup of coffee on Eric's balcony and pictured Bella Trattoria coming to life. Kate loved that restaurant; she loved Charleston and, most of all, she loved Eric Manfredi. Becoming part of his family after so many years on the run felt like heaven.

'We have time for a jog or to hit the pool before heading to Bella.' Eric ruffled his fingers through her hair as he sat down beside her. 'Don't worry. Everything is prepared for the pasta Bolognese, the orecchiette, and the veal tortellini. We'll start with an antipasti platter and finish with Estelle's famous tiramisu.'

Kate shook her head. 'It's not the food I'm concerned about. These people invested a lot of time and energy in training me.'

'And you just saved their lives,' spoke the voice of reason.

'But I've never had this many friends.'

'Who would drop pals with a place they can eat and drink for free?'

'I can't imagine not seeing the Prices or the Galens again. They live so far away.' Kate dropped her chin to her chest.

'Hey, whenever my family gets on our last nerve, we'll take a road trip to New Orleans or Natchez. Turnaround is fair play.'

Kate pondered the logic of a very handsome man. 'Heck with running; let's go straight to the pool. We've got tonight handled.'

That evening, with the table set with Irena's best crystal and china and Bocelli on the sound system, Kate and Eric stood at the door of Bella's private dining room ready to greet their guests, who not surprisingly arrived promptly at six o'clock.

'Hey, guys! OK if I put these over there?' Without explaining what these were, Nate marched past them and set two wrapped boxes on the bar.

'Thanks for letting us bring the ruggies.' Izzy buzzed Kate's cheek with a kiss. 'I made sure Nathan Jr took a long nap this afternoon.'

'Good evening, Kate, Eric,' Hunter greeted, holding his daughter in one arm. 'Very brave of you to include the under-twelve set. Consider yourself forewarned.' He set down Evangeline who immediately bolted toward Nathan.

'Hi, Katie. I hope you don't mind, but I told the staff we needed a card table in the corner with nothing but plastic for these kiddos. A drop-cloth wouldn't hurt either.' Nicki carried a fancy bag and a large bow-tied box to the bar.

Next in line were the Prestons. 'Man, those Galens start giving orders the moment they arrive!' Beth set her gifts on the floor and wrapped both arms around Kate.

'What's with the presents?' Eric asked Michael. 'It's neither of our birthdays and a long time till Christmas.'

Michael smirked over his wife's head. 'You know women. They like to make a fuss over everything. I think it's Canadian Thanksgiving.' Michael winked and wandered away.

'What's up, Beth?' Kate demanded with hands on hips.

'Nothing's up. Izzy said we're supposed to take hostess gifts to a dinner party. And I refuse to be outdone by those Galens.' Beth picked up her packages and joined the others at the bar.

Arching up on tiptoes, Kate hissed in Eric's ear. 'Did you spill the beans, Manfredi?'

'Of course not. I told them this was a reunion of the Elysian survivors. That's it.' Eric held up his hands.

'Stop whispering, you two,' Nate ordered, 'and open the champagne. Contrary to popular opinion, the Price team of private investigators are not as stupid as they look.'

While Bella's bartender opened one bottle, Nicki popped the top on another. 'We know exactly what we're celebrating tonight,' she said over her shoulder.

Once everyone's flute was filled, Nate offered the first toast. 'To Kate Weller who, despite her short tenure with us, will always be the agency's favorite employee. Good luck with your new career.'

'To Kate.' Everyone lifted their glass and sipped.

'Who will always have an open invitation to every retreat,' Izzy added.

'So much for my surprise announcement,' Kate murmured as her friends lifted their glasses a second time.

'Surprises are overrated.' Nicki handed her a gift bag. 'Open this present first.'

Inside was a chef's hat which read: *Be nice or I'll poison you*, along with a full-length apron showing a woman with glass in hand and the caption: *I cook with wine. Sometimes I even add it to the food.*

From Nate and Izzy, Kate received an eight-inch copper skillet, with a whisk and spatula. 'That's to cook breakfast for two,' Izzy explained. 'Best to start small.'

Beth pushed her way to Kate's side. 'I wanted to buy you

an Easy-Bake Oven, but Michael said Aunt Estelle handles the baking. So we thought you needed something of your own.'

Kate shot a glance at Eric, then ripped off the paper. Inside was the cookbook, *Fifty Favorite Southern Appetizers*, which she pressed to her chest. 'My own specialty at Bella? I can only dream.'

'But now you'll have to get to work on time,' Michael teased. 'Appetizers come first.'

'I don't know what to say.' Hot tears stung Kate's eyes. 'Thanks everyone.'

'Hey, did you ever find out why Creery kept you two away from Elysian?' asked Michael.

Eric chose to explain. 'Yeah, my dad cleared that up once I showed him a photo of Jonah Creery. He said that guy used to come in every Thursday with a gorgeous younger blonde woman. She was *unforgettable*, so we knew it had to be Ariana Frazier. Creery probably thought I might remember them as a couple – he would have seen my name on the list of agents and their partners that Nate gave Frazier and realized who I was.'

'OK, now is it time to eat?' Beth playfully punched Kate's arm.

'Let me say it for both of us.' Eric wrapped his arm around her. 'Take your seats, fellow Elysian survivors. It's time to get this dinner started.'

And the meal couldn't have been more perfect. While Nathan Jr and Evangeline enjoyed chicken fingers and spaghetti at their own table, the adults consumed a vast quantity of Alfonzo's and Bernadette's deliciously prepared cuisine. As Kate glanced around at her friends, she finally started to relax . . .

Until Eric tapped his knife against his glass to command attention. 'Kate and I have a second reason to celebrate tonight,' he said when the room grew quiet. 'I asked her to marry me and lo-and-behold, she said yes.' As usual, the ensuing comments ran the gamut: Nicki stood and lifted her glass. 'That gal knows a good deal when she sees one.'

Beth scrambled to her feet next. 'Are we talking about Kate Weller?'

Hunter rose with great dignity. 'It's about time you popped the question, Manfredi. Why leave Preston and me alone on the ledge?'

From Izzy came Kate's favorite reply: 'Thank goodness, because the rest are engagement presents and we hate returning stuff to the store.'

Her former boss, Nate, was last to respond to their announcement: 'Like I said, Kate, the Price team isn't as stupid as it looks. To Kate and Eric. With food and drink this good, I can't wait for the wedding.'